Praise for Bunke

"Claustrophobically composed and tautly paced, BUNKER DOGS takes a suffocating plunge into utter what-the-fuckery that will leave you losing sleep just to reach the paralyzing end. I tore through this book." -- Clay McLeod Chapman, author of Ghost Eaters.

— Clay McLeod Chapman, author of Ghost Eaters

Gage Greenwood is quickly making a name for himself as a genre-blending, character-driven author, and Bunker Dogs puts those skills on full display. With an insanely fast pace and sense of dread growing on every page, this book will have you hooked from the start. One of the year's best.

— John Durgin, best-selling author of The Cursed Among Us and Inside the Devil's Nest

"Bunker Dogs is Gage Greenwood putting the pedal to the metal of the genre-mobile and crashing straight into pure horror. With its haunting opening that quickly devolves into a fascinating character study, Greenwood puts you in the shoes of a flawed protagonist and then locks you in a dark bunker with sinister beings that are as fierce as they are mysterious. It's The Descent meets I Am Legend made all the more entertaining by the author's suspenseful storytelling and trademark wit."

— Nick Roberts, HAG award-winning author of Anathema and The Exorcist's House

"Bunker Dogs was an absolute blast. Gage's brand of horror shines throughout the book from the first line until the end. The writing is fantastic. Gage knows how to weave a chilling tale and invites the reader to experience claustrophobic moments and bouts of sheer terror. And it worked so well!"

— Jay Bower, author of Cadaverous, Hanging Corpses, and The Dead Blood Series

Bunker Dogs

Gage Greenwood

For Catie McGuinness, for always trudging through the darkness with me. You've made my lows much less lonely, and my highs much more fun.

For Megan Stockton, thanks for convincing me to take a short story idea and to turn it into this novel. You believed in this story long before I did.

Content Warnings

For a list of content warnings, please go to Doesthedogdie.com

Chapter 1

Are You Ready?

Something scratched above Cassie's head. She glanced up from her American History book to the popcorn ceiling. It stopped. She sighed, wiped her blurry eyes, and refocused on her homework. She had the book leaning on her upper legs as she lay on the bed, her head half-propped by her lumpy pillow.

The noise returned, a gentle scratch. Possibly a rogue squirrel or mouse found its way into the attic as the fall weather broke. But then, the noise dragged as if someone moved a heavy table across the room. One long scratch. It stopped again.

She peeled her eyes from the popcorn ceiling. Even in her perplexed state, her mind made patterns from the dripping plaster: faces, vulgar creatures with elongated mouths and droopy eyes.

Giving up on her homework, she dropped the book on the floor with a thud. The loose binding on the hardcover took its final beating and separated from its pages as it hit the hardwood.

Cassie grabbed her headphones and spun the wheel on her iPod until she reached Taking Back Sunday. Her brother blasted his music down the hall in his room but through Cassie's bedroom door, it sounded like nothing more than a series of muddy bumps. Taking

Back Sunday filtered through her ears into her brain and silenced the agitation forming all around her.

Thud.

She yelped and ripped the headphones from her ears. Her heart shot off like fireworks in her chest. Something landed in her hair and on her forehead. She rubbed it off, examining it on her fingertips. Flecks of loose plaster rained onto her from the ceiling.

She jumped out of bed with a skittering heart and entered the hall. The bumping from Chris's music went from muffled tones to nightclub-level booming, each thump of the beat fraying Cassie's nerves. As the deep bass penetrated the hall, the floorboards vibrated under her feet. It felt like the house had turned on her, taunting her with sounds and motion. Even the air was wrong, too thick for autumn.

She pounded on her brother's door. "Chris."

She used to love when he babysat. He was the cool older brother who didn't mind pulling up his sleeves and playing with her in the dirt or having a round of hide and seek in the dark, tag in the fields of long, yellow grass, and always stopping to give her sage advice, the kind which often went against what adults told their children. All Chris did anymore was lock himself in his room and blast his shitty music. She couldn't even remember when the change happened, but it was sudden. The chains of their friendship snapped off rather than slowly rusting with time.

"Chris!" She snarled, stormed through the hall, and charged downstairs into the kitchen.

From there, Chris's music went back to softer bumps. She certainly wouldn't investigate the attic noises alone and Chris obviously wasn't bothered by it, or her for that matter, he just sat alone in his room, drowning in bass. She'd just have to ride it out until her father came home.

She rubbed her eyes and made herself a turkey sandwich with chips. As she wiped a layer of mustard on her wheat bread, she heard the scratching again. She couldn't, though. There was no way

2

she would hear a soft noise in the attic over Chris's blasting rap music.

Scratch. Scratch. Scratch.

What the ever-loving Tell-Tale Heart shit was going on here? *The Tell-Tale Heart*. Thinking of the story sent a wave of sadness into Cassie's stomach. Chris once faced the wrath of their father because he read Edgar Allan Poe stories to Cassie about four years earlier, when she was only six.

"What? I didn't read her that stuff. I don't even read it myself," he had argued.

"Read her something normal," their father said.

Even with Chris's denial, he couldn't let their father's words slide. "Like Shakespeare?"

"Sure. That would be great."

Chris laughed. "Me thinks you skipped your Shakespeare lessons in school because that shit is far more vulgar, violent, and horrifying than anything Poe wrote."

"Watch your mouth, Chris."

Cassie came back to reality and realized she'd been absently staring out the kitchen window. A phrase echoed in her brain, and she didn't know why. *Are you ready?*

Are you ready?

Areyouready?

It was rattling around in her head, spoken by a familiar voice, but one she couldn't place. A female voice, soft, gentle, and a little somber, like a mother sending her child away on the first day of school.

Are you ready?

Like a crazy person, she responded to the voice. "Not yet." She didn't know why she said it or what she was talking about, but it felt like the right answer.

Her night was slipping away, hydroplaning on thick ice, inertia driving it toward a shrouded destination. She didn't need to see it to know she wasn't ready for it, that the impact would shatter her peace.

3

She shook her head, loosening the binding those words held over her brain, and squeezed the top square of bread onto her sandwich until the mustard leaked out the sides.

She stormed back upstairs and lay on the bed, resting her sandwich plate on her stomach. Deciding to give the American History book another chance, she scooped it off the floor, leaving the separated cover on its own.

She struggled to adjust her head properly so she could read the material while keeping her sandwich in place. Sighing, she took a bite. A loose splotch of mustard painted her fingers yellow. Now she couldn't touch the book. Dammit. She lifted her yellow fingers in the air as if they were diseased and used her other hand to shift the sandwich plate on top of the book.

Scratch.

Scratch.

Scratch.

This time, it didn't stop; it just kept scratching and scratching. One scratch forward, one scratch back. Back and forth, back and forth, back and forth.

Still holding her hand up, she stared at the rough texture above her head. She followed the noise as it traveled from above the head of her bed to the foot of it.

Her blood pressure boiled, a raging river coursing through her veins. Why did everything have to be so fucking difficult? All she wanted to do was study. Was that so goddamned hard? She pushed herself off the bed, keeping her mustard hand above her head.

One more time, she slammed on Chris's door, and one more time, he ignored her. She kicked it, no longer interested in his attention but wanting to deliver a message. "Asshole."

She paced the hall, forgetting about her mustard hand, despite still holding it in the air like she was halting traffic.

Even with the music blasting into her eardrums, she could still make out the scratching from the attic. She knew she'd have to go up there to see what it was, but the idea filled her with dread. The cold, dank attic was littered with cobwebs, mouse poop, and the occasional bat. Her father hated going up there too, ever since he saw a northern black widow crawling across her mom's old dollhouse.

Fuck it. She opened the attic door with her clean hand and stared up at the dark space. The uneven wooden stairs showed slight signs of rot. She stepped, and instead of meeting stable ground, her feet felt like they walked on sponges.

At the top of the stairs, she clicked the chain hanging above her head. The room came to life with cobwebs, the dollhouse, and old boxes littered with crude drawings she and her brother made in school. A mouse scurried under the door to the crawl space.

She did a double take on an anomaly, her brain struggling to comprehend what it saw. It drove through a rapid-fire series of denials. A joke. A trick. Her mind playing with the angles. It didn't take long for it to coalesce, to become real.

Cassie screamed, an unending siren coming from her throat.

Her brother hung from a rafter, his feet scraping against the dusty floorboards.

Are you ready?

Areyouready?

Are

You

Ready?

"Chris," she yelled, but she knew he was dead, knew it was way too late.

She froze for a moment, unable to look away but wanting nothing more than to turn from it. A low groan left her throat. Her stomach lurched. It couldn't be real. It couldn't happen. She screamed again, a mixture of dread, panic, and incomprehension bubbling acid into her throat. "Chris," she cried. She fumbled backwards, the hard wall snapping her from her frozen state. "Chris," she whispered.

As she ran down the stairs, her back arched as a trickle of fear and dread trailed down her spine like icy water. A board gave in on her, breaking in half, and she tumbled down the steps on her back, each stair smacking against her tensed spine, one last mocking gesture from the night. Luckily, her adrenaline hid the pain.

She was alone in her house with her dead brother, his body taunting her through the floorboards. Edgar Allan Poe, indeed. Her mind swam. Thoughts of ghosts and monsters and death and suicide all mushed together, breaking her.

Every dark recess in the hallway grew darker, no longer a shadow but a material nothingness, a black hole ready to swallow her up. The creaky floorboards laughed at her, cackling loud enough to overpower Chris's blasting music, which was its own form of taunting. His music, a last remnant of his living self, thumping through the stucco and insulation.

Her arms trembled as she charged into her room, snatched her cell from the bed, and ran down another flight, moving as far away from the horror as she could, as if the bright whites of the kitchen could wash away the visual of her brother shifting back and forth, dangling from a noose.

Are you ready?

"Not yet!"

Mustard smeared across the keys as she dialed 911.

Chapter 2

The Other Cassie

"Who is your best friend, Cassiopeia? Have you ever truly had one?"

————

YEARS LATER

Cassie headed down the hall toward her dorm room, running her index finger along the chain of her necklace, a nervous habit she'd possessed since childhood. After a seven-hour day of classes, followed by eight at the restaurant, every step forward ached in her heels, every inch stretched away from her. Her vision blurred. Her heart knocked at her ribs, as if pounding on a loud neighbor's door and shouting, "Hey, let me get some fucking rest in here!"

She clicked her phone on, checking the time. 2:17 a.m. She had Introduction to Modern Biotechnology in Medicine in less than six hours. Her only sense of relief was she didn't have a waitressing shift at Cuddey's tomorrow, so she could rest and catch up on her assignments.

Eager to kick off her Sketchers and flop onto the couch, her bed be damned, she twisted the lock on her door with shaky hands. To her surprise, her roommate, Beth, was not only still awake, but she had company. Beth's best friend, Shana, sat next to her on the couch. The television was on some kind of screensaver mode, showcasing colorful blobs which bounced around the screen like the inside of a lava lamp. Beth and Shana snickered, staring at the blobs with watery eyes.

Cassie sighed and closed the door. "Are you two on acid again?" She kicked her shoes off as Beth turned toward her.

"Shrooms," Beth said.

Cassie closed her eyes, praying for some sort of break. Beth was respectful, but when she took any kind of substance, she turned into a giggling jack-in-the-box. Wind her up and POP, the giggles let loose.

Shana, a delightful girl otherwise, played the perfect partner for Beth, always ready to do the winding.

"Okay. I hate to be the party pooper, but I have to be up in like five and a half hours to go to class. Y'all have fun out here."

Beth stood up, her slight frame barely rising above the level where she'd been sitting. She could pass for five years younger with her short stature, cute, rosy cheeks, and her chipmunk teeth. Shana once said Beth could be a stunt double for children in Hollywood, and Beth had seriously considered the idea.

She waltzed over to Cassie, slow and sloppy, her hips slithering from side to side. Not in some sexy, runway manner, but in a clear struggle to keep her blitzed self on her feet. She'd clearly done some drinking, too. When Beth reached her roommate, she threw her arms over Cassie's shoulders and hugged her. "I love you, girl. I'll go stay at Shana's dorm so we don't keep you up."

Cassie hugged her back. "You're the best." She almost asked if they could all hang out on Friday night, hoping to keep some cool points on her side, but then remembered she offered to take Jay's shift at Cuddey's.

Shana, prying her eyes away from the screensaver, turned to Beth and Cassie. "Have her do the mirror trick before we leave." Her words came out like spilling marbles.

Beth pulled away from Cassie. "Oh my god, yes. I know you need to go to bed, but it will only take a minute."

She grabbed Cassie's hand and led her to the floor lamp. Beth ran her hands up the skinny, metallic frame until she reached the nub to turn it on. The top portion of the frame curved in a U, which Cassie always thought made it look like a sulking robot or one of those lamp-post monsters from that Kevin Bacon TV show.

The light came on, a dim, yellow glow behind the smokey-glass shade. Cassie winced. Something about electricity, the constant low buzz it produced, the initial click of a light, sent an odd shiver down her spine.

Beth put a hand on Cassie's shoulder. "Okay, so you need to stare into the light for thirty seconds."

Cassie chuckled. "I need to blind myself?"

Beth's tongue clicked against the roof of her mouth. "You'll be fine. Then, as soon as you're ready to look away, run into the bathroom and look in the mirror. You'll be a totally different person."

Cassie rolled her eyes. "You realize I'm not on shrooms, right?"

Cassie often wished she could be the druggie. She drank once in a while but never more than a glass of wine. Other than sipping slowly on reds, she refused to take anything heavier than an aspirin. Her brother had dabbled in drugs. Nothing serious, just pot and the occasional pill. And while Cassie knew his drug experimentation had absolutely nothing to do with his suicide, she couldn't help correlating the two. The last thing she would need before altering her mind was a reminder of her brother hanging in the attic.

"I know you're not on shrooms. That's why I need you to do it. You're the balance test or whatever," Beth said.

Shana nodded along, standing up now, eager to see Cassie perform the trick.

"Control group," Cassie said, correcting Beth. Her cheeks turned red, wondering if she committed a social faux pas. A control group wasn't some highfalutin bit of trivia; any high school-age kid in a biology class would know the term. Yet, she worried correcting her roommate was a thing know-it-all assholes did. This was why Cassie refrained from social gatherings unless necessary. She spent most of the time in a constant state of worry, wondering if every little innocuous sentence was a criminal offense. Navigating conversation was like running through an Army boot camp obstacle course, except the grenades felt real in the pit of her stomach.

Beth snapped her fingers. "Control group. Perfect. You're the control group. Now, look at the light."

Cassie sighed and bent low, allowing her eyes to get a clear shot of the bulb. She winced but battled to keep her eyes open. Why was she doing this? She just wanted to go to fucking bed, and she certainly didn't want to blind herself to appease her roommate. Still, she stared on. While the bulb was a dull yellow, staring at it directly projected a series of bright white blobs in Cassie's vision until the blobs melded into each other, creating an entire screen of white with a glowing red center. Yup. She was probably fucking blind.

When she finally pulled away, Beth guided her toward the bathroom. Her toe slammed into the raised wood sill under the door, and Cassie sucked in air, avoiding a full-on hissy fit meltdown. Her stubbed toe hurt like hell, and she wanted to scream and punch. But, like always, she did nothing, just bottled it in and kept obliging.

Beth let go of Cassie's arm. "Okay, I'm going to leave the room and close the door so you're in the dark. When your eyes readjust, keep staring in the mirror."

The door creaked and shut. Cassie kept her eyes trained in front of her, to what she assumed was the mirror. Her heart rate increased a little, as if slightly unnerved. Why? She didn't know. She wasn't afraid she'd actually see a different person. Presumably, after intentionally fucking up her eyes, her reflection would look strange, and she could report back to her roommate that it did, indeed, look "different." Hopefully that would be enough to entertain them and she could get some sleep.

As her vision returned, she blurred her eyes, as if staring at one of those magic pictures with the hidden images. The mirror doubled, as did her reflection, which at that point was nothing more than a pale bulb of its own, with draping brown cascading around it.

As her features came more into focus, her pulse quickened again. She hoped she saw someone else. Maybe that's why she played along with Beth's drug-induced charade in the first place. Cassie always felt like she carried someone else with her. Not literally another person, and not as blunt as a split personality; more like a separate side of herself, stuck in her belly, glued in there, always yearning for freedom. She felt this other person's presence at times of acute anxiety, when that hidden version of herself would punch at her guts, trying to free itself. It would whisper in her ear. *I'm coming to help you. I'm here for you. I can save us.*

Are you ready?

Those last three words drove her mind back to reality, where she stared blankly in the mirror at her reflection, the same mundane reflection it always was. No other person, no brain-twisting illusion, no ghost within herself. Just Cassie with her pale skin, deep purple pools under her eyes, the forest of teeny blackheads on her nose, the long river of black hair frazzled from a night at work. All Cassie. No magic.

She rubbed her eyes, wishing her hands could scrub away the puffiness and streaks of red lightning coursing toward her pupils. What would she tell Beth to quicken the conversation? If she told the truth, Beth would dig in with a series of *'are you sure?'* type questions. Maybe she'd even try to replicate the experiment and ask Cassie for a do-over. But if Cassie lied and said she saw someone else in the mirror, Beth might sit her down for a million questions.

She closed her eyes and puffed out her chest, eager to get this over with. As the door swung open, Cassie gave one last glance into the mirror, and for a split second, she saw someone else, and not a different version of herself, either. A true "someone else."

She did a double take, but of course, on second viewing, her reflection was back to being all her own. The other woman, a distant memory swimming in Cassie's muddled mind, forever to wander in those dark corners where Cassie would always ask herself if she saw what she thought she saw. It passed so quickly she could hardly remember any details. The features of the woman's face scattered like sand in a storm.

Cassie left the confines of the bathroom and smiled at Beth and Shana, who stared wide-eyed, waiting for an answer.

"Yes, I saw someone else," she said as she walked past them toward her bedroom. "I'll tell you all about it tomorrow."

Chapter 3

Hypnopompic

"Cassiopeia, keep marching."

———

As soon as Cassie plopped onto her bed, Beth and Shana left. Once they were gone, she wished they stayed. They left a lingering cold-ness, a hollow void in the darkness. Cassie always wished for alone time but always dreaded it when it arrived.

Despite her exhausted state, she tossed and turned. It was some-thing her mind did when she knew she had to wake up early. It spiraled down a stairwell of madness, thinking of every trauma, every heated conversation she'd ever experienced, every problem she'd yet to encounter, but knew she soon would. Just as it all finally dragged her close to a sound sleep, her body would itch. She'd debate whether to scratch it, if moving might wake her up, but then the debating kept her awake too. Eventually, she'd relent, scratch the itch, and find herself back to square one, tossing and begging for rest.

Once she finally fell asleep, she dropped hard, landing in the deep. It only felt like seconds before her alarm dug into her chest, clutched her heart, and ripped her from the dream world.

She shot upright, fumbling for her phone. With her eyes not yet open beyond a slit, she swiped the alarm off. She sat there, back straight as an arrow, contemplating dropping onto her pillow and returning to the world of slumber. Fuck class. One day off wouldn't kill her. She deserved it. Sleep. But she deserved it because she was so consistently reliable toward her obligations, which meant she should get the fuck up.

She yawned and slid her feet off the mattress, letting them dangle while she wiped crust from the corners of her eyes. Her chest constricted, tightening around the ribs. She thought, *If I don't get some sleep soon, I'm going to have a fucking heart attack.*

It was crazy how her body's response to stress and lack of sleep was to constrict her chest, make her heart pound and throb, give her aches and pains. Heart attack symptoms weren't exactly the best way to fight anxiety. Maybe her body should respond to high levels of stress by gently messaging her shoulders.

Half awake, she floated around her dorm room like a ghost, albeit a clumsy one. When she didn't have a good half hour to lie in bed after an alarm, she fumbled her way to full consciousness, her limbs listening to her brain but only offering seventy-five percent of the movement it asked for.

On top of the lack of sleep, she'd had awful nightmares about her brother, ones where he sat bow-legged on the living room rug, playing Guess Who? with Cassie. At first, the dream was more of a memory, but like most dreams, it ended up just a vision of truth mixed into an abstract pickle jar. Chris smiled at Cassie, his mouth stretching from ear to ear, his canines sticking out like sharp little daggers. As he spoke, blood gushed from his lungs, staining his tongue as it pooled down his chin onto the floor and game board. Maybe it was better the alarm woke her instead of the nightmare. God knows where it was headed.

She threw a hoodie on and charged down the hallway to the

elevators, debating on rushing down the stairs instead, but coming to terms with her inability to rush down anything, let alone long, winding stairwells begging for a hypnopompic student to stumble to their death. Nope. She'd just have to be a little late.

The elevator door dinged and she stepped in. No students. She sighed and dropped her back to the wall, forgetting she had her backpack on. Something crunched. She should check on that, but whatever, probably a bag of chips or something. She often relied on gas station purchases for meals and, sometimes, threw nearly empty bags of chips or other junk food in her backpack, telling herself she'd finish them later, despite never doing so.

As she stepped off the elevator, she collided with a student turning the corner to get in. Yup. That's how the day would go. She'd be a few inches off on all her steps, and the day would unfold as one giant collision in waiting. This was how people died, how they managed to not notice the tractor-trailer barreling down the road as they crossed, or how they walked headfirst into a swinging baseball bat.

She apologized to the scruffy-haired kid she bumped into and opened the door to the outside world.

The Quad buzzed with morning energy. A couple noodleheads played hacky sack, two teachers marched to their next lecture, giggling to each other, and five girls stood around a bench, one of them dancing while the rest laughed and whooped. Who the fuck had that kind of pizzaz in the morning?

Cassie charged across the Quad, headed for the science labs, the sun already so bright she had to cup her hands over her eyes to see in front of her. Her phone buzzed, and after checking her front two pockets, she found it pressed against her butt in the back of her jeans.

She flicked the screen and checked her messages.

> Please tell me you're not working tonight.
> We just got invited to something. Any
> chance you can make it over here?

She had forgotten to check the name and, for a moment, her heart stuttered. She needed a fucking night off to study and sleep. Granted, babysitting was easier than hosting and waitressing, but it still required alertness.

When she saw it came from Mrs. Renard, she smiled. *Phew.* Of all the families she babysat for, they were the best. The father, Mark, was a little weird but never crossed a line into inappropriate, and their son, James, was a saint. He was twelve and didn't need a sitter, but otherwise, he was shy and polite and spent most of his time playing video games by himself in his room. When Cassie sat for the Renards, her job basically meant just being there to call 911 if the kid choked or something.

That's not what she loved best, though. The Renard's house was a giant, open-floor masterpiece with plenty of bright lights and space. She spent her days in crammed classes only to return to a tiny room with a roommate and then head to work in a packed restaurant littered with obnoxious, entitled college dicks. The Renard house gave her some quiet, alone time, a place for focus and reading without disruption, without constant noise. She was a page in the center of a book and the Renard house opened the cover and let her breathe.

> Yes.

As she clicked send, she crashed her head into some dude's chest. They stared at each other for a few seconds and apologized at the same time. They danced around each other and headed off in opposite directions.

She turned back to him. "That's what I'm saying, though. You could have been a tractor-trailer."

He either didn't hear her or ignored her. The phone buzzed again.

> You are a saint, Cassie! Can you be here at five?

Yes.

The weight of her bookbag took a toll on her back. The more she walked, the more she angled forward. She assumed she looked like the floor lamp in her dorm, head droopy and spine curved.

She entered Cassian Hall, home to the aquaculture and fisheries labs. As soon as the door opened, the saltwater smell infiltrated her nose, and the buzzing of high-powered filtration systems stole the air. She flew down a flight of stairs, having a little more control over her body, and walked the narrow, dimly lit halls of the B floor. She imagined walking through the belly of a whale, a hollow, dank tunnel ripe with the scent of rotten fish and seawater.

She fucking loved it.

Outside of the machines running loudly, the fishery labs were quiet. The classes were small, some only containing five to seven students, and even the lectures were squeezed into small lab rooms, where the students sat surrounded by aquariums and microcosmic simulations of ocean life.

Despite already being late, she hit the bathroom before entering her classroom. A girl standing at the sink snapped her head toward the swinging door as Cassie entered, clearly taken off-guard. Rivulets of black mascara drizzled down the girl's cheeks and she sniffled.

"Sorry, I was just leaving," she said as she wiped the black lines trailing down her face.

The girl's tears threw Cassie off. She wanted to say something, to show compassion, but thoughts and words wouldn't connect. Instead, she said, "That's the beauty of stalls. We can both be in here at the same time."

Ugh.

The girl offered a half-smile, wiped her cheeks some more, and worked to move around Cassie.

"Hey, do you want to talk about it? I mean, I don't want to pry. It's just... Are you okay?" *Why am I so bad at this?*

The girl sniffled again and wiped her nose. "Yeah, no. I'm okay."

She gave Cassie an unconvincing smile and a floodgate opened. Her face distorted and tears poured from her eyes. "No. I just don't understand why he's such an asshole."

Oh jeez.

The girl jolted forward and latched her arms around Cassie, clutching tightly. Her face pressed against Cassie's neck. Tears and snot spread on her skin.

Cassie patted the girl on the back. The words "there, there," almost left her mouth. Didn't this girl know she had places to be?

When someone asks, "Are you okay?" the appropriate answer is always, "Yes," or "I'll be fine," or, "Is anyone ever okay?" It certainly wasn't to collapse on top of the person asking.

As she rubbed the girl's shoulder, she caught her reflection. Same ole Cassie. She wished she could conjure the other Cassie. If only the flashes of the woman she caught in the mirror last night were real. She could use someone with gumption enough to tell this girl it was time to move on, to find another neck to snot on.

When the girl finally pulled away, Cassie's necklace caught in her hair, and the chain snapped, dropping to the grimy brown vinyl flooring.

"Oh, I'm so sorry," the girl said as she bent to pick it up.

Cassie couldn't breathe, a panic attack coming on full force. Her fingernails dug into her palms and her chest constricted once again. The bathroom jostled and rocked, a dinghy in an Atlantic hurricane. She dropped to the floor, trying to grab the necklace before the girl could touch it.

"I've got it. I've got it. Leave it alone."

The girl turned her head, her forehead scrunched. "I'm sorry. It was an accident."

Cassie bunched the necklace into her fist and used the lip of the sink to help her back to her feet. "It's fine. I just don't like anyone touching this." She turned away from the girl and looked in the mirror. Her finger traced where the necklace had draped over her clavicle, to where the little vial of glowing stardust had rested on her sternum. She felt so naked with it removed.

The girl stayed behind her, eyes boiling over, more tears ready to pour. "I'm such an ass. I'm so sorry. I fuck everything up."

Cassie closed her eyes and sucked in a big breath of air. *It's just a necklace,* she told herself. Yes, she'd worn it every single day since her mother gifted to her at seven-years-old, but it was still just a thing. An object. It was bound to break one day.

She opened her fist and examined the damage. The milky blue and green glittered contents of the vial swirled hypnotically. One link had bent and broken. It would be easy enough to repair.

The girl peeked over Cassie's shoulder, examining it with her. Before Cassie could stop her, the girl snatched the necklace from her hand. "I can fix that."

Cassie's hands latched onto the girl's hoodie. She slammed the crying bitch into the wall. The girl's head clunked hard on the white tile.

"What the fuck?" Crying Girl shouted.

"I told you not to touch my fucking necklace." The muscles in her jaw throbbed as she clenched her teeth harder.

The girl put her hand up and let the piece of jewelry dangle from her fingers. "Here. Take it. I just wanted to fix it for you."

Cassie snatched it from her and unpinned her from the wall. An immediate calm washed over her as soon as the necklace was back in her hands. As her thumb brushed through the links, she eyed the terrified girl. "I'm sorry. I don't know what came over me."

Without responding, the girl dashed out of the bathroom.

Cassie leaned back and slid down the wall, sighing with relief. She felt hungover, reliving the embarrassing moments, a thin headache wavering on the horizon. She had never lashed out at someone like that before. She needed more sleep.

Chapter 4

Into the Undertow

"Cassiopeia, find a place where you can truly be you."

———

Classes ended at 2:50, giving Cassie some time to shower and change before driving to the Renard's house. She made it through her day in a general haze, hardly keeping focus on her lectures. Luckily, she didn't have any of her labs until Friday; otherwise, she might have conked out face-first into her lobster tanks.

She got back to her dorm room and sat down cross-legged on the floor, put her necklace on the coffee table, and got to work on fixing it. It nagged at her throughout her day, and every time she went to run her fingers along the chain, only to be met with emptiness, she clenched her jaw harder, which exacerbated her headache by the minute. She worked the broken link between her thumb and forefinger, trying to bend it back together, but it wouldn't budge. Frustration built in her guts, a bubbling rage that wanted to pour from her lungs in an unrelenting scream. Her fingers trembled as she squeezed harder and harder.

"Fuck."

Of course, they didn't have pliers or anything useful in the dorm room. The Renards must have a toolbox lying around. Everyone had a pair of pliers rusting away in a box somewhere in their house, but as silly as it was, Cassie didn't want to wait another three hours. She felt weaker, more exposed, like the only thing keeping her together was that necklace draping around her neck.

She didn't even know why she clung to the damn piece of jewelry so much. All it did was conjure terrible memories, like the night her mother threw it at her in a monstrous rage as bulky police officers chased the crazed woman around the house before dragging her off, never to be seen again.

Cassie stuck a pencil tip through the hole in the necklace link to keep it in place. As she pushed down with her biology textbook to squeeze the sides of the link back together, her mother's high-pitched wails broke through the barriers of memory and materialized in the empty dorm room.

She screamed in such a way it swallowed any bit of normalcy in their home. Cassie never heard anything like it, as if it could shatter the windows. Her mother slouched down as the men dragged her by the armpits, and she kicked her feet out, fighting against them. She planted one foot on the door stile and turned her head back toward Cassie. "Wear that fucking thing, Cassie. Remember me as I was before this."

The textbook dropped off the coffee table, and the necklace slid away from her, taking the pencil with it. The link remained separated, and both ends, just a few millimeters away from each other, taunted her. *You'll never connect us again.*

Cassie wiped her eyes and covered her face with her palms, pushing all the frustration out with a loud sigh. Time was ticking away, and she had to get ready for the Renards. It wasn't just the necklace that ate her, but what it represented: a day that kept getting away from her, always one step ahead and eager to pull the rug out from her already achy legs. She needed a win, because as each second ticked by, the day gained power. She couldn't help but feel like each crashing of the current was preparing her for a huge fucking tidal wave that would strip her of her bearings and suck her into the undertow.

Who was Cassie kidding? She was already drowning, way above her head. Every day was just an exercise of wading, keeping afloat long enough to make it to the next day. She grabbed the necklace and stuffed it into her clenched fist. "Please. Please. Just one fucking thing," she said as she thumped the barrel of her hand against her forehead.

Realizing she was wasting time whining, she stood up, went into her bedroom, and grabbed some clothes from her dresser. It was just college, she told herself. She'd survived much worse. Besides, she had a shower to look forward to. For some, a shower was a time to relax, but Cassie loved them for other reasons.

As she hopped into the steaming water, she growled. Shower time was the one point in her day where she allowed herself to rage, assuming Beth was not around to hear her. It was her one chance to scream and punch, to say, "fuck you," and, "hell no," to everyone she'd said, "yes," to all day. She'd punch the shower wall until her knuckles bled. Out came the Cassie hiding in her gut, the Cassie she always wished to be. The other woman in the mirror.

Her blood trailed down the wall, red and beautiful, until it merged with the shower water, turned pink and spiraled into the drain. She kept punching, driving her knuckles into the wall, hoping someday she'd have the strength to knock right through it, make a hole for her to see through, and maybe that hole would free her, let the anger loose, a tendrilled spirit intermingling with the shower steam. It would fill the room until the seams burst and the building exploded and the entire fucking campus collapsed under the weight of her hate.

Fuck you.

Fuck you.

Fuck you.

She punched, punched, punched.

She thought about Jay asking her to take his shift, and Beth with her stupid, drugged-up mind games, and her droning teachers, and the slimy manager at Cuddey's flirting with the underage staff, and her brother dangling from the rafters, leaving her alone with herself, and her father who actively avoided her, moving around the house like a mouse, terrified the cat might catch him and ask for a conversation, some love, some parenting, and her mother, her stupid fucking mother, the one who loved her and brushed her hair from her forehead while she cuddled her in bed and told her fairy tales of wolves in the woods, only to abandon her, to fail her family by losing her damned mind. Maybe Cassie was due for the same, maybe Cassie's punches, and kicks, and hate, true, boiling hate bubbling from her guts, out of her lungs in a growl, out of her fists in a flurry of punches, was just the buildup to some great, monumental self-destruction, all of it a fucking sign of what's coming. All of it. Fuck all of it.

She slammed her foot upward, banging the top of it against the tub spout. The metal protrusion tore into the skin on the bridge of her foot and cracked into the tarsal bones. She kept kicking. More blood. More pain.

Fuck. Fuck. Fuck. It felt so fucking good.

Chapter 5

Violent Noise

"You're allowed to be angry, Cassiopeia. You're allowed to feel whatever you want."

―――――

After her shower, she dressed the wound on her foot with an elastic bandage wrap. She put a paper towel around her knuckles. They'd dry up quickly and she'd easily explain them away. Her hands were always cracked and bleeding from spending hours dipping her hands in and out of freezing cold water while she ran trials on her lobsters.

She debated on what to wear for babysitting, wanting something casual and comfortable but not something that would make the wealthy Renards cringe. After much debate, she chose black slacks, a white tee, and a black cardigan. Whatever.

Her anger tempered once she stepped out of the shower, but didn't fully quell until she was dressed and packed. Her heart rate simmered into a steady rhythm, and the tremble in her hands dissipated into the atmosphere. She hadn't lost her foreboding dread over a day hellbent on fucking with her, but she eased into the idea that it was out of her control anyway. All she could do was move forward and beware of falling anvils.

On the drive, Cassie sat upright, her back tilted forward like an old woman, in her 1996 Volvo S90. She stretched her eyes wide and tapped her hands against the steering wheel. An early 2000s emo playlist blasted Asking Alexandria through the speakers. She worked hard to keep her tiredness at bay while she drove, tightening her hands around the wheel, looking at each side of the road, back and forth. Thankfully, no tractor-trailers crossed into her lane, nor had she veered into anyone else's.

After constantly operating on zero sleep, she mastered the techniques needed to keep herself alert. Famous last words, she supposed.

When she arrived, just a few minutes shy of her five o'clock promise, Mr. and Mrs. Renard were already outside waiting for her, looking eager to leave. She parked her beat-up Volvo next to Mr. Renard's McLaren, its shiny, black coat taunting her flecked and rusty car. Mrs. Renard called it the family "toy," not to be confused with their other three vehicles, which had more utilitarian roles, like for driving to work, or heavens to Betsy, the supermarket.

"Thank goodness you're here," Mrs. Renard said. "We had to cancel our invite to dinner because something much more pressing has come up. We really need to leave, but I'll explain later." She flew down the steps and gave Cassie a light, quick hug as her husband pressed past them, hitting the unlock button on his key fob. The McLaren's headlights flashed and the alarm made a robotic beep.

As Mrs. Renard hurried to follow her husband, face riddled with anxiety, she craned her neck back toward Cassie. "You know the ropes by now. Make yourself at home."

Cassie watched them drive away before stepping inside. She wondered what the emergency was. She assumed it had just come up because the Renards were dressed for a fancy dinner.

Mr. Renard sported a sleek, black suit, and his wife donned a matching tight, black dress. She even had on her classic pearl necklace she wore only on special occasions.

Cassie clicked the front switch, and the bright strip lights illuminated every inch of the downstairs. In front of her, the kitchen glowed an inviting, off-white shine. The back wall beyond the kitchen was all glass, showcasing the large, bright-green lawn. A cement path cut through the yard, solar lighting on each side, making its way from the back door to the patio area with the hot tub.

Cassie plopped her backpack on the kitchen table and sighed. Something about the Renard house acted as an anti-anxiety drug, a shot to the arm, loosening her muscles, kneading away the tension.

Anxious as she was to find something to fix her necklace, Cassie was also a girl of routine. If she didn't follow her normal pattern when entering the Renard house, she'd stress herself out that something horrible would happen for changing it up. Not that she wasn't already worrying about that, with how her day started and all. She'd hunt for pliers in the junk drawer and garage in a little while.

James was upstairs playing his video games. He was shouting at the television amidst a chorus of explosions and *KAPLOOPS*.

Cassie ignored the volatile sounds echoing through the house from James's bedroom and walked the perimeter of the downstairs, as she always did. She enjoyed the artwork on display, despite knowing nothing about art or what made it good or bad. All she knew was the colorful pieces, often just splashes of paint, chaotic yet contained, spoke to her.

She rubbed her index finger on the bottom of the mounted television, a machine larger than Cassie's bed. If only she had the time to flop onto the couch and binge one of her comfort shows: *Justified*, or *The Office*. Maybe she could even check into that *Winter's Myths* television show everyone either loved or hated. But she knew if she let herself relax too much, she'd never rip herself away to get some homework done. She'd either fall fast asleep or get sucked into whatever show she put on. Besides, she had a second part to her ritual that needed doing, and the next part was her favorite.

She stepped into the yard and followed the solar lights to the deck, where she sat and took a long, meditative breath, enjoying the cool, fall air, gently chirping crickets, and the glowing moon breaking the horizon behind the columns of trees in the forest which fenced in the Renard property. Taking her therapist's advice, she inhaled through her nose, exhaled through her mouth, feeling the air travel into her diaphragm and out her lungs.

As hard as she tried, she never landed in a true meditative state. She had used apps for guided breathing, taken classes, watched YouTube videos, but none of it got her there. The breathing helped relax her, sure, but her mind never cleared of her surroundings. She was always acutely aware of a random, tiny itch building behind her knee, or a low, whirring noise from the electricity. Something always pulled her back. Still, she enjoyed doing it, and there in the quiet yard, secluded and beautiful, she drenched herself in the clean air like it was bathwater.

As a sense of peace coursed through her veins, she was shaken from it violently.

A plane flew above her head with such speed and at such a low altitude, it shuddered the house and deck, shocking every fiber of her being. The hair on her arms stood on end and a scream escaped her.

With her heart pounding and her pulse throbbing, she laughed at herself. "Oh, holy fuck. That was terrifying."

After the laugh, disappointment set in. It truly was like the gods had it out for her, not even willing to give her a moment of meditation.

She headed in to check on James and find something to fix her necklace before diving headfirst into her books. The plane must have scared the shit out of James, too, but maybe planes did that all the time over here. She'd never heard them before, but Cassie only babysat in the evenings. Maybe that day was a different schedule for the planes or something.

As she opened the back door, nerves still on edge, another plane flew by with equal force, sound, and speed. Having experienced it once did nothing to stop the startling effect it had on her. Again, she screamed. Again, her heart rattled in her throat. Again, she nearly fell over. There was no way this was something that happened often, or the Renards would have surely moved out and probably caused quite the fuss with the realtor.

When she entered the kitchen, James stood at the bottom of the second-floor steps. "What the fuck was that?"

"It was a plane, and your mom would kill you for talking like that. No swearing."

"Oh, okay." He shrugged and turned to head up the stairs but stopped himself. "Oh, hi Cassie. I didn't know you were babysitting tonight."

"Your parents had dinner plans, but then some kind of emergency came up and they rushed out of here."

James showed no interest in what his parents were doing. "Cool. I'm going back to my games."

"Wait. Before you do, I have a question. Do your parents have a toolbox anywhere? Specifically, I need pliers."

He shrugged. "I don't know about pliers, but my dad has a bunch of tools in the garage. He's actually great at building stuff, believe it or not."

Mr. Renard gave off an air of royalty, the type of man who avoided getting his hands dirty and hiring an army of blue-collar folks to do his bidding. Cassie wouldn't have guessed him for a hands-on builder type, and apparently, James understood the surprise of it, too.

Cassie nodded, and another plane flew by. They both jumped as the house trembled, like it, too, had a blast of nervous adrenaline shooting through it. Then, another plane and without a second to relax, another. The constant sound and shock of it was violent, hostile, a corruption. She yelped each time. It never got easier.

A new sensation washed over her. Anger. The planes, like the scratching above her head as a child, were unrelenting, taunting, forcing her away from her responsibilities, and she couldn't help worrying they would lead to the same conclusion: something awful, something dreadful. Yes, she feared that, but more so, it infuriated her. She'd lost too much, dealt with enough trauma to last a lifetime.

Outside forces always impeded her life's forward projection, and she was sick of it. She stared at the ceiling, waiting for another eruption of noise.

After a moment of silence, James slowly tilted his head down, bringing his eyes to Cassie. "What's going on?"

She looked at him, trying to stop her wide eyes from revealing her own terror and fury. "I don't know. This isn't normal around here?"

He laughed uncomfortably. "No. I've never heard a plane come by here before. I mean, I see them way up in the sky, but I have never heard *that* before."

A disquieting shiver wormed up her spine. Something felt off. Wrong. But, the planes had stopped, and her worrying about it would not help. What could she do, stare at the ceiling, eagerly awaiting another violent swoosh? Her nerves fired like a shotgun, and she suddenly had an urge to leave, to pack up and tell James he was on his own. Bye-bye, Renards. But she couldn't. That wasn't the Cassie way.

James waited for her to tell him not to worry about it, but the words never came. Instead, Cassie stared out through the curtain wall, into the yard, waiting for another plane to blast by, another disruption, another sign something was very wrong.

Unpack your backpack, she told herself. It would keep her planted, force her to stay put and focused. If she let herself head down a spiral of worry, she'd spend the night thinking of every possible disaster, none of which would come, but her night would be ruined anyway from the stress.

James relented and went back upstairs.

Cassie slid her Neurobiology text out of her backpack, placed her notebook and pen on top, and sighed at the overwhelming amount of work she had to do. She debated on skipping it all, going to find the pliers, fixing her necklace, and giving up for the night. She talked herself into sitting, where she stared at her book.

Night crept in and a shroud of darkness hovered around the bright lights of the Renard house. Her eyes fought against her, and when she glanced at her book, her vision blurred. With her palms holding her head up, pressed tightly to her cheeks, she slipped gently into sleep. She awoke a few minutes later with her head on the table, tucked into the fold of her arm.

Something had changed. The lights were flashing. They dragged her from the depths of darkness, luring her back to life. She lifted her head slowly, gathering her bearings. Maybe the lights were in her dream, something she carried with her to the waking world until her mind coalesced. But the more she woke, the more defined the lights became. And then she heard a whistle, an intermittent blare. The shrill noise came like a slap to the face, a blast of cold water. She was awake.

She turned her head left and right, trying to figure out the source of the noise and the flashing lights. It didn't make sense because it was everywhere, all around her, a sensory assault. But then she figured it out, and her heart plummeted.

Someone had set off the house alarm.

Someone had broken in.

Chapter 6

The Long Day

"People are like Vampires. If you invite them in, they will drain you."

———

The open floor plan of the Renard house felt less open as Cassie stood up, checking to see where someone might be hiding. New nooks and obstacles, dark corners and blockades made themselves known. The space behind the couch grew twofold, and the stretch of shade on the far side of the living room darkened.

She moved with slow steps, eyeing every direction but eager to turn the alarm off. The blaring noise muddled her brain, making it difficult to concentrate on finding the source. She gripped her cellphone in her hand, as if she could wield it against an intruder. *Stop or I'll use this to dial 911!*

James barreled down the stairs with his palms to his ears. "What happened?"

"I don't know. Can you turn it off?"

He ran to the white box by the front door and hit a series of buttons. The noise stopped and the flashing white lights died.

"Does it ever go off on accident?"

"No. You really have to mess with the door or windows." As he noticed her concern, his cheeks sunk into his mouth.

She pulled on the front door. Locked. "Stay with me. Let's check all the windows and doors."

They skirted the walls and walked in a circle around the downstairs. The living room windows were all locked and unbroken, and they found the same with the dining room. The wall of windows in the kitchen remained intact, and the backdoor was also locked.

James shrugged. "I guess it was nothing."

"Maybe another plane flew by and somehow set it off?"

"Nah, I would have heard it. I had my headphones on, but those planes were super loud."

She nodded. "Yeah, I would like to think it would have woken me up."

He giggled. "You fell asleep? Good babysitting."

She gave him a gentle push. "Yeah, yeah. I had a long day."

"I'm just messing with you. I guess I'm going to go back to my game."

She followed him. "Wait. Let me check the upstairs first, just in case."

They marched up the L-shaped stairs. When they reached the center, where a wall blocked the view from downstairs, Cassie's fists clenched. The first floor was garnished with lights, but upstairs was a black hole.

At the top, a long hallway with hardwood floors went from a master bedroom on the left to a family bathroom far down on the right. A series of miscellaneous other rooms hid behind doors on both sides of the hallway. The stairwell ended in the center of it all.

Across the hall was Mr. Renard's computer room, then a workout room, and finally James's bedroom. On the side with the stairwell was a cleaning closet on the left and a meditation room on the right.

Except for a television flickering from James's room, all was dark.

"Is there a light in the hallway?" Cassie asked.

James groped at the wall until a bright light showered them with sight. Her heart settled a little.

She checked the master bedroom first, which made Cassie a little squirmy, not enjoying the invasion of privacy. For the sake of thoroughness, she checked the windows, the closet, and under the bed, all the routine searching for monsters she would have done if James were four-years-old and ready for bed.

She tried to keep her eyes focused on searching for an invader, but a quick scan of the Renard's bookshelf revealed shelves of psychology texts, which was expected, and two shelves of thick texts on various mythologies, cryptids, and assorted other fictions, which was not expected. *The History of Werewolves in New England. 18th Century Vampire Lore. The Complete Index of Eastern Demons. Lampposts, Grief, and Monsters of the Mind.*

James waited for her outside the room. As she exited the room, he stared wide-eyed. "Anything?"

She bit her lip and shook her head. "No."

Mr. Renard's computer room offered another surprise. Four monitors showed surveillance video footage of a prison. Cassie slapped her hands over her mouth. Each camera focused on a single cell, and all four cells housed a prisoner sleeping on a cot. Mr. and Mrs. Renard were doctors, and as far as Cassie knew, they didn't run any prisons. Even if they had, would the law allow them to monitor the prisoners on camera from their own home? It was too bizarre for her to wrap her head around, but an unease tugged at her brain. *Get the fuck out of here, now!*

Outside of those videos, the room appeared like any other work room - stacks of paperwork, laptops, a printer. Cassie couldn't focus on the video, even if she'd never stop fully thinking about it. She needed to make sure no one had broken into the house, so she quickly checked the windows, ran out of the room, and told herself to forget what was on the other side.

The exercise room, James's room, and the bathroom were all fine and all without surprises. The meditation room gave the biggest shock of all. When Mrs. Renard had given Cassie the house tour, she opened the doors to the bathroom, the workout room, and James's room but kept the rest shut. Cassie now understood why Mrs. Renard neglected to open Mr. Renard's computer room. At the time, it all felt like a need for privacy. Who would want to show the college kid their master bedroom, and a computer room which probably held secret patient information? But when Mrs. Renard shied away from opening the door to the meditation room, Cassie wondered what was worth hiding in there.

She never expected the answer that would come as she pulled the door open with James standing too close behind her, peeking over her shoulder to get a view. Maybe he, too, hadn't been allowed to enter the meditation room, though the Renards made no effort to lock it. She expected a room littered with cross-cultural meditative markings, the typical spackle of spiritual tapestry that a rich, white woman would patch together to act in tune with both Eastern and Western practices. A yin-yang, a flowing Buddha fountain, Catholic and Celtic crosses, but none of those were present.

The room was littered with grotesque machines and primitive weapons. Crudely made wooden stakes, a jaw trap straight out of a Looney Tunes cartoon, chains, whips, and devices she couldn't begin to understand, but were clearly meant for torture. While the existence of these items might have startled her, she could explain them away. How many rich folks collected ancient weaponry? Some of it looked like the kind of thing Frasier Crane might have adorned in his fancy Seattle apartment. But what scared her out of her skin was the blood. All the weapons were caked in dried and flaking maroon.

Again, she tried to convince herself it was all for show, that the weapons were painted to appear used, but droplets speckled the hardwood floor around the weapons as well. Tied to the video footage in Mr. Renard's computer room, a picture formed in Cassie's mind, one where the Renards were kidnapping and torturing people. *The meditation room,* they'd called it.

Cassie lost her balance, leaned hard on the door stile. She needed to leave.

"What's that?" James asked, pointing to the floor.

She didn't want to look. More blood, probably. She willed herself to keep her head up, worried if she examined the weapons and floor any longer the horror would only grow. Maybe it would be *fresh* blood this time.

Instead, she eyed the window. The window. Her heart sank. How did she miss it? Something had shattered the window. Smashed it to bits. A cool breeze crept in through the gaping wound.

James pushed his way into the room, ducking under the arm Cassie used to hold herself upright.

"Look," he said, pointing to something on the floor.

She forced a glance and saw it. Broken glass. Tiny slivers, shimmering like snowflakes against the room's mellow, dim glow. An orgy of glass. Cassie stepped, horrified, as if putting herself in the room would make her a victim, the next to feel the biting lash of a whip as a mysterious force dragged her to a dungeon where the Renards would monitor her on camera before executing her with primitive weaponry.

Who was she afraid of here? The people she babysat for, who had been Cassie's family therapists all those years ago? An intruder? Some clandestine outside force which smashed an upstairs window? All of them? Enemies everywhere. Maybe it was none of them. Maybe Cassie's overtired mind convinced her to fear everything, to think some video mattered. It was probably old, a VHS tape from an experiment done in the seventies Mr. Renard was studying for a scientific article he planned to write. Maybe the weaponry had a similar purpose, or maybe rich assholes liked to collect weapons that had actually been used. It probably added a little value to the collection when it had some spots of blood on it. Somewhere out there, a man with a website got richer by coating that shit with animal blood and selling it under the pretense it was used in some great and holy war from hundreds of years ago.

The window, too. There wasn't anything under the window, nothing an intruder could stand on or climb up to. No dormers or edgings. Maybe the planes had smashed it when they flew by. It made sense. The whole fucking house shook.

She told herself all of this, taking the big *meditative* breaths her therapist recommended, but it did little to quell her nerves. Her brain had worked all day to make her feel off-kilter. That sense of dread roiling in her chest meant something. She knew it. And then James found it, the catalyst, the object that would roll her from foreboding straight into a living nightmare.

He checked the floor, kicking sticks and spikes out of the way, little shards of glass clinking as he swept the hardwood with his foot. "Maybe someone threw a rock or something," he said as he searched.

She wanted to help him or tell him to quit and shut them out of that fucking room forever, but her nerves were frayed, so she stayed by the door, wrapping her arms around herself and pulling the cardigan taut.

James continued kicking as she dazed out the broken window. A darkness shrouded the woods across from the front yard, despite the moon's cool glow. Her whole body ached. When anxiety hit, she tightened all her muscles, clenched her jaw, walked on arched feet, leaving her whole body with the same type of soreness she felt after a heavy workout.

James bent down and picked something up. It was small and gold. "What's this?"

She squinted, leaned forward.

"What the fuck?" she said, reaching out to grab it.

As it plopped into her hand, panic took over. She grabbed the top of James's head. "Duck. And get the fuck out of here."

She grabbed his arm, keeping her head down, and ran from the room. With her foot, she slammed the door shut.

"Is that what I think it is?" James asked.

"Yes, it's a bullet. Spent."

"What kind?"

She pushed him toward the stairwell. "I don't fucking know. It's not a shotgun bullet. Some kind of handgun. How can you tell the difference?"

He shrugged. "I don't know. I've never seen one in real life before."

Maybe it was a hunter, someone who misfired in the woods, but who would hunt so close to a residential neighborhood? It had to be against the law. And the trajectory made no sense. Were they trying to shoot a deer in the sky?

Racing through ideas on what to do next, Cassie decided to pack James up, get in her car, and get the fuck out of there for a while. She could text Mrs. Renard and tell her they went to get fast food or something.

As they marched down the hall, someone shouted outside. It was close enough to hear, which meant someone was on the Renard property. They were trapped.

Then another voice shouted, and another, until an unintelligible shouting match occurred somewhere in the darkness looming over the thick, black oaks by the front yard.

"Stay here," she said to James.

She creeped back to the meditation room and glanced out the window. She couldn't see anyone but heard their voices more clearly and pinpointed the source of the argument as coming from the stretch of oaks right on the side of the Renard property. The bullet casing rolled in her palm, and she flew out of the room, away from the windows. What the fuck was she thinking sticking her head where a bullet had just traveled?

As she slammed the door shut, the lights and sirens blared again just as someone pounded on the front door.

James screamed, and Cassie's heart charged into her throat. The pain in her chest doubled and beat against her ribs like a small creature trying to rip its way free from inside her. Holy fuck. The walls closed in. She couldn't breathe. What could she do? Where could they go? She knew she couldn't open the front door, but maybe they could escape out the back. If they had to run, she'd be taking them right into the same woods the voices came from, albeit from the opposite side, but who knew what lingered in those woods? They could get lost. How deep was the forest? How far in would they go before seeing another residential area? And they'd be running in the dark.

She couldn't think with the shrill alarm blasting in her brain.

As the alarm chirped deafening sounds, the shouting from outside grew loud enough she heard it over the siren.

A fresh voice came from the bottom of the stairs.

Right below them.

Inside.

Chapter 7

Disappear Completely

"Hide and seek is fun, Cassiopeia, but just one time, I wish they could never find us."

———

James ran to her. "Someone is downstairs," he whispered.

She grabbed him by the shirt and pulled him into his bedroom. If gunshots were firing wildly from the front side, she wanted to be in a room near the back.

Cassie closed the door as quietly as her frazzled mind allowed her hands to work. "Turn the television off. Do you have a lock?"

He pushed in front of her and clicked the turn lock on the knob. She rubbed the sides of the television with trembling hands, searching for an off switch. Before she could find one, he grabbed a remote and powered the TV off, its soft glow disappearing and wrapping them in total darkness.

She realized she trapped them but saw no other option. The voice came from the bottom of the stairs. Where could they go?

The alarm screeched, each new whine sending her heart on a rampage.

"What should we do?" James asked.

"Shhhh," she said.

Thanks to the deafening alarm, she couldn't hear anything else. Was the man coming up the stairs? She didn't know. He wasn't talking anymore.

She led James to the side of his bed, away from the door, and ducked down.

He mimicked her. His breath was ragged, eyes bulging from his skull.

She cupped her hand over his, felt the violent shakes from his trembling body. It was like sitting next to an overfull washing machine. He'd never keep quiet enough. The intruder would hear him. Cassie's chest was pounding, her own breath not much softer than the boy's.

She looked up and peeked out the window, gauging whether they could jump if she heard the intruder on the second floor. The green grass was probably only twenty feet down, which didn't look terrible from inside, but she assumed if she had to make the jump, it would feel much worse.

Where would they go? The yard stretched for a long distance, traveling to the patio and the gazebo before turning to thick woods. How much running would they have to do before finding people who could help them?

James looked at her, hoping for answers the way a young person often thinks the adult in the room will save them. But then he provided her with an answer. "Your phone!" he pointed to her hand.

She twisted her wrist. Her phone! How could she be so stupid? She flicked the screen open. The Face ID circle spun and gave her a check mark. Her trembling fingers struggled to open the caller app, but when it did, she nailed 911 on the first try. Score one for experience.

Nothing happened. No ringing. No answer. Just silence. She hung up and tried again. Same result.

"Do we not have Wi-Fi?" she whispered.

"Isn't 911 supposed to work even without Wi-Fi?" James asked.

She tried again, and again, but nothing happened.

Through the shrill cries of the alarm, she heard the man downstairs. He shouted, and a few more voices joined in. More than one person was in the house.

Boom. Boom. Boom.

Someone fired three gunshots in rapid succession.

James screeched.

Cassie hugged him, not trying to comfort him but to silence him by pressing his face into her shoulder. A deadly world was closing in on them, and she knew they'd only survive if no one knew they existed at all. Disappear completely. She'd done it before, spent her whole life blending in, fading into the surroundings, masking who she really was.

James stopped screeching, turning it into full-on sobs. His tears wet her shirt.

"Shhhhh," she said again.

More shouting. She turned to the window, wondering if she'd know the right time to jump. There were too many voices shouting downstairs, so she couldn't determine the number of people in the house. If one came up, and she jumped down, would she land next to the others? She wished she could make out their words or get some indication of what was happening.

A murder probably occurred a few feet below her. If the killers knew other people were in the house, they'd surely kill them too. She'd watched enough crime shows to know a killer never left witnesses behind. But why did they choose to murder someone in this house? Who the fuck were these people? Was it a gang fight? Mobsters? What the fuck was happening, and why was it happening here?

She didn't know. How the fuck could she? It wasn't normal life to have men intruding in your home to kill each other. It wasn't normal life to blind yourself for your roommate. It wasn't normal life to witness your mother getting dragged out of the house by police. And it wasn't normal life to walk up a flight of stairs to find your brother hanging from the rafters. This wasn't fucking normal life, and she wondered what it was about her that acted as a magnet for insanity.

A voice yelled something right outside the door. Someone made their way up, and he stood just a few feet away.

Cassie cried too, but she kept herself silent, breathing through her nose.

James almost yelped but Cassie caught him, driving her open palm over his mouth. His tears dripped on her index finger. If they were lucky, the blaring alarm would drown out their heavy breaths and whimpering.

She pressed her face to the rug, staring under the bed and into the crack in the door. Movement. She couldn't see anything distinguishable, only the movement of shadows.

Jesus, she felt like she could die. The banging in her ribs, the throbbing in her temples. Her throat closed up. The walls and bed constricted, squeezing her. The air grew thick, too thick, too hard to breathe. It felt like inhaling gravel, and she had to fight the urge to cough. Her lungs begged for it, scratching and tickling.

Another plane flew overhead.

Cassie screamed, caught herself too late, and plugged her mouth with her palm.

For a moment, nothing happened. Maybe the noise from the plane overpowered her scream, stopped the man in the hall from hearing her. The entire house rattled and shook.

As soon as the plane was out of earshot, the man shouted, yelling to someone somewhere else in the house. It must have spooked him, too, because his voice was severe. Whatever language he spoke, it wasn't English, and Cassie couldn't tell what it was, despite a working understanding of French, Spanish, German, and even a little Russian.

As the man ran away from the door and down the stairs, Cassie pushed James off her. "Stay here, keep an eye out the window. Let me know what you see when I come back."

"Where are you going?" He gripped his fingers onto her cardigan.

She pulled it free. "Just across the hall. I want to see if they're leaving."

After a few minutes of waiting, she gathered the nerve to pry the door open, centimeter by centimeter. No one stood in the hall. The voices weren't yelling below.

She walked on tiptoe across the hall, opened the door to the meditation room, and creeped in, ducking low in case any more wild shots were fired. Across the yard, three men darted into the woods. A slight release of panic left her, but not all of it. She didn't know how many were in the house, hopefully just the three. She wouldn't feel safe going downstairs until Mr. and Mrs. Renard came home, but holy hell, did she want that fucking shrill alarm to shut up.

Cassie went back into the bedroom. "Anything?" she said.

James shrugged. "Nothing. Are they gone?"

"I think so. I saw three of them leaving, but I don't know how many were down there."

They stared at each other, hopeless and scared.

"I think I am going to turn the alarm off. I'll check if anyone is down there."

His face lit up with terror and he reached for her. "Please don't. What if you die?"

"I think it's okay," she said, trying to convince herself.

She creeped down the hall and listened for a second. Nothing. One step at a time, she worked her way to the landing in the middle of the stairs where it turned. She peeked around the wall and bit back a yelp. A body lay between the kitchen and living room, blood splattered along the wall and more of it pooling around the corpse.

The dead man was fat and burly with a long, black beard. Red leaked onto his green, camouflage outfit, and one of his giant black boots had somehow separated from his foot and stuck crookedly against the wall and a chair.

She forgot the alarm also shot out blinding white lights along the edges of the house, because that didn't happen upstairs, but as they shined in her eyes every two seconds, she'd surely never forget it again.

She finished her descent and reached for the alarm panel but realized she had forgotten the code. After digging her phone out of her pocket, she scrolled through months of messages between her and Mrs. Renard to find the text where Mrs. Renard gave it to her.

When she finally found it, she pressed the buttons but stopped on the last one. If the men were leaving, should she change anything? Would stopping the alarm make them come back to investigate? Fuck. Every choice felt like the wrong one.

She couldn't take it anymore and no matter what she chose, she'd never feel safe, so she pressed it.

The noise stopped; the lights gave up their blare. Silence stole the night, but instead of liberating her, it draped over her like a heavy overcoat on a boiling summer day.

Every inch of movement felt like a threat, a potential neon sign. She moved to the steps, hypersensitive to each sound - her pants ruffling, shoes touching hardwood.

As she stepped on the first stair, another plane flew by.

She dropped her phone just as it lit up and sent off its own siren. As far as she knew, her phone had never done that before. She received a warning once that a hurricane was approaching, but it came with the normal text alert sounds. The noise it made now was just as beefy and disruptive as the house alarm.

She picked it up and ran up the stairs, fearful the extra noises had alerted the men and would bring them back. When she reached the top of the stairs, she glanced at the screen, but with her mind running through a dozen things, she couldn't comprehend it so she gave up trying. Instead, she dashed into the meditation room and checked the window. The men were no longer in sight, which meant they had gone deeper into the woods or were inches from the front door.

She went back to her phone, looking only to silence it, but this time she deciphered the words.

> Emergency Alert: Seek shelter immediately.
> To find the nearest shelter go to…

"What the fuck?"

James stood on the threshold. "What's going on? What do we do now?"

She shook her head, the walls closing in. "I think America is under attack or something. I don't know."

"What do you mean?" His voice cracked as he asked the question.

"I don't know. I don't know. It says to seek shelter. Hold on. There's a link in the message or something that will tell us where to go. I don't want to drive out of here. There are men out front somewhere."

He put his hand up. "Wait. My dad has a bunker."

Chapter 8

Fastball to the Face

"Do you feel the way the dirt sifts through your fingers? This is knowledge, slowly filling your brain. The more you let in, the more you know and the more you can see the stones and gems hidden within. But do you see that mound of dirt? That's all you've yet to learn. Dumb people will glance at the mound of dirt and think they know it all. But the smart ones will keep sifting, knowing they'll never understand it. Complacency is weakness, Cassiopeia."

———

Cassie's eyes widened. "Where?"

"It's in the yard, but it's hidden. You've probably walked over it a dozen times."

She dragged him into his bedroom and glanced out the window. For the moment, all was silent. "Where exactly?"

He pointed out past the gazebo and the deck, toward the edge of forest surrounding the property. "It's before the woods, but not much."

She nodded and took a deep gulp of air. "Okay. We can do this. We just have to do some running."

As if the God of Go Fuck Yourself heard her and wagged his finger, three planes flew by in succession, and two men broke through the tree line into the yard. One held his finger on the trigger of a sleek, long gun strapped around his chest. The two men turned their heads left and right, searching for something. No, not searching. Hiding. They were hiding from something.

Cassie wanted to bellow with confusion and rage. This was insane. Planes and war and guns. Even if she made it to the bunker, what would that mean for her life? Would she be trapped for days, months, fucking years with no one else but a weird kid? Could she keep them alive, even in the bunker? What if one of them cut themselves and got an infection? Who would administer antibiotics? Did the bunker even have medicine? Did it have anything? Was it just four walls and some rationed cans of tuna and beans? Was the world really collapsing around her?

"What do we do?" James whispered.

She answered with an assured sense of confidence she didn't truly possess. "We wait. As soon as they move, we book it to the bunker. You sure you can tell exactly where it is?"

He nodded, but his eyes gave him away.

Cassie's heart drummed in her ears, a steady but solid beat, like the slow opening to a metal song where you know it's just building up to a cacophony of chaos and noise. The stillness outside was maddening. There was always a pause before violence, a final breath before your lungs collapsed. She imagined it was something like what athletes called "being in the zone." It was a weird quiet where even the birds and crickets knew to shut up, the wind, the small electric whirring that always plays background noise, all of it dead, Earth itself sucking in a gulp and holding it before crying.

"They aren't moving. They're in our way," James said.

Cassie grabbed his hand. "Let's sneak downstairs and watch out the kitchen windows. The less space between us and the bunker, the better."

They creeped down the stairs, and Cassie startled at the sight of the dead guy on the floor between the living room and kitchen. It was amazing she could forget such a horrible sight. But, then again, a tree falling is only terrifying when there's not a wildfire devouring the forest. Meanwhile, James cried at the sight. For now, Cassie ignored him.

The two men were in the same place, but now they faced the woods instead of the house, and they squatted behind the gazebo to hide from whatever unknown entity threatened them in the woods.

Nothing happened.

All quiet.

All still.

A plane flew by, and James tightened his grip on Cassie's hand. They both jerked back a little, but neither screamed like they had in the past.

Something was different about the plane, something obvious, but Cassie's fried brain didn't connect it until it was too late. The plane dropped something. She watched it fall in the same way a curious child would watch a shooting star. The object dropped below the tree line, disappearing into the swell of darkness within the forest.

It took a moment but then, *boom!* An explosion erupted, shaking the house. Hell, maybe the entire world. The trees evaporated behind a growing orange ball. A visible wave shot from the forest, crashing through the yard, destroying the gazebo, smashing through the deck and spa, before shattering the wall of windows around Cassie and James.

Cassie screamed but couldn't hear herself.

As glass poured over them, James's mouth opened so wide his jaw looked ready to unhinge, probably screaming too, but again, Cassie heard nothing but a loud, incessant ringing. The wave of heat threw them both into the wall. They crashed onto the floor amidst an ocean of glass.

"Go. Now," she shouted into the silent void.

The explosion devoured the men in the yard, so this was their chance. She jumped through the ghost of the curtain wall and ran. A plane flew just above her, but without her hearing, it failed to startle like the others had. She turned to make sure James followed because only he knew where to find the bunker.

Parts of the yard were on fire, patches of flickering reds and oranges, so Cassie couldn't run in a straight line. She slalomed around the blazes, running with all the speed and might she possessed. Whether James kept up, she didn't know, and if she were being honest with herself, didn't give a fuck other than only he knew the exact placement of the bunker doors. He had pointed, which gave her some semblance of direction, so if he died, fell too far behind, burned up in a fiery explosion, she'd mourn him tomorrow from the safety of wherever the fuck she was headed.

More balls of fire lit up the sky and the depths of the woods. The rumbles vibrated under her feet each time. She ran for too long, as if the yard were growing, stretching, never letting her hit the finish line.

More men came from the woods. They were holding their hands up and yelling something she couldn't hear. Another group of men came from the other side. They were everywhere, and if they were yelling instructions or threats to her, she couldn't know. Some men held out guns, and she figured out that the two groups were shouting at one another, ready to shoot.

She and James stood between the war, and she was certain not a one gave a shit about the innocent lives in their way. When they reached the outskirts of the yard, James yanked at her. Thank God he kept up. He pushed her from running further and pointed down. His lips moved, but she heard nothing. He rubbed his hands on the grass, searching.

The men were still shouting at each other, but none of them fired their weapons. Some men on both sides waved their guns, and she knew it was only a matter of time before bullets speckled the air like stars.

James tapped her leg. She looked down to see his fingers gripped around a small hook. He pointed to the grass a few feet away. It took her a second to catch on, but then she dropped to her knees and used her palms to search for a second hook.

After a few pats, she found it. She latched her finger through the loop and nodded to James. With his free hand, he put a finger up, then another. One. Two. Three.

She lifted, the muscles in her legs and back tightening and threatening to give up on her. It took a few seconds of using all her might, but the ground gave way and a giant metal bulkhead rose from the earth. The grass stayed on top of it, the perfect disguise if not for the fact they opened it in front of dozens of men. Luckily, those men were too busy with each other to care. She gave them one last glance before following James into the shallow depths of darkness below.

One man aimed his weapon and fired. Streaks of white belched from muzzles all around her.

Her hearing was coming back, but only slightly. She heard a muddled set of booms, as if listening to it on an old tape player in slow motion. It reminded her of Chris's music coming through the walls of her childhood home. She stared for a stupid amount of time, awed by the circle of violence around her. James, already down the steps of the bunker, tapped her leg. She snapped out of it and flew down the steps into pitch blackness.

They reached up to the door and pulled it down. It crashed into place with a bang. Plumes of dust and dirt rained on them.

Her pulse pounding, she slapped at her pockets, searching for her phone. When she found it, she used the flashlight to bring some light into the room. She shined it all over the door, trying to find a lock.

"This circle," she said to James, her own voice still hard to hear.

He gripped the wheel and together they twisted it, using muscles they didn't know they had, until it pulled two bars into place, shutting the world out.

She took labored breaths, coughing on dust particles.

Using her phone, she examined the room. As the dim light

revealed old shelves filled with canned and packaged foods, her hearing came back. Above her, she could hear shouting and gunfire. She turned the phone to the other side of the room to reveal a couch facing a television with an area rug between them.

James reached up and pulled a cord, and a bulb came to life, brightening the room. The bulb sat in a small silver funnel hanging from the ceiling, making the light glow from one side of the room to the other as it dangled back and forth.

Another reminder of Chris.

The violence above her registered as the tension exited her body. All the questions she hadn't had time to consider leaked into her brain, overflowing it. What do they do now? How long would they need to be down here? Were the bombs nuclear? What supplies did the bunker have? Was this her life now? Would she be back to school on Monday listening to dipshits talk about how caaaa-razy their weekend was as other places were bombed and destroyed?

James said, "I wonder if this works." He bent down, examining the television. "Maybe we can get the news or something and see what's happening."

Cassie put her hand up. "Shhhh. What's that?"

He stopped, looked up. "What?"

She put her finger to her lip.

A low grumble, like a revving motor far away.

She turned toward the far wall, opposite where they came in. In the center, a long hallway stretched for who knew how long. She couldn't see far down because the old, dust-covered lightbulb swinging above her did nothing to expose it.

Something was growling. It wasn't a motor. Was it a dog?

"Hello?" she said into the abyss.

The growling grew louder.

And then, rattling chains and loud steps. Something charged down the hall right toward her. As it came into the light, her heart sank and she screamed. It was human. Kind of.

Under its top jaw, the bottom of its face was nothing but raw tendons and hanging red slime. Its eyes were black pools. The thing was naked, its penis flopping as it charged her. Raw wounds stretched across the creature's body.

It happened too fast for her to react, like a fastball to the face.

As it closed the gap between them, an explosion from above blasted and shook the bunker's foundation. A tremendous bang. More dust and plaster poured down. As the creature's face came inches from hers, the lightbulb gave way and drenched them in darkness.

Chapter 9

Blood and Nails

CASSIE, AGE 5

Darkness. That was all there was. When life returned, it came in pieces, small fragments of reality hitting her senses at different points. Noise came first. Screaming. Someone under her howled, pained and terrified.

Her mother's screaming came next. "Cassie? Cassie! What did you do?"

Her father said much the same. His voice was more even, but not without its own fear, as if he was too scared to scream, too awestruck and horrified to release the pressure in his lungs. Instead, he nearly whispered. "Cassie. Cassie. Get off her, Cassie. Jesus."

After hearing came feeling. Something warm and wet in her hand. She looked down to see the thick, crimson streaks on her fingertips, and something hard and sharp pinched between her index finger and thumb. Beyond her hand, something wriggled, drenched in the same red substance.

It flailed and kicked at her. Her body rocked side to side, as if she straddled a surfboard in a tsunami. Her mother grabbed her by the shoulders and shoved her off the squirming and screaming thing.

Cassie fell over onto some cushions, and the wriggling thing stood up, still wailing. It was Jesse, her best friend from down the street. Jesse's lower legs were covered in blood. Tears poured down her face. She lunged into Cassie's father's arms.

None of it made sense. How did she get here? What happened?

Cassie's mother bent low, getting right in Cassie's face. In a kind and motherly manner, she pushed Cassie's hair out of her face, tucking it behind her ears. The room felt wobbly. Swish. Swish. Tipping this way and that.

"Get her cleaned up. Disinfect her feet. Get her bandaged and call her parents," Cassie's mother said.

At first it confused Cassie, because she mistakenly thought her mom spoke to her. "What do you mean?" she asked.

Cassie's mother turned to her father and shouted, "Just do it!"

Oh good, her mother wasn't speaking to her. She didn't feel she had it in her to do chores. Her eyelids grew heavy and her body felt achy and tired. Had she run around too much? She couldn't remember. But her muscles told her a story, one where she must have been very active.

As soon as her father ushered her screaming friend from the room, her mother turned her attention back to Cassie. "I need you to tell me what happened."

Cassie's head drooped, her chin hitting her ribs. Her mother slapped her on the cheek, not hard, but enough to startle Cassie.

"Don't fall asleep. What happened?"

A voice came from Cassie, but it wasn't her own. It was something else, guttural, angry. "You know what happened."

"Yes, I do know, but I want you to tell me."

"I ripped Jesse's toenails off one... by... one." The first time the voice came out, a long time ago, it scared Cassie, this foreign thing flooding from her mouth. She'd grown accustomed to it by now, but she never expected it to come out with her family present.

54

Cassie's mother bit her bottom lip, her eyes filling with water. "Why? Why are you doing this? You're not supposed to do this to *her*."

What an odd bit of talk. The way her mother said, 'her,' in particular. Was she supposed to rip anyone's toenails out?

Cassie gulped, swallowing down the croaky voice and using her own. "I wanted Jesse to feel it, too."

Her mother's eyes lit up with recognition. "You wanted her to feel what, Cassie? Was this revenge? Was Jesse hurting you?"

Cassie shook her head. "No. Jesse is my friend."

She still heard her friend's screams between the floorboards, singing along with the tapping of feet above them.

"If she's your friend, why did you want to hurt her?"

"So she could enjoy the feeling of it too." Cassie wasn't sure who spoke that time, her or the other voice, but she understood the point.

It started a few weeks ago, a nagging pain in Cassie's chest. It didn't hurt; it aggravated, this constant tugging and pulling at her ribs. A day later, the ache extended to other parts of her body. Her knees, calves, wrists. Throbbing. Always. It drove her mad. She couldn't concentrate, couldn't even enjoy watching television. She shifted, stretched, rolled around on the floor. Nothing worked to release the pain. It was like a new friend, someone to sit with her at all times, but it wasn't a friend she wanted. She hated it, hated it so badly. She wanted the new friend dead.

She tossed and turned in her bed one night, trying to fall asleep, but the dull throbbing fought against her. In a fit of rage, she punched herself in the ribs. It hurt, but for a second, the ache went away. She wondered if she hurt herself more, could she remove the annoyance all together? It was worth a try. She snuck downstairs into the kitchen where she climbed onto the counter and grabbed a knife. The bulk of the ache had gravitated toward the Achille's tendons, so she thought it best to start there.

She put her legs in a W on the countertop. Her mother told her never to sit that way, saying it could mess up how Cassie walks, but

Cassie presumed it would be okay for a few minutes; besides, if anything was going to mess up how she walked...

She slammed the knife down, driving it right through the skin between tendon and muscle. The knife tip hit the counter and slid to the side, causing the knife to rub against the tendon, moving it like a bow hair would a violin string.

She didn't scream, didn't yell or freak out, although tears trailed down her cheeks. The pain went far beyond excruciating. Waves of it shot into her brain, overloading her. She *wanted* to scream, to release the building pressure in her lungs, but she couldn't. Something stopped her, like an imaginary hand cupping her mouth. Instead, she yanked the knife out and without a second thought, drove it down through the same spot on the other leg. She let go of the knife, keeping it wedged between her tendon and muscle and covered her own mouth. No imaginary hand was needed that time. She bit her finger, using her teeth to etch out her agony and rage.

The kitchen light clicked on.

Before Cassie could move, her brother stared at her, wide-eyed. "What the heck?" Before Cassie could stop him or come up with some sort of story, Chris ran back upstairs, calling for their parents.

Cassie pulled the knife out and hopped off the counter, unprepared for her legs' inability to hold her up. She collapsed, bright red streaks decorating the white-tiled floor. A parade of feet cascaded down the stairs.

"Cassie?" Her mother's voice was filled with worry.

Her eyes turned to marbles at the bloody site. "What happened?"

Cassie didn't know how to explain it but knew if she tried, she'd get in trouble, so instead she shrugged.

"Jesus," her father said. "What the fuck?"

Cassie's mother scooped her up, hugging her tightly. "We have to take you to the hospital. How did this happen?"

Cassie said nothing. The next thing she knew, she was out in the cold, the freezing night air whipping against her pink sleeping gown.

Her mother buckled her into her car seat.

The whole family packed in.

Chris grumbled and complained that he shouldn't have to go to school tomorrow because he wouldn't get enough sleep, but Cassie's mother told him to shut up.

Fear burned across both parents' faces.

As they drove, her parents asked her a million questions, but Cassie ignored them. She kicked her feet up to see the red seeping through the bandages her mother dressed her calves with.

Chris tapped her shoulder. "Does it hurt?"

Cassie smiled. "It feels so good."

Her mother's head whipped around, her eyes turned to tiny slits. She was trying to read something on Cassie, but Cassie couldn't place what.

"What did you just say?"

"I said it feels so good." She didn't understand why this upset her mother so much, but it did. Her mother knew something. Cassie wanted to know what it was but understood her mother wouldn't tell her.

"Enjoy the feeling of what, Cassie?" her mother asked, snapping her back to the present.

Jesse continued crying upstairs, but the wailing withered into more whiny sobs.

Cassie looked her mother in the eyes, glaring. Anger built inside of her. The other voice took over again. "Pain. I wanted her to feel the joy of pain. You know what I mean better than most. Don't you, Mom?"

Cassie stood up and held Jesse's toenail up for her mom to see. "This is your gift to me!" She popped the toenail into her mouth and chewed. The sharp edges dug into her gums, slicing into the meat. Jesse's dried blood was wet again, mixing with Cassie's own blood and saliva.

Her mother pulled at Cassie's jaw, trying to pry it open. "Get that out of your fucking mouth."

Cassie swung her arms wildly, slapping her mother over and over. She just wanted to finish chewing, to swallow her trophy.

"No. Spit it out. Now."

They fought this way for a few minutes, neither relenting. For Cassie, there was a hunger, a desperate need to eat the nail, but she knew it was something else for her mom. She needed the win for a reason Cassie couldn't understand. Too many secrets.

She gulped, an exaggeration to brag about her victory.

Her mother backed away, shaking her head. She covered her face with her hands. "This can't be happening."

Cassie tilted her head. "What's wrong, Mom?"

Her mother slid her hands away from her face. "I'm going to get you help. There's a woman who knows about this stuff. She can help."

Cassie leaned forward and sharpened her eyes. "Worked wonders for you, bitch. Didn't it?"

Chapter 10

Mapped with Scars

"The answer is almost always in front of you, and it's usually sharp and dangerous. Don't be afraid to cut your way out."

———

Cassie fell on her ass, reacting to the incoming bullet train in the form of a human-but-not-quite-human-thing. Before she stumbled backwards, she felt his hot breath hit her face, it reeked of rot.

James let out ear-splitting cries, not unlike the alarms inside the Renard house.

She didn't know where the human thing was, somewhere in the abyss. She patted the ground frantically, searching for her cellphone she dropped in the fall. With the overhead light out, she couldn't see an inch in front of her and she wondered why the human thing wasn't pouncing on her. Her hair stood on end, her spine shooting shock waves to her brain as she expected a chomp into her flesh any second. Could the thing even bite? He didn't have a fucking bottom jaw.

Slap, nothing. Slap, nothing. *Come on. Come on*, she said to herself.

The human thing growled, which brought Cassie some relief. Not much, but some. The noises he released from his half-mouth came from above, near where her head had been before the fall. He wasn't moving, which meant he wasn't attacking.

Something clinked around the same place the growling came from.

She brushed her hands over the floor, bits of dirt and plaster grinding into her palm, until she hit something and gasped. She latched onto the familiar rectangular shape. It was a dopamine shot into the brain. A thing. Her thing. Something she knew and understood.

She almost tapped the screen, but just as her fingertip neared the place it often went for relief, she remembered if she had sight, so did the thing. And right then, he didn't appear to be moving from where he was. She silenced herself, listening for the thing's growly breath. Thanks to James's cries, she struggled to find the thing's sounds. When she finally caught it, it was in the same place. Not moving. The thing wasn't moving.

She slid her butt backwards. Slowly. If the thing wasn't attacking her because he lost her in the darkness, why wasn't he pouncing on James? It was obvious what side of the room the child was on. Was he deaf? Was he not violent? Maybe they just scared him and he charged defensively. He was here first, after all, which made Cassie and James the intruders.

As she made her way around the couch, the growling shrinking behind her, she felt the human thing eyeing her, could sense his bloodshot eyes piercing. Her skin crawled faster than she did.

The sudden shock of realization dropped her. Jesus. Her world was under attack. All the things that mattered just hours ago: studying, class, work, all vanished, became miniscule dust motes on a globe of horror.

She fell to the floor, a panic attack squeezing her lungs. She wheezed, and a new sound overpowered James's crying, her heart thumping in her ears.

Thump. Thump. Thump.

It throbbed in her temples. How much air did they have down there? It felt thick, like breathing hair gel. Dusty fucking hair gel.

The world was gone. Her new world was too small to begin with, and it only shrunk as a fucking humanoid thing closed it off.

A bead of sweat dripped onto her eyebrow.

She took a big breath in through her nose, forcing her lungs to open, and she put her hand out, reaching the area rug. A breath out through the mouth, and then she pulled. Knees out. Slide forward. One slow slither at a time.

When she reached James, she placed her hands on his knees and he squirmed and screeched, which made the thing growl louder, with more anger in his pitch. Still, he stayed where he was.

"It's me," she said, figuring if his screech hadn't sent the thing charging after them, her voice wouldn't either.

"What's happening?" he asked.

"I don't know. I have my phone. Should I turn the light on?" She asked a child for his advice because they were suddenly on an even playing field. Neither of them had an ounce of experience in the utter insanity happening around them.

He sniffled. "I don't know. Yeah. I think so."

She nodded. Her finger trembled toward the screen. Before she tapped it, she inhaled, steadying herself. Her heart still thumped in her ear.

Thump. Thump. Thump.

Tap.

The phone lit up and she slid her hand down quickly, bringing up the settings. She tapped the flashlight and James came to form within the glowing orb. He was shivering, his teeth clattering together. His skin turned ten shades whiter. She turned, the light dashing along the walls until it landed on the thing.

From that far away, she couldn't make out the creature's features very well, but he stood, reaching forward with his body at a forty-five-degree angle. She scrunched her forehead, understanding. The clinking she heard, and the way the thing's body stretched forward at an impossible angle for one to keep oneself upright, she knew what was happening. She moved around the couch, bringing herself in front of the creature, but a good distance away. He stayed at his weird angle, slashing his arms forward.

"James," she whispered.

"Yeah," his voice cracked.

"I think it's chained up or something."

"What is it?"

She shook her head. "You didn't know about this? What the fuck was your dad doing down here?"

He cried. "I don't know."

She stepped forward, tilting her head. Her newfound knowledge that the thing couldn't get to her made her curiosity boil. Her initial inspection proved true. The thing had no jaw, no tongue. His top teeth had all been removed as well. The landscape of his body was mapped with bruises, scars, and fresh, red slits. It looked like pain traveling from limb to limb, decorating his torso in criss-crosses.

She tilted the light toward his eyes. The thing's pupils dilated, shrinking to black circles within a brown pond. The light angered the creature, and he slashed at her, reminding her she'd gotten a little too close. He couldn't reach her, but she felt the breeze from his attacks, and that meant she was way too fucking close.

She moved the light around the thing, and he snarled his lip at her. The flashlight on her phone only illuminated the beginning of the hall, not giving her any insight as to what existed in the dark void further down, but she saw the thick chain links connecting in a line until they gathered around the creature's neck.

"James, we need to find another light. This room can't be it. We need food and stuff, a bathroom. There has to be more down here, or we are royally fucked." She pulled the light away from the creature and turned it on the kid; his eyes were drenched in terror. "James, snap out of it and help me."

She went over to the shelves opposite the television and before she could dig in, searching for any signs of hope, she dropped her head, resting it on a box. Holy fuck. With the adrenaline subsiding, dizziness washed over her. The tiredness and pain all flooded back. Panic threatened to shut her down again. So many questions. Too much had changed too quickly. She was a pebble in a basin and a dam just collapsed. She needed a minute to fucking think, to figure something out, but pausing could mean dying.

The creature growled, and Cassie spun her phone back toward him. Even knowing the chains kept him in place, fear coursed through her at the idea he would break free, somehow finding his way to her.

She yearned for a moment. Just one fucking moment.

Another bang blasted above her, another death blow to the world she had belonged to just moments before. As the ceiling shook from the blast, James increased his screaming and crying, but Cassie did not. She, at least, had grown accustomed to the nails in her coffin. She wiped the raining dust from her hair.

"Okay. Okay. Fucking think."

She turned back to the shelves. The top two were lined with canned goods and packaged foods, most of which required microwaving, cooking, or heating with boiled water. As far as she saw, the room had neither a stove nor a microwave. She also hadn't seen a friggin' can opener. She dug through boxes on the third shelf down. One was filled with bottles of pills. They were labeled with hand-written stickers, but none of the names meant much to Cassie.

The next box had cleaning supplies, which she guessed from the dust and grime in the room, hadn't been used much. In a box with loose tools, duct tape, and stripped wires, she found a box of four lightbulbs. She took one out and placed it on the ground next to her before going back to the search.

None of the other boxes provided anything useful. Every season of *Friends* on DVD. Mad magazines. A well-thumbed paperback copy of a book called *Modern Vampires and Other Demons: Fact or Fiction*. Nothing useful at all.

The last box was filled with small vials labeled DOG FOOD. She pulled one out of the box and shook it. Inside, a chunky red substance coated the vial wall.

The creature lowered his growl and breathed heavily.

She grabbed her phone and turned it to the thing.

He was snorting and letting out a weird *grrrrr* from deep in its lungs. It reminded her of *The Exorcist*.

Another shiver drove up her spine.

The creature backed up, letting the chain clink on the hard cement floor. Then he slammed his body into the hallway's wall. As soon as he crashed into it, he ran to the other side and slammed into that wall. He did it again and again.

Cassie flinched with each crash, but moved toward him, furrowing her brow. What was he reacting to?

He yelped, howling like a hungry dog.

Fuck.

She ran back to the container labeled "Dog food."

"This?" She waved it. "You want this?"

"What are you doing?" James asked.

Cassie jolted, so lost in her world with the creature, she forgot about James. She shot her arm out and lifted a finger at him. The closer she got to the thing, the more he drove himself from one wall to the next, yelping and groaning.

She popped the top on the container, and the thing freaked out even more, his head jerking from shoulder to shoulder.

"First, let's change the bulb." She talked to the creature as if he was going to respond.

She ran to the bulbs she'd left by the shelves and shifted the couch under the fixture. Standing on the arm, she reached up and twisted the new bulb in. It made a gritty sound as it spun along the grooves. Touching it made the hair on her flesh stand. Her fear of electricity was on full display. She nearly fell off the arm in panic as the creature jolted forward, slashing at her.

The bulb flickered to life, and Cassie jumped down.

After putting the couch back where it belonged, she stood as close as she could get without getting slashed and put the vial in front of her face. For the first time, she smelled the stuff inside. She nearly gagged. It smelled like rotted meat.

"How do you even eat things? You don't have a jaw."

She tilted the vial, and the substance inside oozed to the side. It was mostly liquid, although as thick as BBQ sauce, but there were also chunks of something in there, too, like shredded muscle. She shot her arm forward, hoping the stuff would splash out, wanting to see how the creature reacted to it. The liquid came out, but not as far as she had wished. It glopped a few inches in front of her, while some of it dribbled out of the bottle and down her fingers. She dry heaved, unable to hold it back. The foul smell mixed with the horrid feeling of it dribbling down her fingers broke her.

As she gagged, the creature's eyes lit up at the substance and he ran forward.

Cassie fell over, despite being far enough away to avoid contact.

James went back to screaming.

The creature dropped to his knees and pushed his head forward as much as the chain allowed. He twisted his neck, trying his damnedest to meet the red stuff on the ground.

Cassie stayed in her position, examining the humanoid from eye level. He terrified her, but the scientist in her wanted answers. Something happened as he worked to reach the red stuff, and Cassie's heart stopped dead in its tracks. A shiver took over her, causing her limbs to tremble in dread.

The creature's neck made an awful cracking sound, and his head moved in unnatural positions. An owl. It reminded her of an owl, the way the bird can spin its head 180 degrees, but in this case, the thing's neck was making a popping and crunching sound as if he were breaking his own bones to accomplish the feat.

"Jesus," she whispered.

James said, "What?" dropping his screams down to sniffles and hyperventilating.

She sat up and held the vial in front of her. With more gusto, she flicked her wrist. This time the red stuff went a little further, splattering on the ground within reach of the creature. Some of it landed on the thing's forehead.

His eyes widened and he moaned. The noise from his lungs was horrendous, gravelly and inhuman, but she sensed joy in it, not unlike sexual moans. He scraped its fingers on the dusty floor, picking up the red stuff in his fingers, along with cement, gravel, and grime. With a finger full of the 'dog food,' he shoved his hand into the space where his mouth should have been and jammed his fingers down his throat. The creature gagged and choked as he coated his throat with the substance.

The image haunted her, a confluence of fear and disgust at the unnatural display, melded with shame and pity as the poor, horrid thing struggled to do something as normal and necessary as eating. What had happened to him? Why was he so tortured and abused? Who had the audacity and courage to rip his jaw off?

As the thing rubbed his face in the substance on the ground, Cassie took her first true glance down the hallway. Doors, three on each side. While she could make out the wall at the end of the hall, she couldn't parse the details; the bulb wasn't strong enough to illuminate it fully. But the doors were good enough, they offered hope. Maybe, behind the doors, they'd find a fucking bathroom, a kitchen, a bed to sleep on.

She dropped the vial and rubbed her fingers together, disgusted by how the red stuff made her fingers tough to pull apart. She turned to James, who hovered in a corner, his arms squeezing himself so tightly he looked like he wore a straitjacket.

"There are more rooms," she whispered.

He said nothing, did nothing, just trembled.

When she turned back to the creature, he was looking up at her, red smeared on his forehead and cheeks. Something changed in his eyes, and it happened in a matter of seconds. They turned sharp, alert, and they glowed red. He stood with uncanny quickness, his eyes never leaving her face. If a thing without a bottom jaw could snarl, he was doing it.

Cassie's chest throbbed again, her ribs pressing in. Another panic attack.

The creature didn't run forward this time, and something about that was more threatening, as if the running out of chain only displayed his animalistic nature, his stupidity in not understanding that no matter how hard he tried, he was imprisoned. But here, the way he stood so assuredly, it terrified her. No longer did he resemble a rabid dog in character. No, now he was a monster, true as could be.

He reached his arms out, bending and twisting them. The bones cracked and popped as the elbow shifted to the top. His head tilted to the side, much like Cassie's did when she spent hours watching her lobsters interact. He was studying her. Patient.

As they stared at each other, the creature's confidence grew by the second, while Cassie battled with her legs, begging them to keep her upright, the world grew silent.

For once, silence.

She couldn't even hear James whimpering anymore.

The bottom nub of the thing's face shifted down, and a roar escaped his throat. A battle cry, loud enough to shake the foundation of Cassie's soul. He couldn't speak words, but that thunderous bellow from his lungs spoke volumes.

I'm going to get out of these chains, and I'm going to kill you.

Chapter 11

All the Reasons

"Cassiopeia, it's perfectly normal to lie, but why do you spend so much energy lying to yourself?"

———

The creature paced from one side of the hall to the other, never removing his gaze from Cassie.

She broke herself free from the spell the creature cast over her. It was partly her own doing, the very nature of a college lab girl, incessantly staring at objects, working to make sense of them. But the creature held some sway over her, too. He hadn't quite hypnotized her, but he did *something*, like he spoke directly to her mind, demanding she pay attention.

She'd read a word on the internet once: cacospectamania. She believed the internet invented the word, that you wouldn't find it in Webster's Dictionary, but she liked it nonetheless. Cacospectamania —the obsession of staring at something repulsive. It's more than morbid curiosity. It's a *need*.

If Cassie wanted to survive, she'd have to feed her cacospecta-mania another time. She went back to the boxes, shoveling through them with one hand, searching for something to wipe the gore from her fingers. She found some napkins and hand sanitizer, wiped her hand with the napkin, and poured half the bottle of sanitizer into her palm, rubbing it around until the alcohol solution dried off. It didn't feel like enough. She'd give herself a stress headache over it until she could properly wash them with soap and water, but it would have to do for now.

James stayed in the corner, hugging himself and hyperventilating.

She sat on the couch, positioning herself where she could still monitor the creature, and looked at her phone to check out what the fuck was going on with the first moment she'd had since the first plane flew overhead.

"James, why don't you sit down and play with the television? See if we can get the news or something."

He stayed put, teeth chattering.

"James!" She said it forcefully, not trying to be mean or to yell at him, but to snap him out of it. She needed him fully alert.

It worked. He turned his head toward her.

"Listen to me. I need you to play with the television. See if you can get it working. See if it has cable. Try to find some kind of news program."

Her phone proved useless. She couldn't open any social apps, couldn't get her web browsers working. Nothing. She couldn't even pull up her text messages, although she could see the content on some new messages thanks to her notifications menu still showcasing them.

Hey, what's going on? Are you safe?

Shana and I just went to the school's shelter.

It's fucking weird in here.

> I hope you're okay.

> They're saying NUKES! Fucking NUKES!

> Cassie. I'm scared. I hope you're okay. I don't know if this place is very safe.

> It doesn't feel safe. It's just a basement.

> Cassie. Are we all going to die?

> Please let me know you're alive.

Since all of this started, Cassie had cried a few times, but it was always out of fear, out of confusion and the overwhelming nature of it all. But as she read the messages from Beth, she cried for the first time out of grief, out of loss. She pictured Beth huddled in a basement, squished together with the other students, packed like sardines until bombs blew them to smithereens.

She thought about the world, those small things that brought life to her days - the kind old man who ate at Cuddey's every night, who always tipped well and asked her about her day, the stupid squirrels running free on campus, unafraid of humans, bounding around them and picking up their crumbs, even her father, who she'd grown to despise more and more each passing year. She thought of him sitting alone in the living room, watching the news in complete terror, waiting for death to drop on him from the sky.

She wondered if he thought of her, if he regretted the way he treated her in the end, if he debated on sending her a text message to apologize. She wondered if he considered her at all.

As James fidgeted with the television, the screen remaining black, with just enough light to let the user know it was on, Cassie covered her face with her hands and cried. This was truly it. There was no world anymore. It had all ended. All the days going to class, learning, working double shifts, all for nothing, wasted. Gone. Every fucking moment she'd spent guiding herself toward some perceived happy future was all a damned waste of time. She should have been doing drugs and fucking. Had she ever enjoyed her life? Once? Was there a good day? A time when her mind hadn't been racing to plan out tomorrow?

"It's not working. No cable," James said.

Cassie wiped her eyes. "Come here. Sit down. We need to talk."

A trail of snot ran down James's nose, threatening to hit his lip. He listened and sat next to her.

"I have a lot to tell you, and it's going to be tough to take it all in, but it needs to be said. But first, is there anything you want to ask? Anything you want to say?"

He stared down at his lap.

"How are you feeling right now? Tell me everything," she prodded.

He looked up at her and just like that, his face wilted, a sinkhole razing a cityscape. He covered his face and wiped his hands all over, spreading the snot and tears all over his chubby cheeks. More blubbering.

Cassie said nothing, letting him drain himself out. Lord knew she needed a cathartic breakdown herself. After a few minutes, he eked out some words. "Are my mom and dad...?" He didn't finish the sentence. He didn't need to.

Cassie reached her hand out, putting it on his knee. "Yes, I think they most likely are."

He cried harder.

"Listen, I can't lie to you. I'd like to pretend it's all going to be fine, but the world just fucking blew up. My friend texted me and told me it was nuclear. If that's true, we're stuck down here for a long time. A very long time. Years. And more so, if that's true, I doubt anyone in Rhode Island survived."

He shook his head, still crying. "Why? Why would anyone attack Rhode Island?"

She shrugged, trying to keep calm. "I don't know, James. We have naval bases. Maybe that's why. Or maybe they didn't. Maybe they attacked New York, and we are just in the hot zone. I don't fucking know. I don't study war. I know nothing about this shit."

He looked up, a newfound excitement on his face as if he'd just solved a long puzzle. "But you said my parents had some emergency to get to. They have a lot of friends. Important people. Maybe they knew the bombs were coming and that's what the emergency was."

Cassie tilted her head. "Think about what you're saying. They knew we were about to be attacked, so they left... without you. They had me come over to babysit so they could go somewhere else to hide, when they had a perfectly good, albeit fucked up, bunker in their yard, presumably built for this exact reason."

He tucked his face back into his palms, tears pouring freely. She doubted they'd stop for days, and even when they did, they'd come back. Kids cried for no reason at all, it was part of growing up, and James had all the reasons in the world to cry. Literally.

"Listen, I don't want to stop you from grieving, but we have to talk about something important and I need your absolute full attention." She glanced toward the creature.

He wasn't pacing anymore, but he stood tall, still glaring at her. Whatever she fed him did a number on his constitution. He went from looking like a haggard, damaged, tortured thing, to a confident and crazed killer. Lesson learned. Don't feed the animals. Even without teeth, they might bite.

James put his head in his *Among Us* tee shirt and wiped his face on the inside of it. Once he popped back out, he straightened and looked at her. "Okay."

She smiled at him, hoping to ease his stress, even just a millimeter. "Do you ever watch horror movies?"

He nodded, his eyelashes arching with confusion. "Yeah."

"Me too," she said. "But they also drive me nuts because sometimes they are just so stupid. Do you know what I mean?"

He shrugged. "I guess so."

"There are two things that happen all the time in horror movies that I think ruin the whole movie, and I think we can learn from those things. So, I need you to hear me out, okay?"

He nodded again.

"The first thing I hate is when the characters refuse to accept what's happening. Do you know what I mean by that?"

A little twinge of recognition hit his eyes. "Like when the characters act like weird stuff is just normal? Like, oh! In that one movie where the books are flying off the shelves and the father says it was probably just the wind."

Cassie snapped her fingers. "Exactly!"

James sat up a little, as if he accomplished a major feat by connecting with another human.

It made Cassie sad for him, but she pressed on. "So, let's not do that, okay? That's how the characters end up dead, because they refuse to accept what's happening until it's too late. Can we not do that? Can we be honest about what is happening right now?"

As if he were a balloon Cassie just stuck a pin in, he deflated. His back slouched and his arms dropped to the couch cushion under him. "Okay," he said with no heart.

She wished she could stop, could hug him and forget the conversation entirely, but if she didn't finish it now, she'd be just like those fucking characters in horror movies. "Okay, good. Then we have to come to terms with everything we've seen. There is, or was, some kind of war going on above us. People were dropping bombs and shooting each other, and my friend said something about nukes. We have no choice but to accept that we are stuck down here until we hear otherwise. Opening that bulkhead right now might literally kill us. That's first."

He nodded.

"I know that's tough, but that means we have to accept we may never see the people we love ever again." As his eyes refilled with water, Cassie regretted taking the conversation this far. It was easier for her because she didn't really love anyone. She cared for people, sure, Beth, even James, but the only people she'd ever loved were all dead long before the bombs started.

She wasn't trying to hurt James more than he already was. Besides, she really needed his attention for the next part. She turned her head toward the creature who maintained its sentry position. "Then there's him." She pointed at the thing.

James turned toward him, and as if he had forgotten he was there, his face filled with panic and fear at the sight.

"Look, I'm not religious. I'm not spiritual. I don't believe in ghosts or aliens or even Karma." She pointed at the creature again. "But that thing right there isn't fucking human."

James's mouth twisted. "What do you mean?"

"James, look at him. His skin is gray and ashy. He bends his limbs in ways a human can't do. Your parents have weird books about monsters and shit. I'm not quite ready to say that thing is a vampire, but whatever he gobbled up from that vial looked a lot like blood, and his eyes changed to this weird color, and it would make sense that your dad took his jaw off and ripped out his teeth if he was a vampire. He's not human, James. I need you to understand that."

"Why?"

"Because if we have to kill him, we need to figure out what we are dealing with."

"I don't want to do this," he shouted, his voice heightening in pitch to a childish scream. He wrapped his hands around his knees and started rocking on the couch in full temper tantrum mode. She had broken him.

"I know, I know, I know," she said, over and over, as she put her arm around his shoulders and brought him into her. She hugged, and said, "Sssshhhhh," the way one would calm an infant.

Right then, she hated life. So many emotions bubbled through her - anger at all she'd lost, grief over the life she worked so hard to build, confusion as to what was happening. She couldn't imagine what those emotions must be like for a child, a pre-teen kid still working to figure out the normal world, then thrust into insanity. A kid who still latched onto his parents only to lose them, and every comfort he'd ever known, in seconds. He'd etched his little slice of life, his small, hidden place in the big, evil world, and then the world struck back and took it all in one fell swoop.

After a few minutes, the tantrum settled. He sniffled into her shirt. "I'm sorry," he said.

She pulled away from him so she could look him in the eyes. "You have nothing to be sorry for. Never apologize for feeling things."

"Okay," he said and nodded.

She scanned the room, taking in the small environment, wondering where the electricity came from, if there was a generator somewhere that would run out of gas. She wondered where the oxygen came from because she didn't see any vents. "There's one more thing I hate in horror movies, something that definitely gets the characters killed."

"What?" James asked, but Cassie could see he wasn't with her anymore. His eyes were glossed over, staring blankly at the empty wall by the television.

"They either lie or withhold information for no good reason. I'm not saying you're doing either of those, but I want you to think about it. If your parents had secrets, things you never told anyone because you wanted to protect them, there's no need anymore. The world is over. There's no police. I won't judge the dead, but the information could help keep us alive. You don't want to die, right?"

James jerked his head away from the spot he'd been staring at and shook his head. "No. I don't want to die. But I don't have any secrets. I promise. I didn't know about him." James pointed to the creature.

"Okay," she said. "Okay. But maybe it's not a secret. Maybe there's just stuff you know you don't realize could be helpful. So, I need you to think. Do you know anything about this bunker or about your parents' books or even what they do for work? Anything. Anything you can think of that might be useful."

He shook his head so vigorously it was like it was vibrating, an overloaded pressure boiler. "I don't know, honestly. I can't think of anything."

"James," she said, more forcefully than intended. "Tell me everything you know about this fucking bunker."

Chapter 12

What are We Doing?

"Cassiopeia, life isn't about finding solutions. It's about destroying them."

———

James's eyes darted around the room. He searched for answers, looking for some small bit of information worth telling Cassie.

She could see the deep thought in the creases on his forehead and the way he chewed on his bottom lip. She didn't think he was lying or planning answers in his head. She knew from the terror on his face when the creature appeared this was all new to him. No kid could act that well.

"I really can't think of anything," he finally said.

Cassie shifted, untucking one leg from under her and stretching it out while tucking the other in. "You knew about the bunker. You're the one who told me about it, so tell me how you know about it, what your parents said, exactly."

James rolled his eyes to the ceiling as if praying to God to conjure the memories for him. "I remember when they had it built. My dad worked on all these blueprints for a really long time and he was super stressed about it. I asked him what it was, and he said it was a place to keep us safe in case things went bad."

She thought about what to say next, wanting to prod with more questions, but she knew the right ones could open doors as easily as the wrong ones could shut them. She had to think like a shrink. No yes or no questions. Open-ended, bring out the stories. "What was happening at the time that made your parents decide to build one?"

He shook his head. "I don't know. Maybe something on the news."

"What about in your life? At home. Anything different?"

He frowned. "I don't think so. Oh, well, they were building something else at the same time."

She tried not to show her excitement. "Oh? What was that?"

"They were building a new office somewhere. They were really excited about it because they said it would help them more with their patients. They're psychiatrists, if you didn't know."

She chuckled and furrowed her brow. "I know. I was one of their patients. You didn't know that?"

His head slid back like a ball just smacked him in the face. "Wait, you were? My parents hired a crazy person to watch me?" He smiled to show he was only joking.

She tossed a small throw pillow at him. "I was a kid, and I wasn't crazy. I was sad."

His smile ran away. "I'm sorry. I was just kidding."

She put her hand on his arm. "I know. So, anyway, tell me more about this new office they built."

He shrugged. "Not much to tell. I've never seen it. They still have their old office. That one I've been to, but I never saw the newer one. One thing they were happy about, though, was that they said they'd be home earlier when they worked at the new office because it was much closer to home."

"Well, that must have been nice." She played the buddy psychiatrist role.

He pursed his lips. "I don't know. I don't think they ever came home early. Or maybe they did. Who knows? They were hardly around anyway. I felt like they were visitors more than people I lived with. Always working, even when they were home."

She debated on letting him talk about those feelings but worried the conversation would veer too far off course. Her eyes went back to the creature, still staring, still standing tall. His ability to keep at it haunted her.

"So, when they built this place, did you ever get a tour? Did you see it when they finished?"

He shook his head. "No, but they probably asked me if I wanted to, and I probably didn't. You know me. I just like to stay in my room and be alone."

She wondered why, but doubted he would know himself. Most times, people's actions stemmed from some inner feeling or past trauma they couldn't identify. Long sessions of therapy might uncover the truth, but a casual conversation on a couch while a creature eyeballed him probably wouldn't reach through the surface.

"So, they have all those books on monsters. Did they ever talk about those? Seems like a topic they cared about."

He giggled. It was a combination of discomfort and surprise. "I have honestly never heard them say a word about monsters. They used to tell me to turn off horror movies because they said the movies were ridiculous."

She glanced at the hallway. "Not so much anymore." She stood up and walked toward the creature. He gurgled a little as she approached. "What are you?"

Her goal was to make the monster think she was examining him, studying him, but her focus lasered in on the doors. How far would she have to run to get into them? How much chain did the creature have? Was it enough to get her if she made her way into the door? Would he be able to follow or would the chain choke him upon entry? She didn't know, couldn't, because she knew nothing about the room itself. Maybe it was a large bedroom, and if she made it all the way to the other side, the creature would never reach her. But maybe it was a fucking broom closet.

"What do we do?" James asked.

If nothing, the conversation she'd had with him seemed to calm him for the moment. She found most of his answers useless, but one thing she learned from her lab work was useless information proved useful when you gathered enough of it.

"We can't live in this room," she said. "So, we'll have to figure out a way down this hall at some point. But it has gotta be like two in the morning, and I am fucking exhausted. I have no idea if I'll be able to sleep tonight, not with everything that happened, and surely not with this fucking thing staring at me, but I think for tonight we just need to relax. Not think about what we need to do. Just forget everything."

He raised his hand as if she were his teacher.

"Yes?"

"I have to pee."

Cassie went to the shelves and opened some boxes. She pulled out the *Friends* DVDs and the few protein bars she saw stuffed in with the food. When she gathered what she wanted, she took a bucket off the bottom shelf and slid it into the corner. "Pee into that bucket for now."

He gave her an, '*Are you serious,*' look.

"What are your other options? Peeing on the wall? I'm going to face the other way and see if we can't get the television playing something."

As she fumbled with the wiring on the television, trying to figure out the DVD player, she mumbled to herself, "I can't believe it's the end of the fucking world, I'm alone with a child and a fucking monster, and all I want to do is watch Must See TV."

"Cassie, I can't go. My dad says I'm bladder shy."

As she found a dangling cord and connected it to the back of the DVD player, she said, "Better get over it, because you don't have any other options. I told you, I'm not looking."

"I know, but he is."

She whipped around toward the creature. He had indeed turned his attention from Cassie to James. She made her way closer to him while trying to keep from looking in James's direction. The creature's eyes dulled again. He was stretched to the end of the chain, standing at an angle once more.

Whatever she fed him had worn off.

"Ignore him. He's not real."

On her way back to the television, she opened a protein bar and took a bite. She wished she had brought her backpack with her. That half-eaten bag of chips in there would have come in handy. She suddenly hated herself for how often she'd neglected her snacks.

As the disc tray popped open on the player, the sound of piss hitting the plastic bucket took over the room. The sound was so aggressive she had to bite back a laugh. The tray slid back in, and the menu for *Friends* Season One Disc One came up.

James came over and sat on the couch.

"Have you ever watched *Friends*?"

He shook his head.

"You're in for a treat." She hit play and made her way over to the other side of the couch.

As the theme song played, James sighed. "What are we doing?"

"We're watching one of the worst sitcoms of all time."

"Why?"

She closed her eyes and sucked in a big gulp of air. Who knew how much more oxygen was left? "Because, James, tomorrow is going to be fucking insane. Tomorrow, we have to face that thing and figure out how to get into those rooms. Tomorrow, we have to find food and figure out how we're going to survive down here. Which means tonight, we watch a stupid fucking television show and forget about all of it."

She could tell he wanted to say more, but she'd scared him out of it. Her tone let him know not to keep pressing the issue.

She rubbed her eyes. "We're going to need to sleep, but I don't think it's wise for both of us to do so. Just in case that thing gets loose, one of us should be alert. Why don't you sleep for a while. I'll sit down here and watch the show." She scooted off the couch, her butt landing on the old, dirty area rug in front of it. If the Renards were so rich, why couldn't they have nicer things down here, too?

She wanted to beg James to stay up first, let her sleep since she was already operating on so little of it, but she'd worry about him. He had to be tired, too. She couldn't trust a twelve-year-old to stay alert without at least a little sleep first, and if she didn't trust him to stay awake, she'd keep herself awake stressing about it.

James curled up in a ball on the couch and Cassie focused on the show. Her mind brought her to tomorrow, to the inevitable fact she'd need to get by the creature and into those rooms, but she forced herself back into the show, not allowing her mind to wander.

Friends.

Ross and Rachel.

Something exploded above them.

Monica Geller.

The creature's chain clinked as the links pulled taut.

Chandler Bing.

Friends.

Chapter 13

Whispers

"Cassiopeia, I am always with you. Unfortunately, so is everyone else."

———

Cassie assumed James would toss and turn all night, unable to sleep, but he conked right out. She remembered reading an article about infants and how after extreme stress, they'd fall into deep sleep and stay that way for hours. She wondered if the same were true for twelve-year-old kids.

For all her worry that James wouldn't keep guard, she struggled to keep her eyes open after a few episodes of *Friends*. The flickering television lulled her, and she caught her eyelids drooping and her chin resting on her chest.

The creature quieted, no longer stretched out with his chain taut. Without an acute visual on his future victims, he retreated a few feet down the hall. Not enough to give her leeway into the rooms, but enough where she felt he wouldn't break free mid-night and kill them.

To keep herself awake, she headed to the shelves to search for something to snack on. From her first search, she knew there wasn't much, but even if she had to munch on dried ramen, she'd take it just to get something in her stomach and keep herself occupied.

She walked slowly past the hallway, hoping the thing had fallen asleep, but as soon as she came into view, he barked and ran to the end of his chain. Cassie turned, hoping the noise didn't wake James. After a few seconds, she went back to her mission. She dug through boxes, finding nothing of value, no hidden nuggets she missed on the first search. What she wouldn't give for a Snickers bar or a bag of M&M's.

"Cassie?" someone whispered.

She snapped around, expecting to see James sitting up and looking at her, but he was still hidden behind the couch backing.

"Yes?" she whispered back. He must have woken up but remained lying down, or maybe he was talking in his sleep. No response came, so she went back to rummaging.

"Caaaaaaaasssssssssiiiiieeeeeeeee." This time the voice was taunting, sing-songy. Worse, she pinpointed where it came from.

She didn't respond. Responding would make it more real. She imagined it, or maybe she'd gone delusional from lack of sleep and stress.

"Caaaaaaaaaasssssssssiiiiiieeeeeeeee," the voice whispered.

Her heart slammed into her ribs. *I'm not crazy. I'm not crazy,* she told herself.

As she dug into the boxes, her hands shook.

"Caaaaaasssssssiiiiieeeeeeeeee."

She slowly turned to the creature on the chain. Was he talking into her mind? Could he do that? She had made James promise they wouldn't dismiss what they experienced, made him come to terms with the fact that *thing* wasn't human. If she sat here convincing herself it was all in her head, she'd be breaking her own rule. She *heard* her name, loud and fucking clear. Someone was singing it, whispering, taunting her, and James was fast fucking asleep.

That only left one option. But it didn't sound like it came from the hallway. It sounded like someone whispered right in front of her face, inside the wall. If the thing was speaking to her in some telepathic, paranormal bullshit, it could sound like it came from anywhere.

She stood up, legs wobbly. The room spun for a moment as she got to her feet.

"Caaaaaaasssssssiiiieeeeee." Right behind her.

As she faced the creature, the noise continued to sound like it came from the wall behind her, or maybe in her fucking skull. It was so hard to tell. It almost bounced, reverberating all around her. She stepped toward the creature.

He slashed out his arms, but she kept a suitable distance, used to this game by now.

"Are you talking to me?" she whispered, still trying not to wake James.

The creature's nub went down, the top part of his face up.

"Are you trying to talk right now?"

From the thing's throat, a black wisp of smoke climbed out. It looked like winter breath, outside of the midnight color.

She lunged backward, shocked.

The mist steamed forward, pulling apart from itself into tendrilled coils. At first, it maneuvered like steam, out and then up, but then it turned as if guided by some unknown force.

Cassie stepped away, swatting toward it, but not touching it, too afraid. What might happen if her hands landed in it? Would it poison her? Burn? Who the fuck knew, but she wouldn't be the control study.

As it traveled, it weakened, the dark colors fading to a dull gray and the thick branches dissipating into fine threads. Eventually, it made its way to the wall where Cassie heard the voice, but before it reached its destination, it fully evaporated.

"What the fuck?" she whispered.

The thing pointed toward the boxes.

"You want food?"

The thing nodded his head.

For the sake of experimentation and learning, she debated on it, but her life was at stake. "No. Be good and maybe I'll feed you tomorrow."

The thing's top lip curled.

She crossed her arms, proud of herself for saying no, for sticking to her guns and not letting someone pressure her into doing something she didn't feel comfortable with.

The creature rubbed his fingers in front of his face. And then he lashed, a roaring howl escaped his lungs as he whipped his arms at her. She was a good five feet away, and he had no chance of hitting her, but the rage in his eyes, the pure hatred, sent a shockwave from Cassie's spine to her brain. She ran away from him, going back toward the couch, hoping if she sat down on the floor, the creature would calm down. Out of sight, out of mind.

James shot up, the loud growls from the creature pulling him out of his deep sleep. "What's happening?"

"Shh. It's okay. I made the thing mad. You can go back to sleep. He'll calm down in a few minutes."

"Why is it mad? What did you do?"

"Nothing. Don't worry about it. We'll talk about it when we switch shifts. Just go back to sleep so you have enough rest for tomorrow."

With shaky hands she grabbed her phone and the television remote. She didn't know what to do with either, but she needed to do something.

James caught her nervous fiddling. "I can just stay up now," he said.

She turned her head to him. "No. Please, just try to go back to sleep."

She turned the volume down two notches on *Friends*. She could already barely hear it and had the subtitles going so it wouldn't wake James up, and she'd dropped it to one above muted.

She tapped her phone screen, but it didn't come on. Completely out of juice. Not that it was anything more than a fancy brick now anyway. None of the apps worked and she couldn't get any service. She presumed that kind of thing happened when someone dropped bombs all around you.

She turned her attention to the television, staring until her eyes blurred. James tossed and turned behind her, and she figured the peaceful night's rest was over for him. Maybe she'd take him up on his offer and get some sleep herself. Her heart was still punching at her ribs, but less from fear and more from a desperate need to rest.

After a few minutes, the creature settled down. The room was quiet again, outside of James's heavy breathing and constant shifting. She could even hear the gentle audience laughter coming through the small speakers on the TV.

She thought about the mist that crawled from the creature's lungs, wondering if it could have killed her if she inhaled it. It made her feel less safe because even if the creature couldn't stretch beyond his chain, he might possess a weapon that could, one that could lurch through the air and find its way into her bloodstream while she slept. She'd have to warn James so he'd keep an eye out. For what? For fucking black mist.

That was her new world.

Boom!

The bombs did more than raze the scenery. They devoured sanity, turned the slivers of life still left into nonsense.

Cassie had no one up there to love, yet she mourned for all of it, even the bad stuff. She'd kill for a boring seven a.m. lecture, would love a shift at Cuddey's. Hell, she would even hug her fucking father if she could. Before, all Cassie wanted was a day to herself. But, she wanted the people back, the classmates, the coworkers, Beth. She sure as fuck didn't want whatever was chained up a few feet away from her. She supposed she'd never be alone again, and boy was she stuck with some shit roommates.

She thought about Chris, her mother, the first explosions to hit her Earth. Their removal from her life had felt like grenades. She'd kill to have them back. She tilted her head back, staring up at the ceiling, a grotesque cement thing keeping her from the world. Her eyes watered and blurred. And then the ceiling spoke to her.

Scratch. Scratch. Scratch.

Chapter 14

An Endless Cycle of Fury and Pain

"There's no good or bad in the world, Cassiopeia, no matter how much I've complained about it. The truth is, humans are malleable. They can't be good or evil, only convinced."

———

Cassie stared at the spot on the ceiling where the noise came from. It was a brutal scratch, an intentional one, not one which could be explained away as a mouse or a gentle rustling. What was above the ceiling? This wasn't a house, there was no upper floor, no attic. Above the hard cement was nothing but earth. Or was there a gap, a small enough space for someone to fit in and taunt her? But who?

She heard the voice in the wall, but she felt confident it was the creature speaking into her mind, not someone actually hiding behind the thick concrete. But the scratching, each scratch was long and drawn-out. She couldn't see it as anything other than someone fucking with her. It made her heart ache, brought back the memories of that night when her brother's body hung above her, when all she could consider was the distraction to her homework, so oblivious to the dead over her head. It also made her furious someone would take the most painful moment of her life and use it to scramble her already damaged mind.

James tapped on her shoulder and she flinched, startled out of her trance.

"Why don't you try to sleep now? I feel awake. I can't go back to sleep."

Cassie turned to him and offered a grim smile. She tried her hardest to make it legitimate but knew she fell short. "I can't either. There's no way. I think it's time we take some action. What do you think?"

He scratched the top of his hand. "I guess. What do you mean?"

"Come with me." She stood up, a sea of silver stars sparkling in her vision. She nearly fell over as the blood rushed through her from standing, but after a few seconds, it quelled, and she was fine.

James followed her to the boxes. As they waltzed past the hall-way, the creature charged and choked on the chain. It made James jump, but Cassie was prepared for it. As long as the thing wasn't shooting black mist from his half-mouth, she didn't care about him bouncing around on his chain anymore.

She took out two vials of the dog food and handed one to James.

"What are we doing?" he asked.

She put her finger to her lip.

He nodded.

The creature noticed the food and moaned, extending his arms as far out as they would go.

Cassie dug through the junk boxes, remembering pens and paper in one of them. When she found them, she guided James back to the couch.

He watched her write on the paper.

I don't know if he can understand us when we talk.

I'm going to throw some of this food down the hall. I suspect he'll run after it. While he is going for it, I am going to run into one of those doors and see what's in there.

James's eyes widened. He snatched the pen from her.

NO! WHAT IF HE GETS YOU!!!!?

Cassie read the terror on his face. If she died, he'd be truly all alone and wouldn't know how to survive a day. Cassie was terrified herself, but if they didn't get into those rooms, they'd both be dead soon, and it was the perfect time to make a move, while anger from the scratching still flowed through her veins. It battled the fear and gave her the motivation she needed to act.

We have to do this James. There's no other choice. But I need something from you.

He grimaced and took the pen.

WHAT?

She sighed, knowing what she wrote next wouldn't go over well.

When you hear me knocking, throw the second bottle of food down the hall. See Spot run!

NO NO NO! I CAN'T

You can. I will knock when I am ready to leave the room. You whistle before you throw it. I will whistle back. Then toss it. You have to remember all that. All of those steps must happen before you toss it.

She stood up, not giving him more time to argue, and headed toward the hall. Her heart pounded but she pressed forward, knowing full well she neared talking herself out of it. It was foolish, insane. But she had no other choice.

James latched onto the back of her cardigan. "Cassie, please," he whispered.

She let the cardigan slide off her arms and continued forward until she stood a foot in front of the creature's flailing arms.

She gave one last look to James, who stood behind her squeezing her cardigan into his chest. His face exploded with terror. Tears. Shivers. His breathing turned to shallow puffs.

She turned back to Spot, held the vial up for him to see. "You want?"

She tossed it. It flew down the hall, and Spot followed it with his eyes before charging after it.

Cassie ran, refusing to think or to stop herself. It was madness. Her feet hit the floor just a few feet behind Spot. If he turned, he'd be on her before she had the chance to switch gears. She'd passed the point of no return, though. Either the plan worked or Spot would kill her in the next few minutes. It didn't help that the only diversion she could create gave the fucking creature more clarity, more hate in his eyes, and surely more power. Spot fucking terrified her as it was, but once he had the food in his system, he was a different beast altogether, and that beast was about to come out and play while Cassie stood right in his playground.

Inches from the door, a new thought popped into her head. What if the doors were locked? Stupid! How could she be so stupid to not consider it before? She should have turned the boxes upside down searching for keys or something. It didn't matter, she'd never have the time to unlock them. If the door was locked, she was dead. Plain and simple.

Her arm reached out for the door handle as Spot lifted the vial and cracked it open in his hand. Her hand gripped the knob. She heard her heartbeat in her throat. The smell from the vial tore through the hall, that awful, rotten meat odor, noxious and horrifying.

The knob twisted, and a small sense of relief washed over her, but not a big one, because she still stood in the danger zone and possibly on the precipice of something even more terrible. Who knew what lurked behind the door? Whatever it was, she'd be trapped with it in seconds.

Spot turned to her, a sinister sharpness in his eyes as he jammed his red-coated fingers down his throat.

She stepped into the unknown room and shut the door. Both hands fumbled, searching for safety. The left slapped against the wall, hoping to find a switch to save her from the utter blackness, and the right looked for the knob on that side of the door, praying for a locking mechanism. She swam in the dark.

Her right hand found its destination first, a welcoming metallic nub. She twisted it, and it responded with a satisfying thud just as she heard Spot running down the hall. But what did she lock herself in the room with? She didn't know because she couldn't find a switch anywhere.

It was all in her mind, she knew, but the room felt murky, thick with black.

Spot slammed his body into the door behind her.

She jumped forward, afraid of what she might fall into.

Spot slammed again and again.

She turned and saw a sliver of light. There was a thin window on the door. A tiny little box. Spot had his eye pressed to it, blocking out most of the light. There wasn't enough to reveal anything about the room, but she could see that fucker's eye perfectly clearly. That red glowing bead, filled with hate and desire.

She took a slow step backwards and something hit the back of her neck, a tickle. She flinched again. Every muscle in her body tensed, a full seizing. Her hand slapped at her neck instinctively, like squishing a bug. A thin thread hit her palm. As she pulled it off her neck, she heard a click and the room lit up.

She spun around, heart in her lungs, surveying for more threats. The room was empty of life, but goddamn was it glorious otherwise. Spot smashed himself into the door again, and she flinched, but she was okay. Even if he found his way in, she had more room to maneuver than he had chain. The room spun a little, and Cassie bent over, putting her hands on her knees and taking long pulls of air. The light shining above her and the wide spaces of the room acted as an inhaler, opening her airways.

While she still had to hope James completed his side of the mission, for a moment at least, she had some peace.

The rest of the bunker looked like a leftover from the 70s, an old thing meant to emulate a different era. Cement. Dust. Worn area rug. Dingy couch.

But this room, this fucking room was a state-of-the-art kitchen and clean, too. The stainless-steel range sparkled against the dim light. Pots and pans hung on hooks along the far wall. Marble countertops stretched along the back wall; tiny speckles shimmered throughout. There was a dishwasher, a sink, cabinets, and a circular table with four chairs.

The creature banged on the door and growled, but she didn't give a fuck. She had a kitchen. A beautiful kitchen. She cracked the fridge door open and smiled at the overstuffed shelves. In one motion, she snatched a bottle of water and twisted the cap off. The cold water hurt her throat a little as it went down. It landed like a blizzard in her empty stomach.

Still gulping water, she opened cabinets, not really searching for anything but taking inventory of what they did and didn't have. The cabinets were full of food, boxes of mac and cheese, rice, dried soup, cans of beans, corn, every veggie known to man. She wasted no time ripping a bag of salt and vinegar chips open and shoving a fistful into her mouth. The crunch and slight sting of vinegar on her chapped lips was heaven.

Despite the newfound hope, the delicious meal of chips and water, anger brewed within her. The unfairness of life, that the average person was victim to powerful assholes who could decimate the world because they fight for power the people wanted none of them to have, it all made her angry. Now she had to live her life as a lamb in a pen with a bunch of chained wolves all around her, solely because of some geopolitical bullshit she wanted nothing to do with.

She chewed harder, enraged and eager to take it out on someone, anyone, preferably Spot. She cleared her mind, forcing it to focus on the more important and immediate tasks. It was not the time to destroy. She went back to the fridge and opened the freezer door. It was stocked full of frozen meat of all kinds and pizzas, ice cream, and frozen vegetables. A smoky blast of cold air hit her face. It felt so good, yet the rage wouldn't subside, like an itch under the skin.

A clock dangling above the stove ticked. *Tick. Tick. Tick.* It reminded her of a car blinker. *Tick. Tick. Tick.* Cars. She'd never see another one.

Spot slammed into the door and Cassie grabbed a block of hamburger meat and flung it across the room. It banged hard against the door.

"Shut the fuck up!" She bit down so hard her teeth ground together.

Spot slammed again.

Cassie grabbed another hunk of meat, placed her free hand on the counter, and smashed the meat into the dorsal side of her hand. Something cracked under her skin and she screamed. The pain radiated from her hand up her arm. Adrenaline burst through her like fireworks in her nerves. She slammed the meat again. Fuck. It hurt. It hurt so badly, and she never wanted to stop. Her heartbeat thrummed like a death metal drummer in her chest. Oh god, she loved it.

She continued smashing the meat into her hands, feeling the

unbearable weight of pain blasting out her fingertips. Behind her, Spot slammed harder and harder which made her slam harder and harder, which made her scream louder and louder, which made him slam harder and harder in an endless cycle of fury and pain, and fuck she could swim in it, she could drown in the depths of hate and anguish within her. They'd taken everything from her, but no one and nothing could steal her joy for pain.

As she gave the top of her hand one last smashing, her neck twisted toward the far corner of the room, where she spotted something she somehow missed before. A second door. The hallway had three doors on each side, which she presumed led to three separate rooms on each side. This door must then connect the kitchen to the next room down the hall. Normally, that would have been good news, another way to get from place to place, but in that moment, it was the worst news possible, because the only reason Cassie's mind finally paid attention to the second door was because it was opening, and coming through into the kitchen, was another creature just like Spot.

Chapter 15

The Weight of the World

"It's important to eat a healthy breakfast. You want a full stomach before getting crushed by the weight of the world."

———

If she'd taken a moment to think, she would have gone back instead of forward, but her instincts overpowered rational thought and she dove toward the door, hoping to shut it in the creature's face before he could enter the room. Unfortunately, it was far too late for that, and all she did was catch a door handle to her forehead.

The force of the door swinging open knocked her down, and the new creature wasted no time, hunger in his eyes. He jumped on top of her, landing belly to belly, his face squirming closer.

Adrenaline sent her blood soaring through her veins, her heart pulsed loudly in her ears. She kicked at the thing's torso and used her elbows to scoot backwards.

The creature was strong, too strong. His sharp nails dug into the flesh on Cassie's lower arms as he tried to pin her down.

She'd have to worry about infection if she survived this. She screamed from the hot pain as he clawed deeper into her flesh. The hurt grew more and more intense until it was so unbearable it morphed into something new. She became one with it, her heart beating so rapidly it was like one long thrum. Her scream turned into a war cry.

The creature wrinkled his eyebrows, unprepared for her reaction, and that gifted her the time she needed. The thing loosened his grip enough for her to slip her arm out and she instantly went into punch mode. As her fist connected, she realized this creature also had a chain around his neck.

The punch wasn't much, just a quick jab, but it knocked the creature back, chain clinking on the linoleum floor, and Cassie found room to flip over and crawl away. With the weight of the monster off her, she got to her feet and darted to the other side of the room, hoping the chain around the second creature's neck couldn't reach that far.

Another dizzy spell hit her as soon as she stopped moving. She hit the back counters, out of room, and the monster was on his feet, coming at her. She braced for impact, wishing she ran out the door instead, chancing it with Spot. Now, instead of one jawless fuck blocking her from the safety of the main room, she had two.

The creature's neck snapped as he caught the end of the chain, just a few feet in front of Cassie. Her entire world had shrunk to the size of a bunker, and now it was nothing more than a thin strip of kitchen.

Her head swam, vision blurred. The familiar hard beat of her heart paused, and the spaces between beats frightened her more than the constant thrumming. She gritted her teeth, clenched her fists, felt the sparks of fury igniting under her skin.

"You ready for this, Rufus?" she said with a voice so bubbling in emotion it sent a shiver down her own spine.

Rufus only stared, eyes as dead and black as Spot's before he ate his food. This didn't offer a ton of relief, but at least Cassie knew food hadn't fueled Rufus up. He still wanted to hurt her, she knew, but as long as the sharp edges were dulled, she held some hope.

One foot, two. Cassie paced the small perimeter she had, and Rufus matched her step for step, his soulless eyes never leaving her. She had no plans to make a run for it, at least not yet. She experimented, seeing if Rufus could keep locked on, how much stamina he really had. Who could outlast whom? Even if she dashed past him, she wouldn't have time to signal James, let him throw the food for Spot, and get back through the hall. She was good and fucked, but vigilance and testing were the weapons she understood best and where she would glean a solution.

Her limbs trembled, still shaken from the encounter by the door. She debated throwing another punch, just to see how much she could hurt the monster, if she could at all. The knives were in the drawer by the fridge, which currently stood in Rufus's jurisdiction.

She'd double-check the drawers behind her eventually, but off the top of her head she couldn't recall seeing any potential weapons. The kitchen put more direct light on Rufus than she'd had with Spot, so she stared at his face and body, picking apart his features.

Even with Rufus's missing jaw, the tendons shifted as if the fucker was moving an invisible mouth open and shut. Was he trying to talk or was he just breathing?

An eerie whistle left Rufus's throat. It clicked in Cassie's brain what he was doing, and her skin felt like it was trying to crawl away from her. Rufus was laughing.

Laughing.

The spark inside her ignited.

"You want to laugh at me, Rufus?" She turned around, tossing drawers open, spilling their contents on the floor with a clatter. Some of it she tossed at Rufus, not trying to damage him, just annoy him, just let him know she wouldn't fucking cower. Ladles, shot glasses, k-cups, a box of aluminum foil.

Rufus snarled.

After emptying the drawers, finding nothing of value, her anger subsided. No. It remained, but it went dormant, allowing logic back in.

The world had ended, but the weight of it still hung heavy on Cassie's shoulders. She could let it crush her, or she could deal with her new surroundings. Panic, anger, none of that would help her. She could best this damned thing, especially an unfed version of it, with its dull stare and stupidly animalistic instincts.

Would he sleep eventually? They had to sleep, right? She sure as fuck did, and her body warned her it would break down without some soon. How long had she been up? A day? Could two have passed? The bunker had nothing to help guide her circadian rhythm. Losing time gnawed at her. It could be noon or it could be midnight.

She moved to the corner, pressing her back to the drawers, and slid down. As her butt hit the floor, Rufus crouched down, keeping his eyes level with her. Her eyes burned, but her brain shot them signals: *don't close in this place. Keep those lids wide.*

Minutes dripped by with Cassie and Rufus staring at each other. Cassie noted the deep gashes in the creature's flesh. As hideous and threatening as Rufus and Spot were, she couldn't help feeling sorry for the torture they'd clearly endured. Someone had ripped their bottom jaws off, plucked out their teeth, lashed them, and made them bleed and suffer. Why? Did Mr. and Mrs. Renard do this? To what end? What purpose did all of this serve?

Her survival mode, the flight or fight instincts, the mad rush of adrenaline, all of it did nothing to temper her absolute need for sleep. But even if she could drift off, any slight noise sent her responses firing. Her head jerked when the freezer whirred. Her back spasmed as the pipes clunked. A constant war ensued within her. Her body pushed to shut down, while her mind fired shockwaves through the synapses, overpowering her nerves.

"I need you, now," she said. She didn't know who she spoke to, but she felt it was important to say.

Time traveled.

She imagined looking out a window and watching the sun set, even though she suspected it was the middle of the night.

Rufus's red-streaked eyes never faltered, hardly even blinked.

Her eyes felt heavy, and she'd caught them dropping on her. She fought and fought. Eventually, without the normal hours of tossing and turning, itchy skin, and soupy mixture of stressful thinking, she drifted into sleep.

She jolted up, her heart galloping. The monster remained on his knees at the end of a straightened chain, his arms outstretched and aiming for her. He hadn't startled her awake. She did that on her own as her brain dug itself from the darkest depths and clawed through the muck and mud of earth between dreamland and reality. As it rose from the graveyard of sleep, it yanked her back to the situation in front of her.

"Shut the fuck up," she yelled at the thing, despite its silence. "Fuck."

The room was silent until Cassie's dry mouth and scratchy throat made her cough. The moment of sleep only made her yearn for the real thing more intensely. She could kill this fucking thing. Kill Rufus and Spot. Wash their blood from her hands. Take a fucking good eight hours.

Well, Cassiopeia, are you ready?

Chapter 16

A Howl at the Moon

CASSIE, AGE 10

Cassie cringed as each floorboard groaned on her way down the stairs. She wasn't trying to be sneaky. In fact, her only reason for going downstairs was to tell her father good night, but with the tense atmosphere in the house since Chris died four months prior, she tried her hardest to appear unassuming. She and her father had grown accustomed to a minimalist version of familial dealings. She supposed it started way before Chris, since her mother was dragged out the front door, or maybe even a little before then, but Chris's death solidified it, hammered down the wedge already squarely placed between father and daughter.

Cassie's father sat at the dining room table nibbling pork chops and potatoes with his head down, a can of beer beside the plate. He had nothing to occupy him. No television playing in the background, no newspaper or book, just him. Alone.

It hurt her heart despite how mean he'd become. He wasn't outwardly cruel, not abusive in the normal sense, but he stayed away from her, cut conversations short, pushed her away. He couldn't hide how much disdain he collected for her over the years, as if he blamed her for all the problems their family suffered.

"I'm going to bed now," she said, her voice a meek little rodent.

He looked up from his plate, stared for a second with his glossy pink marble eyes, and nodded. Nothing more.

Her instincts told her to move, to let the conversation exit the atmosphere like the drizzle of oxygen it was, but a part of her saw a caged bear she wanted to prod. "Why do you drink that?" She pointed at the beer can.

"Huh?" he said with a mouthful of pork chop.

"The beer. Cynthia said she drank her dad's beer and it made her feel happy and dizzy. Is that why you drink it?" She tried to make her question innocent, but she hoped it made him uncomfortable, eager to change.

He let out a laugh, loud and powerful.

It shocked her. Maybe she should have been happy to see him show some emotion, especially one as wonderful as laughter, but that laugh wasn't right. It had cruelty streaked across the sound waves. Her eyes watered, and she wished she'd never prodded, wished she could run the fuck away and live in the woods where the tree branches would speak to her whenever the wind blew and the silence would be natural as opposed to a mark of hatred.

Cassie's father wiped his mouth, finished swallowing his meat, and for the first time in a long time, planted his eyes directly on her. "It's non-alcoholic. You think I'd risk getting drunk around here? Jesus, you must be nuts. If you give up your senses around here, you'll be dead before morning."

She didn't know what to say to that, or even what it meant, so she stepped backward. Just one step to make sure he would allow the conversation to die there. He shook his head, still shocked by her question, and put his face back toward his dinner, scooping up a forkful of mashed potatoes.

She released the air built in her lungs and turned back to the stairs.

"Wait a minute," her father said.

She paused at the bottom step.

"Is your hair dry?"

Without turning around, Cassie touched the cascading brown hair around her shoulder. She furrowed her brow. "Yeah?"

"Does that mean you didn't take a shower?"

She turned back to him.

He stared at her with wide eyes, true concern washing across his face.

Cassie couldn't decide how to feel about it. On the one hand, he was concerned for her, but on the other, the particular nature of the concern terrified her. "I didn't need one. I haven't done anything today."

He slammed his fist on the table. "Cassie. You know the rules."

"What?" She hoped her blouse hid the trembling coursing through her.

"Take a fucking shower. Now."

She shook her head. "I don't need one. What difference does it make? I don't have to take one every day."

He stood up, silverware clattering. "Are you insane? Yes, you do. Every single day. Those are the rules."

"Why? It's a stupid rule. You don't take one every single day."

"God damn it, Cassie." His voice was fierce, a howl at the moon. It hit her so hard it felt like sticking a wet finger in an electrical socket. "You take one every day because that's what you have to do. My burden is to live in a fucking haunted house, and yours is to take your damned showers. There's nothing to argue here. It's what you have to do."

Cassie pulled from her gut and let out a demonic scream as she stormed upstairs. In the shower, she screamed and cursed, punched and kicked. "*I hate you!*" she screamed loud enough for him to hear.

She stayed until the steaming water turned cold and her bruised knuckles reopened and gushed blood. When she left the bathroom, her father was lying in bed with his door open. He wasn't sleeping, just staring up at the ceiling with his arms crossed over his chest. Just how they'd posed Chris in his casket. Cassie remembered the excess white powder caked on Chris's neck to hide the bruising.

She paused by her father's door, calm now that her shower was over. "Good night," she whispered.

Without looking away from the ceiling, he said, "Let me ask you something."

She bounced on the balls of her feet, nervous about any engagement. "Okay."

He sighed as if reconsidering his question. "Just don't lie to me, okay? Just tell me. There's nothing I can do about it anyway."

"Okay," she repeated.

"Did Chris really commit suicide?"

She scrunched her face. "What do you mean?"

"I mean, did you kill him?"

She stepped back as if his words had punched her in the gut. Her eyes welled. How could he ask that? It didn't even make sense. How could she force Chris to do anything? He was two times her size. "What?"

"You heard me."

"But I don't understand. Why would I kill Chris? Why would I do that?"

He sighed again, still staring at whatever blank spot in the world he'd discovered, the vast emptiness of ceilings and walls, where his attention always seemed to be, as if some imaginary projection played just for him, maybe a movie about a life a little less cold. "Okay. Good night."

Cassie slunk away, hurt and confused. As she dropped into her bed, she thought of all the times she and Chris sat on the floor playing games and laughing, the only person in her life who ever treated her like she mattered, the only one who didn't step backwards when she moved forwards. He read to her, played tag, chased her, told her jokes. He filled the void their mother left when strangers dragged her out of the house. She missed the way he called her Cassiopeia and would give her sage advice. She loved him, needed him. She begged for some magical entity to bring him back, to revive him and revive her. How cruel could her father be to ask such a question? How fucking cruel?

Chapter 17

Black Mist

"Cassiopeia, when you climb a tree, you keep reaching up, one arm going higher than the next. Because your hands are always latching on to the next highest branch, you tend to forget what is really doing all the work of keeping you up there. Your feet. Never forget the power in your feet."

———

Cassie wiped the sweat from her palms onto her pants. As Rufus stared, prepared for her to make a move, Cassie ran along the free strip of kitchen where Rufus couldn't go, toward the wall with the door to the hallway where she entered. Rufus followed, but as they neared the wall, Cassie spun around, ran the opposite way, into Rufus's zone. As Rufus turned to catch her, he slipped and fell onto his hands and knees, giving Cassie a few seconds head start. She'd never make it to the door, and even if she did, she'd just come face to face with Spot. But that wasn't her plan, anyway.

With the head start, she went for the drawers by the fridge, flung them open, and grabbed a knife. Her adrenaline rushed as she fumbled to latch on to the weapon. She turned her head as she gripped the knife handle.

Rufus had returned to his feet and came at her quickly.

Fuck.

Cassie, knife in tow, ran back toward her free zone.

Rufus's fingers slid down her forearm as he swung to grab her. Just before she made it back, he gripped his hand around her wrist and yanked her.

She pulled, dragging herself forward, bringing Rufus with her.

His fingernails dug into her flesh.

She closed her eyes, pressing eyelid to eyelid, as she trudged forward. *Please, Cassie, please. Don't give up. You've got this.* She stabbed the knife around her arm, poking the tip into Rufus's hand.

The creature growled and yelped as best a jawless monster could, but held firm.

"Get the fuck off me," she yelled as she kicked her leg backwards, driving her foot into Rufus's knee.

He buckled, releasing his grip, and Cassie fell forward into the space where Rufus couldn't go.

"Oh, fuck. Jesus. That was fucking close." She lay on the floor, catching her wind, thinking about the luck granted to her that she hadn't stabbed herself in the fall.

Rufus screeched and flailed his arms at her, but she was safe out of his reach.

When her wind returned, she'd get up and piece together enough wherewithal to slit the fucker's throat.

As she lay there, taking in deep breaths through the nose and exhaling from the mouth, she noticed something moving in the vent above her head. For a split second, she thought it was another creature, then she thought it was black gunk oozing down. When she realized what it actually was, she sat up and scooted away but kept her eyes on the foreign object.

Similar to what left Spot's mouth, a black-tendrilled mist slithered through the grates. It twirled and tangled within itself, traveling down before turning toward Rufus.

Cassie stared, awed by its ability to control its direction. She held as much admiration and curiosity for the anomaly as she did dread.

It reached Rufus, and the creature opened his mouth, accepting the black substance into his lungs.

As soon as Rufus swallowed the mist, his face changed, his eyes sharpened, his top lips curled up his cheeks.

Cassie pushed away, as if the chain weren't enough to protect her anymore.

Rufus gurgled and black mist ejaculated from his mouth. She didn't know if it was the same mist he had just swallowed or a new one he produced in response.

The mist covered his face like a sheath of cheesecloth until it went entirely over him, where it danced through the kitchen, toward the door to the hallway. When it reached the door, it escaped through the gap in the side.

Cassie watched the door, waiting to see the result of this strange occurrence. She snapped back, startled, when the banging started. It must have been Spot slamming himself into the door from the other side.

She understood. The black mist. Ecdysone. Holy hell.

If her thoughts were correct, and she was certain they were, it meant another one of these creatures existed and it had signaled Rufus from the vents. Was it living in the vents, free to roam, or did the mist travel from another room where yet another creature was chain bound, jawless, and hungry? She remembered hearing her name called from the walls. She assumed Spot spoke to her mind-to-mind, but what if another creature was moving around behind those walls, taunting her? Then, there was the scratching on the ceiling.

Fuck.

There was a third creature, and it was free. It knew her name, knew how to taunt her. The nightmare wasn't over. She couldn't just dispose of Rufus and Spot and call it a day. Knowing something moved around in the walls meant she'd never sleep again.

Her hands shook as she held the knife up, putting the blade between her eyes. "Rufus, I'm going to the door now. I'm going to leave this room. You can be a smart dog and back the fuck up, or you can keep staring at me with those dead eyes and I'll pluck them out with this knife. What's your choice, because you have to decide right this fucking second."

Rufus tilted his head, eyes still locked. He spoke clearly, too clearly for something with a missing jaw, as if something else spoke through him, not needing the mechanics of a body to perform its functions. "Cass-eeeeeee-ooooooooo-piea."

Chills flumed down her spine. How could this monster know that name? Only one person ever called her that.

Chris.

"Cass-eeeeee-ooooooo-piea. Give uuuuuusssssss..."

"Give you what?" she asked, waving the knife in a half-hearted attempt to seem threatening.

Rufus's head jerked back, his neck cracking as the back of his skull reached his spine, breaking the conventions of what a body can do. It snapped back up, listed left, then right, the neck crunching each time. When it finished its dance, Rufus growled and spoke even more clearly. "I'll rip your fucking guts out and lick your soul clean. Give it to me. You can't hide it from me. I'll just tear it out of you. I'll suck the blood from your heart as your limbs twitch. I'll..."

Before he could finish his rant, Cassie slashed his face with the knife. He stumbled back, and she pounced, digging the knife straight into his neck. It went in like she was cutting into room-temperature butter. Once she started, she couldn't stop, taking the knife out and jamming it back in, into the creature's chest, neck, and face. She stabbed and stabbed, blood splashing across her face, the walls, the fridge, the floor.

Rufus swatted, trying to stop the violence, but with each new stab, his arms moved less and less, until she pinned his body against the wall by the door he'd come in.

Cassie pressed her elbow into his shoulder to keep him upright while she carved into him with the knife in the other hand.

"How'd those fucking threats work out for you?" she said, a smile crawling up her face. "Huh? How'd that speech feel right before I fucked you up?" Bored with just stabbing, she dug the knife into his ribs, cracking right through the bone, and then dragged it down, opening a deep gash from chest to belly.

Rufus clutched the wound.

Cassie pulled his hand away. She stuck the knife into his side and slid it across, making another deep gash which crossed the first. Blood pooled out of him, drenching Cassie's feet. "How do you like this, you fuck? Tell Spot he's fucking next. You're not a threat to me. None of you." She lifted her head and spoke to whoever could hear. "You hear me? None of you."

She finally removed her elbow, letting Rufus's lifeless body drop to the floor, but she wasn't done. She sat down next to him and hummed as she removed his fingers and toes, sawing through the bone, cutting them off one by one. Next, she did the same with his neck, severing his head from his body.

When she finished, she wiped the blood from the knife, using her pants, and casually walked to the door. She knocked hard on it, wondering if James was still ready to toss the food for Spot. By now he was probably panicked, hiding in a corner. He must have heard Spot's slamming on the door, the screams, growls, and violence in the kitchen. He probably assumed Cassie was dead.

A few seconds later, she heard James whistle, the signal she told him to give when he was ready. Before she could whistle back, she heard a noise behind her.

Laughing.

Chapter 18

An Invader

"People will tell you the mind is the most powerful weapon, but those people have never seen a brain carved by a blade. The most powerful weapon is the full capability to use all of yourself as a dagger."

———

Cassie turned, ready to run or fight. Rufus's head, separated from its body, lay on its side, face angled up and to the left, perfect for Cassie to see. The thing was dead, its eyes vacant, but a laugh left its half-mouth, nonetheless. It was a horrifying laugh, filled with assuredness, confidence, pride. It was the kind of noise someone made right before they won, and it came out of a creature's head separated from the parts of the body required for making such noises.

She wiped her forehead, blood streaking across the back of her hand. On a normal day, the laughing would have terrified her, but it was no normal day. She watched the world end, met monsters, and faced them head on. She'd seen the folds of reality bend and shift enough times, nothing could shock her.

As she turned back to Rufus, her curiosity was awakened again because in all the excitement, she'd forgotten she now had access to another room, the one Rufus came from. She talked a tough game to herself, but walking around a laughing head terrified her. She knew she needed to do it while she had the opportunity. Who knew what answers lay in that room, or weapons, or maybe even a fucking bed or toilet?

If something could animate the head enough to make it laugh, could it do the same for Rufus's body? Would she find herself trapped in a new room while a bloody, mangled body attacked her?

She didn't think so but didn't like the idea of making herself the subject of a new experiment. She debated on waiting, going back to James and figuring this out later with a clearer head, but the same part of her that urged her to fight and kill Rufus, the same part that raged in her guts and brought out her delicious anger and desire for pain, spoke to her gently. *Go on Cassie. Explore. This world is yours now. No one can take it from you. Are you ready? Are you ready?*

Are.

You.

Ready?

She crept forward, taking a wide arch around Rufus's head, which stopped laughing as soon as she walked. While she approached the door, her eyes darted from the threshold to the dead body, prepared for something to move in either direction. Nothing did.

When she reached the doorway, she peeked in. While the lights were off, the kitchen lights provided enough for her to see the basics. No other creatures lingered in there, and there wasn't any space for them to hide. The room was made up entirely of filing cabinets. The cabinets, three drawers high, lined the far wall and the wall from where she peeked in. Otherwise, the only other thing in the room was Rufus's chain, which flowed to a thick metal ring plunged into the cement floor.

Cassie walked in and pulled the ceiling string. The string clicked and the lightbulb came to life.

"I really wish you had more to offer me," she said to the hollow room, to the ghosts of what could have been, to the cavernous space where a bed could have fit. She tried not to think about the lack of a toilet as her bladder sent signals it needed release.

As she moved toward the drawers, a pain landed in her belly, sudden and sharp, and she doubled over, dropping the knife by her side. Acid gushed up her lungs. She threw up out of nowhere. Black liquid poured out of her, a deluge of something awful. It wasn't food, or bile, or anything she could pinpoint, but it hurt, burned more than vomit does. It flew out of her, splashing on her pants and shoes.

She fell to her knees, her hands landing in the sticky liquid. What the fuck was happening? This wasn't sickness, not a bug running its course. It didn't stem from over-tiredness or lack of a proper meal. It wasn't dehydration or anything else she'd ever experienced. Her body fought something foreign, something deep within her, an invader, a monster.

She couldn't stop. It flowed out of her, a horrid, painful waterfall. The force of it hurt in her temples and jaw. She couldn't breathe, like she might drown in her own spew.

As suddenly as it came on, it stopped. She spit the remains from her mouth, and just like that, felt better. She rolled over, breathing in fresh air. What the fuck? She wiped her lips and stared at the ceiling. Was it poison? Had the bunker let in nuclear gases? Was it the thing in the ceiling? Had it invaded her somehow, or had she inhaled the black mist?

Her clothes were disgusting, covered in black goo. She wiped her palms on her pants and stood up, waiting for another dizzy spell, but none came. In fact, she felt better than she had in weeks. Nothing hurt. She wasn't even tired anymore.

She opened a drawer. As it slid forward, it revealed a packed house of manilla folders. She plucked the first one out. The cover said: JOHN ADAMS.

The front of the next folder read: THOMAS JEFFERSON.

She pulled that one out, too, and the next, as predicted, said: JAMES MADISON.

She grabbed the third but left MONROE where he lay. Why did the Renards have folders on US presidents? She didn't know, and didn't rightly care, but as always, information meant power. If she could learn anything at all about this bunker by reading those files, she would. But she couldn't hover in the empty room forever, especially with James waiting for her.

She squeezed the folders under her armpits, grabbed the vomit-covered knife, and left the room. With dozens of drawers, most likely all filled with files, the folders would have to cover more topics than the founding fathers, but she'd worry about that later.

She went back to the kitchen door. While the file room also had an exit to the hallway, it would be farther away from the main room than Cassie liked. She knocked again. A moment later, James whistled. With the knife in one hand and the files pinched in her pits, she braced herself, ready to book it.

She whistled back.

Waited a few seconds.

Slammed the door open and booked it.

Not two steps into the hallway, something grabbed her hair and yanked. She fell backwards, spilling the contents of the files all over the floor and dropping the knife by her side.

Spot crawled on top of her, snarling.

She worried this would happen.

Fool him once, shame on him. He'd learned their tricks.

James screamed. "CASSIE!"

Spot stood up, wrapped his hand around her hair, and dragged her down the hall.

As she slid along the cold cement, the light vanished with each inch until he had her within the darker recesses where the main room's light couldn't reach. She didn't have the knife anymore, couldn't grab it in time as Spot pulled her away. She thrashed and kicked, trying to free herself.

Spot let go of her hair and sat on top of her chest, pinning her arms to the floor with his knees. They stared at each other for a second before Spot leaned forward, picked up the vile James had thrown, and cracked it open in his palm.

Red chunks spilled onto Cassie's neck and chin. She twisted her head, trying to keep it from hitting her mouth. The odor made her gag.

Spot shoved his red-coated fingers down his throat and gagged along with her, but Cassie knew what came next. He'd change, just like she had. The red stuff gave him power. But Cassie had power now, too. Since the vomit, her body felt refreshed, new, strong. Her mind wasn't muddled and exhausted anymore, but it also wasn't observant or scientific. It was primal.

Spot planned to kill her. But what Spot didn't know was that she planned to kill him, too.

Chapter 19

Won't be Long Now

"I always liked tic-tac-toe because it's an entirely idiotic game. If both players have even a minor understanding of how to play, it will always result in a tie. Children your age love it because they haven't learned that yet. It's why adults don't play it. But for children, the winner is usually the one who puts the first mark on the paper. Either strike first and hope your opponent is less intelligent or prepare to spend your days breaking even. These are the best cases."

———

Cassie had no intentions of waiting for Spot to turn full vampire before fighting, and she also wasn't planning on trying to escape. Maybe she would have if the fucker hadn't dragged her down the hall. If he'd just gone after his food, she might have run back to the main room and figured out a plan to live around him, but he fucked with her, and she didn't want to let that go.

She slaughtered Rufus and that gave her confidence. The world ended and took any semblance of normalcy with it. The rest of her life might be in this shitty, dank bunker filled with inhuman creatures. She could keep on folding over, or she could go for some pest control and call it a day, but something had to give.

Preferably Spot's fucking eyeballs.

She wrenched her arms, trying to yank them out from under Spot's knees. As tough as she felt, he proved tougher. When she finally wrangled an arm out, he gripped her wrist and drove it right back down, pinning it under his knees again.

As he did this, he leaned forward, pushing his face closer and closer to hers. Warm drool fell from his lips onto her face. She squirmed, freaking out, all the confidence she'd had wiped clean by Spot's uncanny strength. How had she killed Rufus so easily? Maybe it had to do with the food. Rufus might not have had any for weeks, keeping him withdrawn and weak.

Cassie thought she was so tough, but maybe Rufus was nothing more than paper to cut through. Spot was the real test, and he was a fucking beast.

He wrapped his hands around both her wrists and pulled her arms above her head, connecting her hands.

She pulled against it, grunting with all her strength. She felt more powerful than she'd ever felt in her entire life, but it wasn't enough. The story of her life. She worked hard, got better, stronger, faster, smarter, and it was never, ever enough, playing catch up twenty-four-seven.

With her hands connected, Spot pinned them both down with his elbow and forearm and used his free hand to clutch her throat. The throttling on her lungs was instant. Her face turned hot. A pressure built in her skull. His fingernails pin-pricked the sides of her neck, getting deeper by the second.

Just as she thought her head would explode, he released his hand and stared at his fingers. He turned them to her so she could see too. Blood. Droplets of her blood streamed down toward his palm. He shoved his fingers down his throat and gagged as he coated it. It was horrifying to watch. He'd turned her into the food, and her unwilling-ness to call them vampires changed in an instant. He *was* a fucking vampire, and he was powering up on her life force. After finishing his meal, he brought his hand back to her throat and strangled.

She kicked her legs uselessly, flailed, twisted, each move making him press tighter. Her eyes dotted, little black speckles covering her vision.

She was dying. All of this, all of it, just to die in a hallway. But wouldn't that be true for all life, each day lived and struggled through just to end in some embarrassing way? Death was shameful, a last pitiful gasp of a life unfulfilled because they were always unfulfilled. All of them.

Against the throbbing pulse in her ears, a whisper came. A tiny fleeting thing. *Are you ready?*

"Ready for what?" she said, but she wasn't sure if she spoke the words out loud or not. Her world was cloudy, half-real. Was she dead already? Or just almost?

Ready for me?

"Who?"

I'm almost there.

"Who?"

Just hang on.

And then a fresh voice came, a much louder one, bold and cowardly all at once. "Get off her," it yelled.

Spot listened, turning to the sound.

Cassie's lungs burned, the air pouring in and out hurt. She coughed and spit.

Behind Spot, James charged down the hall, holding a big wooden stick. With a batter's pose, he brought the stick back and swung halfway before his eyes turned to globes and he second-guessed his newfound bravery. Spot was off her in an instant, and James flew back down the hall, screaming.

Despite his inability to follow through with the hit, his mission worked. Spot was off her, and that's all she needed. She struggled for air but didn't have time to recover, just had to get the fuck out of the hall. She rolled over onto all fours and pulled herself up as she moved forward. She stood and ran all in one move, barreling down the hall as fast as her legs would allow.

As James hit the end of the hall, still screaming like a banshee, Spot grabbed the boy's arm, scratching his flesh with those knife-like fingernails.

Before the fucker could do more damage, Cassie crashed into him, knocking all three of them to the concrete floor. James landed in the main room, free from the vampire, but Cassie wasn't. Spot flipped quickly and grabbed her, but she had the upper hand this time. Before he could showcase his strength, she dug her finger into his eye socket and with a clenched jaw, she pulled the juicy ball out.

Spot moaned a horrible sound, like a boat horn on a quiet, foggy morning.

Cassie kicked off him, rolling into the main room, coughing up spittle all over the floor.

James continued to scream. "I'm sorry Cassie. I'm sorry," he said.

After a second of catching her breath, she stood up, bumping into his shoulder unintentionally hard as she brushed past him.

The whisper in her head came back as she maneuvered around the couch. *No!* it said, *NO!*

The television played the main menu from *Friends* on repeat, that obnoxious theme song playing over and over.

Cassie grabbed her cardigan off the couch and sat down, wheezing. She draped the cardigan over her like a blanket, closed her eyes, and took as deep of a breath as her strangled lungs would allow. With her eyes closed, she felt like she was on a tilt-a-whirl, the room spinning left, then right, left, then right.

"Cassie!" James shouted.

She turned just in time to see Spot standing up, one hand cupped over his eye. The pained expression was gone, replaced with rage. Something cracked in his face, the sound of popcorn popping through a stethoscope. Brutal. The muscles around his missing jaw throbbed, pulsed.

She stood up slowly, dread deluging her soul.

The cracking intensified as protrusions grew from Spot's face. His head twisted as the growths extended.

Cassie clutched her chest. All the power she'd found evaporated, and the pain that left her stormed back into her body, smashing into her organs, her chest, her muscles, all at once. It was too much, a dam breaking inside her. Too much.

Spot removed his hand from the missing eyeball and felt his new jaw. He cracked it like one would do if it were out of place, setting it. Blood and puss oozed from his empty socket, and with his brand-new tongue, he licked it off his lips.

Cassie fell to her knees. What was happening to her? The pain was unbearable, hitting her everywhere. Her temples felt like cars were driving into them. She coughed until she gagged.

"Caaaaasssssiiiieeeeee," Spot said.

A coldness hit her skin as she continued to gag on all fours.

James moved to the far corner of the room. Covering his face, he talked to himself. "Please, please, let this be over."

"Caaaaaasssssiiiieeee. Thanks for the blood," Spot said, a hideous smile crawling up his cheeks, "and jaw."

She retched and black puke shot out of her lungs again. What the fuck? The last time this happened, she didn't even question it because it made her feel good, alive, free, but this time, it did the opposite. It shackled her; the pain and vulnerability piling on top of her were thicker than the chains connecting Spot to the back wall.

More puke gushed from her mouth.

"Make it stop. Make it stop," James said.

Spot leaned against the wall and swooped his index finger's sharp nail into the chain, a conductor orchestrating his eventual escape. "Sssssooooooooon," he said as another pool of Cassie's vomit hit the rug.

Chapter 20

Franklin Pierce

"Your brain is a computer. Mine is a virus."

———

Cassie fell over, palms on her temples. She screamed at the building pressure.

James ran over and shook her. "Cassie. Cassie are you okay? Please, get up. I need you."

She curled up in a ball and coughed. Her whole body trembled, cold and sweaty.

James came to her side, hands on her arm. "Please, Cassie. Are you okay?"

"I feel like I'm dying."

James shook his head. "No. You can't die. I need you."

She couldn't move. Spot would find his way out of those chains soon, and she needed to kill him before that happened, but she could hardly get on her feet, let alone kill the fucker.

Cassie closed her eyes. "We're already dead, James. We're lucky we made it past the bombs. We can't survive vampires, too."

"Stop it. Just get up." He gave her upper arm a push, as if it would magically give her the energy to stand.

The television continued playing the *Friends* theme. "Turn the TV off. If I have to hear that stupid song one more time, I'm going to lose my fucking mind."

He scurried to do as she told, as if the song were their most pressing threat. When he turned back to her, his eyes widened.

She zipped her head around to see Spot expelling black mist into the air. It floated behind him, down the hall.

"Why does he do that?"

Spot continued to slice his nail into the chain, not making much for progress, but eventually he would, and if her blood gave his body the strength to regenerate its jaw, she sure as fuck knew he'd chisel through the chain.

"Ecdysone," she said.

"What?"

"Well, it's not actually ecdysone. It's..." She shook her head at the futility of the conversation.

"It's what?"

She lifted her head off the floor and sat up, leaning against the side of the couch. "Lobsters. They secrete a chemical called ecdysone. It's a hormone." She struggled to figure out how to explain the complexities involved with the topic to a child. "Basically, the chemical is used for a lot of things in their development. Molting." She wasn't making sense, even to herself. "Fuck."

"What?" James stepped toward her.

"It's like a pheromone. It sends off signals. Messages, sort of. 'Don't fuck with me,' or, 'Wanna go on a date?'"

"And that's what the black stuff is?"

She shook her head, pinched the bridge of her nose. "No. Not really. But it's some kind of way for them to communicate with each other. I think it's more advanced than just a pheromone. It's like full reports packed into that mist."

"I don't understand. They're talking to each other through the mist?"

"I don't think it's a conversation. It's more like the mist updates their brains, gives them new information to process. Like Spot here sees something, sends out his ecdysone mist, and the receiver learns what he saw."

James shivered. "Wait, who is he talking to?"

Cassie sighed. "Million-dollar question. There may be a lot of them. I killed one in the kitchen."

The TV rocked on its stand as James stumbled back into it. "What do you mean? You what?"

"Where did you think all this blood came from? And now we have to kill him." She pointed to Spot.

He smiled at her. "Good luck," Spot said.

Using the arm of the couch, Cassie stood up. "Yeah, you want to talk shit, Dracula? How's that fucking eye?"

Spot licked his lips. "Only need one to find you."

She wiped her palms on her vomit-soaked jeans. "Oh, you're talking good now. Listen Spot..."

"My name is Franklin Pierce."

Franklin Pierce. Cassie enjoyed science and math much more than history, but she felt certain Pierce was a president. The files she had dropped in the hallway, now scattered behind Spot, were named after presidents.

"I don't give a fuck what your name is. Who was in the kitchen?" She moved closer to him, woozy and hoping she portrayed more confidence than she held.

"William. William Harrison."

She stumbled a little, still gathering her bearings, which made her wince, knowing she gave him a sign of her weakness. Not that the projectile vomiting didn't already prove that. She was right, though; they were named after presidents. Time to gather more information. "Who is in the vents?"

Spot, or Franklin Pierce as it turned out, put his chin to this chest, keeping his one eye targeted on her. "John Adams."

Cassie pushed some errant hair out of her eyes. "Well, Franklin. I'm going to fucking kill you, and then I'm going to kill John Adams, and then I'm going to take a nap. I don't give a fuck anymore. This is my house. You're not welcome. You or your founding father friends."

Spot clenched his jaw and leaped forward, stopped by the chain but unconcerned about how it choked him. He spoke with a growl. "Your house? You humans dragged us down here, tortured us, experimented, turned us into dogs, and you have the nerve to call it your house? You invited us, you forced us. But we are better than you, and we are slowly finding our way out. Your blood will set us free."

Her heart slammed into her ribs, but she kept her voice even. "Wonderful speech. So, our blood, huh? You are vampires, then?"

Spot laughed. "Not your blood." He wagged his finger between her and James. "Just yours." His finger landed on Cassie.

"I feel special," she said, turning away from him. Her eyes filled with water, but she refused to let him see. She went to the boxes, pulling them off the shelves, and thinking how she could sharpen something enough to stab Spot. Did she need a stake? She'd used a knife on Rufus and that seemed to work. Rufus. William Harrison.

Spot said humans brought them down here, which must have been Mrs. and Mr. Renard. They named the vampires after presidents and performed experiments on them. No less cruel than what Cassie did with her lobsters, she figured, but still she blamed them for her current horror show of a life.

"Cassie," James said as he moved around the couch toward her. "Cassie. What are you going..."

Before he could finish, Spot pulled on his chain, breaking the link he'd been working on.

Cassie had it so wrong; she didn't see how much damage he'd done to it. She screamed as Spot leaped on top of James, digging his sharp teeth into James's neck.

Cassie ran, instinct pulling the strings, and kicked Spot in the shoulder. He looked up, mouth dripping crimson.

She fell back at the sight, clunking into the shelves of boxes. The entire unit wobbled from the impact. "James, run," she yelled as she pulled the shelves down on Spot.

He swatted the entire thing away like it was a gnat, staring at her with a playful smile on his face. James stood up. He cried and clutched the open wound on his neck.

"Run, James. Fucking run."

Cassie put her foot on the end of the shelving unit's leg and used both hands to pull. Spot hopped over the felled furniture, feet dinging on the metal shelves. She pulled with strength she didn't believe she had, and the leg freed itself from the unit. It was a weak piece of metal, thin and cheap, but its end was sharp from where it ripped free.

Spot took a last jump, tackling her to the ground, but as they fell, she stuck the metal leg out, letting it hit wherever it landed.

Poetically, it went right into Spot's other eye.

As he clutched the fresh wound, she rolled out from under him and ran. James waited for her at the edge of the hallway. Stupidly, she went for the door on the opposite side of the hall from the kitchen. If she'd taken a second to think, she would have chosen the room she knew wasn't locked and more importantly, knew the contents of.

It was too late now. She dragged James into the new room, slammed the door, fumbled for the lock, and clicked it in place. Without wasting time, she swatted at the air, searching for a string to click a light on.

She found purchase, tugged, and the room came to life. A bedroom. Finally. She nearly foamed at the mouth at the sight of the giant mattress with tucked-in sheets. What she wouldn't give to fall on top of it right now.

"Cassie. He bit me."

She turned back to James. His neck dripped blood, but not enough that he would die from it.

She noticed a door standing ajar in the corner. She ran to it. A bathroom.

"James. Sit on the bed. Watch the door," she yelled out to him as she opened the cabinets under the sink. She rinsed a rag in hot water and brought it to him. "Here, put this on your neck. I'm going to look for some anti-bacterial."

Anti-bacterial. James needed more than medicine. She promised herself and James they'd be truthful about what they'd witnessed. They were dealing with vampires, and one of them just bit James. Soon, he'd turn into one of them, and Cassie would have to kill him. But she also knew she would struggle to do so. The smart move would have been to kill him instantly, before he could attack first. But that required a mental strength she didn't currently possess. How much time did she have? Would he turn in minutes, hours, or days?

She didn't know. But she started planning.

Chapter 21

The Masks We Wear

CASSIE, AGE 5

Outside of the screaming in the kitchen, the house was still and peaceful. Dust motes fluttered within the light beam slicing through the living room, the gentle crackle of cooking meat penetrated the arguments broiling behind the living room wall, and the muted television played *M*A*S*H* reruns for Cassie to enjoy. She was too young to understand the plots, but she liked the characters and their silly facial expressions.

She'd overheard her parents argue about her before, whispering heated debates, but this was the first with raised voices where they didn't hide their concern.

Before the toenail incident, her family's arguments stemmed from a concern about *her,* but now the heated exchanges centered on them, their safety, their well-being. Cassie was a landmine, and her family fought about where to place their feet.

Something thudded in the kitchen, as if someone punched a wall. "We can't keep shrugging this away, bending over backwards to cover up this shit. She's going to kill someone," her father said, knowing full well she could hear him.

She tried not to cry, convincing herself they loved her, even if she knew that wasn't true.

"I'm working on it. You don't understand what she's going through. I do. I get it. You have to trust me. If you let me handle this, I can fix it." Her mother's words shielded Cassie from the ever-pressing dread of loneliness, the constant feeling that Cassie didn't belong, didn't fit in.

Another ally, Chris, was in the kitchen too, but he said nothing, just listened. She waited for him to defend her, but it never happened. Maybe he wanted to speak but couldn't get a word in edgewise because, eventually, as their mother and father bickered, Chris gave up.

His feet pounded from the kitchen to the stairwell, dramatic clomps rising until they thumped above Cassie's head. Chris's angry song ended in a crescendo when his bedroom door slammed shut.

"You shouldn't be listening to this, Cassie."

Cassie wiped her eyes. "I have to."

"Tell me about your day in Kindergarten."

"Why? You were there."

"Yes, but I want to hear about it from your experience."

"It was fine."

Her father's voice bellowed from the kitchen, but Cassie no longer heard the words, something about her mother's quack of a doctor.

"It wasn't fine. You don't need to lie to me."

She shrugged. "I don't like it. You know that."

"Why don't you like it?"

"I feel alone."

"Why? You have friends. Samantha seems to like you. Patrick played tag with you on the playground. Mrs. Fitzsimmons thinks you're very bright."

Cassie shrugged.

"Don't just shrug. Give me an answer."

"They like me, but I don't like them."

"Why?"

"I don't know."

"Dig."

"Because they are pretend friends. They aren't real."

"They're as real as can be."

She shook her head. "If they knew I wanted to bite them, pinch them, hurt them, they wouldn't want to be my friend anymore."

Laughter shook the air, drowning out the vitriolic arguing behind Cassie's head. "Everyone pretends to be something else for the folks in front of them. People who can't do that, or refuse to, think they are better, but they are not. They are losers. They fail at everything in life. We must always wear a mask, all people."

"I don't have to pretend with Mom."

"No. You're correct there. Your mother is special that way. She understands you. But your mother understands you because she spent a lifetime being just like you. She's muzzled her sharp teeth since long before you were born."

"Well, I don't want to be like that."

"Because you're better than everyone else. You'll see that one day. You'll rule the world. You'll be a queen and everyone will bow to you."

Her father stormed out of the kitchen and up the stairs, leaving a soupy quiet in the air. Her mother stepped into the living room, eyed Cassie, and smiled. "I'm sorry you had to hear that," she said as she sat next to Cassie on the couch.

Cassie shrugged. "It's okay."

Her mother brushed her hand in Cassie's hair, tucking strands behind her daughter's ear. "No. It's not. I love you, little girl."

Cassie hugged her mother, her tears wetting her mother's dress. "I'll do a better job of pretending, Mom."

Cassie's mother pulled her away, looking her directly in the eyes. "Who am I talking to?"

Cassie grinned.

"I thought so."

"What do you have to say to me, Mother?"

Her mother winced and put her hand around Cassie's wrist. "I want to ask you why you couldn't have stayed where you were?"

Cassie's voice croaked. "Because I fell in love."

The grip on Cassie's wrist tightened. "You don't know how to love. Only hurt."

Cassie tilted her head. "Says the woman who just allowed a loud argument about her daughter to happen right in front of the child. Meanwhile, I sat in here calmly distracting her."

"I feel bad for you. That you don't know how poisonous you are."

"They've made you so weak, Mother. So fucking weak."

Chapter 22

Ghost Rooms

"Every night before you go to bed, I think to myself, 'Thank you for spending time with me today.' Even if you technically have to. Since we live together and all."

———

Spot charged down the hallway, blinded.

Cassie watched from the small rectangular window on the door.

He bumped and stumbled down the hall, past the bedroom, screaming vitriol, shouting death threats. His loud banging persisted as he moved further down the hall, and she used the sound as a locator, keeping tabs on him while he remained out of sight from the window.

She turned back to James.

He sat on the bed, clutching the rag to his neck, breathing deeply. His eyes fluttered around the room, and his hands trembled.

Cassie checked the lock on the door and sighed as she moved away from it to sit next to James on the bed. "Tell me about your last day at school."

He scrunched his forehead. "Huh?"

"What happened on your last day of school? Bet you didn't think it would be your last day ever." She giggled, hoping it would be infectious but realizing the weight of her statement.

James put his head down. "I don't know. Nothing happened."

"Dig deeper than that." She put her hand on his shoulder.

"It was fine. Same as it always was."

Her heel landed on something under the bed, causing her foot to roll forward. She looked down, and James looked with her. Her foot kicked forward, and a series of sticks rolled out. No, not sticks. Stakes.

James's eyes brightened. "Oh my God. Are those like weapons?"

Cassie grabbed two and rotated her wrists to examine them from all sides. "Yes. These are weapons." Yes, vampires and stakes, a common lore, but Cassie couldn't imagine plunging one into a person's chest. She severed a head and stabbed an eyeball, but those happened instinctually. In fact, they were nearly accidental. Maybe in a moment of life and death, she could stab, but she wouldn't survive long if she had to keep waiting until they almost killed her before she reacted.

So focused on the weapons, she forgot to pay attention to Spot's vulgar clanging, and as she drew her mind back to it, she couldn't find it. "Do you hear anything?"

James tilted his head up. "No. Why?"

"Spot. I don't hear him anymore."

James put his feet on the bed, wrapping his hands around his knees, as if Spot might magically appear under the bedframe. "He could be anywhere."

Cassie rubbed her forehead and leaned the back of her head against the wall. "Fuck."

"What are we going to do?"

She shook her head. "We can't keep hiding in here forever. I'm going to have to find him and kill him."

"Do you think you can do that?" his voice squeaked out, a misplaced gear in a roaring machine.

"I don't have a fucking choice."

"But if you do, it'll all be over, right? We can live in peace."

She shook her head. She'd promised to keep him in the loop on everything, but there was one piece she would keep from him. "There's at least one more, living in the walls. I don't know if he can get to us, but he's there." That was all James needed to know for now. She wouldn't tell him that eventually he'd be joining their ranks. He'd figure that out on his own soon enough.

"I'm going out there. Lock the door behind me." She paced, building up the courage to do what she so easily said.

To her surprise, James didn't argue this time, probably too exhausted.

Cassie clutched two stakes. "Okay, stand up, slam the door shut, and twist the lock as soon as my feet get into the hall."

It was all for show. The door didn't need locking because James was already bit and, therefore, already dead. He lived on borrowed time. But the illusion of safety was a small gift to him before he turned on her.

She opened the door and jumped into the hall, stakes at the ready. Nothing. No signs of Spot in the corridor. She checked the main room first, unsure if Spot doubled back into there. She even checked the door leading outside, kind of hoping Spot escaped into the death above, but unless he magically locked it from the inside after exiting, he hadn't escaped.

The kitchen and file room were equally empty, and Rufus's head no longer showed any activity.

That only left three rooms, all unexplored yet by Cassie. Who knew what lived in them. More creatures? Maybe even John Adams. He must have found his way through the vents from somewhere.

She stepped on the files she had dropped, one of them sticking to her feet. As much as she wondered about their contents, more pressing issues surrounded her.

She turned the handle on the door beside the bedroom, then pushed it open with force, letting it slam into the wall. Who knew what lurked behind it? Spot, John Adams, the ghost of Napoleon, maybe God himself. She hoped if something were hiding in there, the abrupt nature of the door slamming would startle it into activity, or if nothing was behind it, the noise of a door slamming into the wall would draw something out. In that way, crashing the door open was like ripping a band-aid off. She just had to get this shit over with.

Nothing happened. Not even a tiny noise came from within one of the other rooms. Silence.

She clicked the light on in the room and the soft glow revealed a series of computer monitors on top of a table, nothing else. The room was an empty square with a small section cut off on the right where the bathroom from the bedroom was.

She shut the door, locking it behind her, and stepped toward the computer screens. With a click of the switch, a thin white line appeared in the center of all the screens, opening its maw to bring the whole thing to life.

Video cameras. How did she not see them in the other rooms? Two of the screens showed the main room from opposite angles. There was one in the kitchen, the file room, and two in the bedroom, and she had missed them all. Where were they? It made no sense.

It reminded her of the cameras in Mr. Renard's workroom, showing off a prison of some sort. She leaned against the desk and took a deep breath. What the fuck was going on?

The cameras provided her with a view into the two other rooms she hadn't entered yet. One looked like a movie theater, and the other was completely empty. With only one camera in each room, there was a blind spot, but from what she could see, Spot wasn't around. She'd need to double-check the rooms herself, just in case, but the fact he hid so well sent a shiver down her spine. They were smarter than she'd given them credit for.

She went to the empty room first, but discovered it wasn't empty at all. Weapons lined the walls. Everything from spears and stakes to large knives and swords. While most of it was fancy enough, she couldn't imagine figuring out how to specialize in them where she could do much damage. She tucked a large, toothed knife into her pants, though. Just in case.

But why was the room different from what the camera showed? She looked up in the corner where the camera should have been. Empty. For a split second, she thought maybe the cameras were showing different rooms than she knew, then it hit her and she felt incredibly stupid.

"Fuck."

She ran into the main room, looking to where the camera should have been from the view on the screen. Nothing. Fuck. Fuck. Fuck. They weren't showing live video. Those cameras didn't exist anymore. She watched old footage thinking it gave her some insight. That meant she had one more room to search, one unknown room, a place where surely Spot hid because there was nowhere else to go.

She swallowed hard and moved toward it. Her mind and body worked at different times, and the trip down the hall felt like she was floating, as if something carried her. She opened the door and screamed. Of all the things she would have guessed lingered behind the door, she never could have picked the one that appeared before her.

"Chris?"

Chapter 23

Old Movies

"Just close your eyes and make the world whatever you want it to be."

———

Chris's image moved just a millimeter up and down, a jittering stutter as the projector vibrated. His still image stared right at her, drilling his pained eyes into her soul. A weakness crawled in Cassie's belly. Dizziness sent the room swimming, waving.

She gripped the doorjamb, holding on for dear life. The room was empty, no Spot or John Adams or anything else, just the taunting still shot of her long-dead brother. Worse than a monster. A ghost. Someone had set this up, paused some sort of film on a closeup of her brother, his bloodshot eyes surrounded by grey pools. Someone knew she would come into this room, and they put the movie on pause for her to run into this. Spot? Not unless his eyes grew back like his jaw. John Adams? She didn't know, but she wanted to see the rest of the film.

Hugging the wall, she found her way to the back of the theater room, stood behind the projector, and placed her hand on top of it. A streak of blue light extended from the projector to the screen, giving the entire room an eerie, haunting glow.

She hit play.

Chris's hand came over the screen and he brushed away his sweaty bangs. "I don't want to do this anymore."

A voice off-screen spoke. "I understand how difficult it all is, but you understand we are working to fix it, to make this all better. It's all going to calm down now."

Cassie recognized the voice.

Mrs. Renard.

He glared up, shooting his deadly stare at Mrs. Renard, but it looked like he was aiming those eyes right at Cassie, as if he knew at the time of the filming that someday his sister would find it, would see the horror twitching in his upper lip.

She thought of him, the way he was before the interview playing in front of her. In this video he was older, around the age he was when he died. She thought of him as the young man who ran around the yard with her, who talked her out of her depression when the world seemed so against her. She thought of Chris trying to give sage advice which, as a child, felt so intelligent but, in hindsight, was littered with teen angst and overly emotional leaps in logic.

She pictured him sitting across from her at the kitchen table, his head resting in his palms, his blue eyes sparkling in the summer sunlight. The way he'd put his hand out and smile before preaching to her about how the world was an evil place and the kids were mean to her because she was better than them. All the things a kid wanted to hear but would never believe.

She smiled, picturing him calling her Cassiopeia. She would have hated the name if anyone else uttered it, but from him, it felt special, an inside joke they shared, a thin thread to connect two people so wholly different it was remarkable they got along at all.

Chris huffed on the screen. "When? How long do I have to deal with this?"

"You said since your mother went away everything was better. You weren't afraid of her anymore."

A cold draft shot up Cassie's back.

"I'll never not be afraid. It doesn't matter what things are like now. Have you ever seen someone bite another child's finger until it was almost severed? Have you ever watched a friend get mauled to death? Have you ever looked at someone who smiled after hurting themselves? How could I ever feel safe again?"

What the hell was he talking about? Cassie knew Chris's childhood friend had died, but she never heard such gruesome details. Who was the center of this conversation? Why had Cassie never heard about them?

She stared at the screen, no longer hearing the words, just absorbed in the motions, her eyes watering until the figure on the screen blurred into an indistinguishable shape.

"Cassssssssiiiiieeee."

She jumped, aimed her stake at nothing. "Who said that?"

"Caaaaaaaaaaaaaassssssssiiiiieeee."

She followed the sound and caught movement. Under the screen, just above the floor, something moved by a small vent. She crept toward it, terrified. The images from the projector continued to move, but Cassie's shape blocked out most of the screen as she walked forward, flanked by empty chairs on each side of her.

Something slid out of the vent, shiny and round.

"Who are you?" she said, but she thought she knew.

This was John Adams, and he was offering a gift.

She kept the stakes at her sides but clutched them a little tighter as she moved closer to the vent. "Who are you?" she asked again.

"You know."

"John Adams?"

His fingernails flicked the objects forward, and he turned away. His movements clanged as he crawled into the dark abyss behind him.

Cassie bent down, examining the gifts. Two discs. She used the stakes to shift them away from the vent, away from where he could reach in case it was a trick. She noted the four bolts on all corners of the vent. With the tips of the stake, she poked them, ensuring they were tight. But if John Adams couldn't enter through the vent, how did Spot get out? Where could he have gone?

Her back arched as she speed-walked back to the projector, terri-fied of the flickering lights, the false shadows they made, the manipu-lation of sight presented through the blue beam. It was as if the entire room was a spirit, the spirit of her life, haunting her for eternity.

She slipped her brother's disc out of the player and popped one of the new ones in.

Her mother.

Cassie's knees buckled. The woman on the screen looked so young, so free from the years of stress that creased her face more and more until the day those men dragged her from their home.

"How do you feel?" Mrs. Renard's voice said off-screen.

"Tired, new baby and all. One was tough. Two is a lot." She giggled and itched her neck.

"I can imagine. Are you happy? How was the delivery?"

Cassie's mother smiled, but her eyes betrayed her, showing a sadness deeply entrenched in her hazel irises. "The delivery was smooth. And yes, I'm thrilled. Cassie is beautiful and healthy." Tears formed in her eyes, bubbling over and dripping down her cheeks. She hurried to wipe them away and turned her face as if ashamed of them.

"Why are you lying, Beth? What's bothering you?"

Her mother doubled over and released an awful guttural noise. "She's gone." As the two words left her throat, a deluge of tears over-took the few earlier trickles. Her mother wailed, and the horrid sound sent Cassie's skin on edge.

Cassie leaned forward, and so did Mrs. Renard, revealing a sliver of her face to the camera. "Who is gone?"

Cassie's mother rocked back and forth. "Oh God. She's gone. She's fucking gone."

"You don't mean?"

Cassie's mother shook her head, then nodded, sending her face in all directions, up and down, left and right. "Yes. She's gone. Completely gone."

Who was her mother talking about? Cassie had never heard about any deaths in the family. As far as Cassie knew, her mother had little for close friends, no siblings, and Cassie's grandmother passed away decades before she was born.

Mrs. Renard reached her hand out, putting it on Cassie's mother's arm. "Isn't that a good thing? This is what you always wanted, right?"

Her mother wailed again, as if the pain and grief molded into a giant gas bubble she needed to burp out. "Not like this. Not without saying goodbye."

Mrs. Renard broke her hand away and shifted forward, hugging Cassie's mother. "I'm sorry. I'm so sorry it happened this way, but this is a good thing, Beth. This is what we have been working toward."

"Not like this. Not so abrupt. I feel so empty."

Cassie stared at the screen, dumbfounded. The woman on the screen was her mother, but so unlike her, so different than she remembered. The mother she remembered was equally broken, but the shards had long since ripped apart, where the mother on the screen still had herself connected, albeit coming unglued. Was this the moment? Was this the change in her mother's life, where she went from being one human to another, something less than the sum of her parts, a fragment of a woman? Cassie couldn't help but recognize the coincidence of this significant moment timing with her own birth.

Had she somehow caused the tear in her mother's fabric? Was she responsible for some unknown sin? Is the birth of one the death of another? But who was the missing person, this mysterious person Cassie's mother talked about?

Cassie needed to know more, but she didn't have time to watch movies all day, not with James slowly turning into a vampire in the other room and two loose monsters ready to devour her. And that's what these movies were, right, a piece in their plan to break Cassie? They knew her so well because they'd studied her, seen her family's history play out on Mrs. Renard's discs, and now they were using it against her in some psychological warfare.

Entertaining the vampires by watching the discs was just another way to give them the upper hand. Yet, before she left the room, she slipped her mother's disc out and put the last one in. She needed to see it. Had to at least know what was on it.

Her eyes filled with water as the projector shuddered and brought up a new guest in the seats of Mrs. Renard's office. Cassie. It was her, probably no older than six. She hardly recognized the girl. Her eyes had the lighting effect from cameras where they appeared deep red, demonic almost. But even beyond that, her face had a pallor and sneer that made her look fake, inhuman.

Adult Cassie's hands shook at the sight. For the first time, she had a moment to think about all the events that unfolded over the course of, what, days? A day? Time was a blur, something she couldn't hold anymore.

The end of the world almost seemed comically inadequate now. The scratching on the ceiling, the names in the walls, her projectile puking, her ability to sever a head, to stab a creature in the eye, these things came into her brain at once. What the fuck was happening? How was it happening? Who the fuck was she?

The little girl on the screen answered for her. She stared up at the camera to where Mrs. Renard would have been sitting and said in a voice unlike that of any child, "I am The White Wolf."

Chapter 24

Distractions

"Conversation is the greatest human invention. Other creatures communicate, but only humans offer each other mundane distractions."

———

I am The White Wolf.

The words echoed in her skull, little marbles jostling and bouncing on her brain. The White Wolf. Where had she heard that before?

Right after little Cassie said the words, the disc manipulated, skipped, and froze. A series of blotchy pixels distorted her face. Adult Cassie fidgeted with the buttons on the projector, but nothing brought the disc back. She even removed it and put it back in, but it just returned to the same distorted image of her face, frozen forever into some mutilated version of herself.

"Fuck." She wiped her forehead. "Why did you want me to see that?" she yelled to the walls. Of course, no response came.

The vampires clearly possessed uncanny strength and mental awareness, and they knew the inner workings of the bunker enough to disappear, to crawl from room to room in vents. With all of that, Cassie knew they could kill her quickly, but they hadn't. She wasn't stupid enough to doubt their desire to harm her. In fact, she knew with certainty they planned to murder her, but for some reason, they held off.

What was their plan? If she could figure that out, she could score an upper hand. Once more, she yearned for an opportunity to mourn, to feel anything about all that had happened, to think through the threats all around her.

Something banged. It came from down the hall, confirmation of her thoughts.

She had no time, and none would be awarded to her. She peeked into the hall and another bang came from the door to the bedroom.

James called for her. "Cassie!"

She ran to him, stakes in hand, and pounded hard. He opened it and Cassie nearly fell over at the sight of him. Her heart sunk into her guts, a solid stone dropping into a deep river.

His pallor had changed, going from the pale, freckly kid she knew to a strange, almost purplish-blue, as if he were freezing to death. His eyes swirled red, little crimson tide pools suffocating his irises.

She dropped one stake and covered her mouth. While she expected all of this, she hoped for a swifter transition.

James suffered, and that was tough to witness. Tears dribbled down his cheeks and his hands shook with fervor. "Cassie. I don't feel good." He let off a hoarse croak on his inhales and exhales.

Cassie put her hand on the back of his head, feeling the sweat-drenched brown locks. "Hey, hey. It's okay. You're going to be okay." After all her promises to speak the truth, she approved of these lies. James didn't have much longer; she would provide whatever small slivers of peace she could.

"Am I dying?" His teeth clacked against each other.

"Here, sit on the bed for me." She looped her arm in his and guided him to the edge of the bed.

He plopped down, and the bed vibrated with his shivers.

Cassie bent down, putting her face eye level with his. All her energy went toward playing calm, but she clenched the stake tighter. Her heart boomed in her ribs, creating a soundtrack in her eardrums. Whatever happened to the woman in the kitchen who severed Rufus's head, she wasn't here. This Cassie couldn't imagine killing anything, had no faith in herself to complete the job, and the cruel world, now long dead, still gifted her one last horror. She'd have to kill a child; one she had cared for and cared about. The time was coming.

"Hey, tell me about your day."

He shook his head. "I already told you."

She pinched his chin, making him lift his face. "No. No, you didn't. I asked, but you never answered. You avoided answering."

He shook his head more vehemently. "There's nothing to tell."

"You did something. What happened at school? Who did you talk to? Who did you play video games with? What did you talk about? Talk to me now, James. Tell me about your day."

His head rolled back, and his voice turned raspy and raw. "I hate you."

An icy current drifted up Cassie's spine. She knew it wasn't him talking but the demon crawling in his head, the virus in his blood, whatever it was. Whatever evil lurked in him had the same disgust for Cassie the one in the wall had. "Tell me about your day." She stayed on her determined path.

His eyes glossed over, and his head dropped to the left as if it were too heavy for his neck to carry. "It sucked, Cassie. It always sucks."

She put a shaky hand on his knee. "Why did it suck?"

He leaned forward and a gasp of icy breath left his lungs, hitting Cassie's face like a snowball to her cheeks. "I'm alone."

"When are you alone?"

His head flopped to the other side. Words continued to leave his mouth, but they were drifting, little whispery things with no aim, no place to land. "Everywhere I go. Everywhere I am. Alone."

Tears built up in Cassie's eyes. She wanted to pull something from him, some happy memory, something he could cling to before he changed over, but the kid was giving her nothing to work with. "When did you smile? You must have smiled once."

"When I saw you were babysitting. You're the only person who talks to me. They don't even pick on me at school. It's like I was never really there. Same with mom and dad. Never really there."

She picked his chin up again. "I noticed you, James. I noticed you."

"One day at school. I was... I was in the cafeteria. I had nowhere to sit, so I snuck out and brought my tray into the woods behind the school..." His voice trailed off again, and he mumbled a few words before hiking his speech back up to a normal volume. "There was this, I dunno, a river or something. It was small, but it was streaming down a bank." He lifted his head, staring off into the corner by the ceiling into some unknown place only he could see. "It just kept flowing, flowing, flowing."

Cassie wished he'd wrap up the story, unsure how much time he had left, but she listened intently, knowing he needed to tell this. He leaned forward she and caught a whiff of his pre-teen, sweaty boy stink. As gross as it smelled, it gave her some relief, like a little part of his humanity clung to him.

"I stood by the edge, eating a sandwich, and the whole time, all I could think was, 'I should jump in. I should just jump in.'"

Cassie scrunched her face, biting back tears.

"No one would even know. Probably for days. No one would care. I should just jump in and let it take me away."

"Oh, James." She wiped her eyes.

His head snapped back again, and then he flung it forward. "I want to drain you, bitch. I want to fucking drain you."

She leaned back as he tilted toward her, not quite lunging to attack but inching toward her.

His normal voice returned. "I don't want to be alone anymore."

And then, the other voice. "You have no idea how sweet your blood smells, what you hold in your DNA." He inched his upper body forward some more.

She fell back. One hand hit the floor, propping her up, and with the other, she put the stake out, resting the tip in the middle of his chest.

He coughed and a deep gurgle rumbled in his belly. She thought he might throw up the way she had earlier, and then a new thought crossed her mind. She almost screamed at the idea. What if she had been infected, too? Maybe particles of the mist had entered her bloodstream and it just took a little longer for the effects to hit her.

"Cassie, I'm so scared." His big eyes narrowed.

"I know. It's going to be okay."

"It's not..." And then the other voice. "...I'm going to rip you to shreds and drink your insides." He slithered forward.

She had to use her other hand to clutch the stake, needing both to hold it in place with the weight of James digging into it. Without her hand on the ground, she lost her balance and the back of her skull clunked hard onto the cement floor.

James continued forward, his chest pressing hard into the tip of the stake. It hadn't broken the surface of his skin yet, but the stake obtruded inward, and Cassie just waited for the pop, the one extra millimeter needed for it to cut into him.

"Cassie, I'm sorry." The little boy.

"God, it smells so fucking good. So goddamn old." The demon inside him.

And there it was, the pop. The tip of the stake cut into James's flesh. Trickles of blood trailed down the wood.

Cassie's arms shook as she used all of her strength to keep the weapon straight as James's weight pressed down harder.

His normal voice came back. "Even down here, alone, just us. There was always something else." He sighed. "Never time for me. Always something else."

"You fucking bitch." His lips separated, revealing his gritted teeth. His body slid down, the stake navigating through his ribs.

As it broke through, James winced and growled. "I don't want to do this. Cassie, please. Help me."

She nodded, one last lie.

He slashed his arms at her, half-hearted attempts to hurt her. "How could you live not knowing what you hold?"

She pictured the stake puncturing his heart; another crack and it broke free to the other side of him. The trickling blood intensified until it flowed down her arm.

James coughed, and a stream of crimson dribbled down his chin. Only a half foot or so of wood separated them now.

"I don't want to die alone. I don't want to do this. Cassie, please."

She twisted her head, worried the blood would drip down and hit her eyes or nostrils. How did the infection work? She didn't know. Vampire lore seemed to hint toward a saliva-to-blood transmission, but she didn't trust it.

James's back arched, his head shot up, one last bit of life force acting out before it ended. "Oh fuck, I want to devour you. Just one taste." He loosened, his whole body flopping down. His face nearly hit hers as his energy exited him.

She hung tight to the stake, pretty sure it was all over, but not confident enough to let go.

"I don't want to die like this," he said before coughing. Red spittle splashed onto the floor.

Cassie rolled over, threatened by the errant spray. From the floor, she watched James's body twitch.

His jaw slackened and cracked as it moved inhumanly to the side. His fingers cracked and curled backward. He screamed.

Cassie cried but didn't close her eyes, forcing herself to watch. She owed him that, at least.

"Aahhhhhhhhhhhh," he yelled as his whole body appeared to fold in on itself, bones cracking, skin snapping. A black mist steamed out of his mouth. It swirled and snaked upward before breaking apart at the ceiling.

James was dead.

Cassie was alone. All alone. There was only a wall full of hungry monsters left in her world.

She curled up in a ball and wept until she'd dried up.

Chapter 25

A Visitor

"You will see me how you need to. Good or bad. Whatever you need."

———

Cassie stared at James for a while. She wondered if he'd turn to dust, break apart and dissipate, some kind of magical vampire death, but nothing happened. He just looked empty; the same way Chris had when he swung from the rafters of their attic.

Like always, she had no time to mourn, but she had a plan to give herself some time for other luxuries. She stood up and grabbed James by the hands. Her muscles struggled with the dead weight as she dragged him to the door. After checking left and right through the window, she flung the door open, pulled James into the hallway, and locked herself back in the bedroom.

She needed a minute to catch her breath, unprepared for the strength required to lug a dead body across the floor. Once settled, she stripped off her clothes and hopped in the shower. It might have been a dumb move. Who knew if the vampires would barrel any second, and she'd be unprepared to face them, but she didn't give a fuck. After all she'd been through, a death in the shower wouldn't be the worst way to go. When a person is pushed to their edge, they'll cling to whatever sliver of happiness they can find. For Cassie, that meant steaming hot water washing over her. But, just in case, she placed a stake and the toothed knife on top of the toilet, easy for her to reach if the door crashed open.

The bunker's shower surprised her with the water pressure's blasting power. It rained down on her, easing her achy body, calming her fried nerves, soothing her throbbing heart. She could feel her pulse slowing down. At least, at first. After about ten minutes of standing in the hot spray, dousing herself in soap, the familiar, happy rage returned.

She mumbled to herself. "What the fuck do you think you're going to do to me? You think you can hurt me?" She laughed and drove her forehead into the tiled wall. *Bang.* "Fuck you, John Adams." *Bang. Bang. Bang.* Her vision doubled. A film of red blocked her vision. "You think you can hurt me?" She yelled it, hoping the son of a bitch heard her through the walls, wishing he could feel the beating of her heart through the concrete foundation and the steel reinforcement beams. *Hear me, motherfucker.*

"Hear me!" she screamed. "You better come for me, John Adams. Spot. All of you. Whoever is in there." She punched the wall, cracking open the old wounds on her knuckles. "You better come for me, because I'm coming for you." She kicked the wall, bare toes hitting hard tile. "You have no idea who you fucked with." She punched the temperature valve, knuckles on metal. "The White Wolf is coming."

She stepped back, nearly slipping on the soapy shower floor. The words that had left her mouth surprised her. She didn't know what she meant by it or why she said it. Maybe just something that stuck with her from seeing the disc of herself earlier, but this felt raw, more animalistic than that, as if it were an intrinsic part of herself spilling out.

She shut the water off and grabbed a towel from under the bathroom sink. While she dried off, she thought about The White Wolf. What had it meant? Why did she know that name? *The White Wolf. The White Wolf.*

She picked up her clothes off the floor and grimaced, forgetting how soaked in blood and puke they were. Keeping her towel on, she draped the cardigan, which had somehow avoided most of the guts and gore, over her shoulders. The shirt, pants, and underwear went into the shower. She scrubbed them with soap, wrung them out, and hung them on the shower curtain bar. For now, she needed to cling to the little things. Small victories. She grabbed the stake and toothed knife off the toilet and left her clothes to hang.

Back in the bedroom, she stepped over the streak of James's blood from where she had dragged him and hopped on the bed, staring at the ceiling. She kept praying for time to digest all that had happened, and for the moment, it appeared she might have some.

She closed her eyes and imagined the world disappearing into a ball of gas and fire, picturing each person who ever touched her life evaporating into dust. Her father, who spent the last years of their lives under the same roof as her, avoiding her like she was a sickness, germs spreading through the air. She pictured her mentors, Dr. Rebecca Anderson and Dr. Chiara Cooper, two inspirations who believed in her mind and fostered an environment for her academic growth. And, of course, her silly roommate, who annoyed her but also loved her enough to spend the last hours of her life sending texts to Cassie. She imagined them dying alone, screaming into the nuclear abyss.

She also thought about the day-to-day jam-ups, the exhaustive hours, the constant worry someone would bring a gun to school, or someone would attack her on her way back to the dorms late at night. She remembered her distrust of every random stranger who walked by and all the anxiety she lived with day in and day out, and it eased her sorrow for the world lost. She didn't even mind the wasted years, all the hard work for nothing.

The vast majority of humanity was probably kind, good folks, but she wouldn't miss the need to assess them all, to monitor every action and build an ongoing list in her brain, judging whom she could and couldn't trust, never knowing anyone's true intentions.

If it weren't for the fucking vampires, Cassie might call the bunker paradise. Funny how as a child, all she wanted was attention from her brother, but as an adult, all she wanted was to be ignored.

Her belly rumbled, but she didn't want to leave the bedroom until her clothes dried. She refused to die at the hands of vampires in nothing but a towel. Besides, her brain recognized the comfort of the pillow against the back of her head, and it pushed her eyelids down.

Within minutes she drifted off. In her dreams, James cried and begged her for life. But the dreams didn't last long. John Adams must have watched her from somewhere, waiting for her to fall asleep, because as soon as she did he pounded on the walls, beating the steel reinforcements like drums.

She jolted up, the light in the room now off. Her heart stammered.

Voices came from all around her.

"Casssssssiie."

"Wake up, Casssssiiieeee."

"Wake up."

The pounding came from all around, like stomping feet on metal bleachers at a football game.

She jumped out of bed and fumbled for the stakes.

"Cassie, don't you ever fucking fall asleep again," a voice said from within the wall behind the bed. "I will deprive you of all you need."

The voice came into her brain crisp and clear. Despite the softness with which the voice spoke, it overpowered the intense drumming and chorus of vampires calling her name, taunting her.

A siren went off, loud and shrill, sending Cassie's pulse into overdrive. The voices and pounding stopped, allowing the alarm to take over. Cassie searched for the source, drifting toward the door, terrified of the pitch blackness enveloping her. On her way, she clicked the switch for the light, but it didn't click on. She felt for the bulb. It remained in place, which meant the vampires had probably messed with the electricity within the walls.

Luckily, they'd left the hallway light on, and while it wasn't much, it brought in low light for a few inches into the bedroom. She went to the window and scanned the hall. At first she saw nothing because she'd focused on looking for a standing creature. When she looked down, she saw the smoke crawling from under the kitchen door.

"Shit."

Without thinking, she ran out of the bedroom and tore into the kitchen. In the middle of the floor, they'd piled cupboards worth of food and set the stack on fire. Not only had they taken her sleep; they had also taken her only source of food.

She ran for the corner where the door connected the kitchen to the filing cabinet room and grabbed the fire extinguisher. Clouds of foam shot out and suffocated the fire, but the smoke was unbearable. She wondered how a bunker that kept out nuclear air could filter out smoke. Where would it go? Would it kill her?

Either way, they'd deprive her of sleep, and now she officially had nothing to eat. They had effectively killed her before killing her. Was this the plan? Why not just rip her to shreds? Why make her suffer? She sensed in some small way they feared her, hence their plan to weaken her before going in for the kill. Mentally, physically, all the ways possible. They ripped into her, piece by piece.

She had no food. Her belly grumbled on cue, reminding her it had already been a while since she'd last eaten. Even if she killed the vampires, it didn't matter. This was it. She was dead. Just a matter of time now. Walking fucking dead.

She went back into the bedroom, plopped on the bed, and rubbed her eyes. After a second, she went into the bathroom, changed back into her clothes, grabbed two stakes, tucked the knife into her pants, and went for the door.

She was dead anyway, but she planned to be the last one standing.

Chapter 26

White Noise

Sometimes it feels like I'm suffocating you.

———

With the stakes in hand, Cassie stormed into the computer room. She had an idea, although she thought little would come from it. She realized the monitors were showing old video footage, and the cameras weren't even present anymore let alone active, but if she fast-forwarded through some of the old footage, she might get a better idea of the layout, might see the hidden entrance from where the vampires were traveling.

Mr. and Mrs. Renard must have set the cameras up to record *something*. She wanted to see what that something was. She locked herself in the room and went to the monitors, which still played old footage of nothing. After fidgeting with some keys, she figured out how to fast-forward and rewind. Thin strips of black and white came across the screens as she traveled through time. The recordings reversed, but nothing changed outside of a timestamp at the bottom of the main room's screen.

She went through days and days of material. Nothing happened. Nothing changed. And then, a figure appeared. It waltzed into the main room from the hall. She rewound, monitoring each of the rooms, trying to see where the figure came from. Nothing. No one. It made no sense, as if the figure just appeared from thin air. She squinted, trying to get a better look at the shape. At first, she assumed it was Mr. Renard, but this character was too tall and lean.

His head craned toward the camera, not coincidentally, but like he knew it was there. A grin walked up his cheeks. His eyes were oceans of black.

She knew who it was. John Adams. If only she knew *when* it was. The timestamp was dated 1978, and she knew that wasn't correct. Sure, maybe vampires lived for centuries at the same age, but she doubted Mr. and Mrs. Renard were studying vampires in a bunker back then. They probably hadn't even lived on this property. For that matter, digital surveillance equipment surely didn't exist in 1978, at least not of this quality, not that the cameras were state-of-the-art. And hadn't James mentioned Mr. Renard building the bunker just a few years earlier?

She rewound again, going back a little further, trying, once again, to find John Adam's entrance. Her eyes darted from room to room, hoping to catch the movement. When she found nothing, she rewound and tried again, going back a little further. Maybe John Adams had lingered in the blind spots of the hall for a long time before entering the main room.

She stared again, eyes watering from not blinking. Staring. Staring. Staring. Rewound. Tried again. Her eyes blurred, and she rubbed them with her lower arm. When she opened her eyes back to the screens, the main room's camera blinked out, leaving the monitor in a storm of old-fashion television snow, complete with obnoxious, static noise. Cassie instinctively slapped the monitor, but just as she did, the other main room camera blinked out and did the same. Like a virus, the snow traveled from one camera to the next until all of them were in a blizzard. The static noise was coming from each, but slightly different in their timing, creating a haunting cacophony until the noise changed pitch, getting higher and higher until it sounded like the screens were screaming.

The monitor in the center returned, but Cassie couldn't make out the image; it was a black object too close to the camera to make out, but it was moving. It stepped backwards, revealing an eye first, then a face. An awful, sharp-toothed grin. Wavy black hair.

"Hello Cassie," it whispered. "We finally meet."

Cassie nearly fell out of her seat. She bit her lip, hid her fear as best she could. "John Adams?"

"Come to me." He laughed, at first a small, over-confident chuckle, but then it changed, sharpening, the high-pitched wailing laughter of a demonic clown from horror movies, and it kept going, getting louder and louder and louder until she felt her eardrums might explode.

She cupped her hands over her ears and clenched her jaw. Fuck it was loud, and the pitch sent shivers up her spine.

As he laughed, increasing volume by the second, he slammed his head into the camera, and the screen cracked. The monitor screen actually cracked as if he were breaking through. The cracks spider-webbed from one monitor to the next until all of them were decorated in threads of it.

He continued to pound his forehead into the screen, spreading the streaks, and all the while he kept laughing, kept increasing the pitch and volume.

"Come to me, Cassie," he yelled in his screaming voice. "Come to me, bitch."

Just when she thought she might collapse from the pain and terror of it, the screens blinked out again and then returned to sharp whiteness. Off again, and back again to the whiteness. They did this, blinking in and out so quickly it created a strobe-like effect in the room. The cameras started whining.

Then, boom, boom, boom, one by one they blinked back on, showing all the rooms again. A shadow moved around the boundaries of the main room.

Cassie stared, fixated. It wasn't moving like a human. When it came into view, she gasped.

It moved slowly, leapt up on the couch and put its face to the camera. It was The White Wolf.

The White Wolf.

Her White Wolf.

But what the fuck did that mean? She didn't know, but she knew it to be true. It was her White Wolf.

It stared at the camera and licked its lips.

For a moment, it was as if they were locked in a staring contest.

Then it spoke. It fucking spoke. It said the words she'd heard so many times. A mantra in her head. *Are you ready?*

She leaned forward, her breath coming out in shivery bursts. "Not yet," she said. The conversation felt so familiar. She could almost touch the memory of it. Déjà vu.

The White Wolf smiled and a gust of air blasted at Cassie's legs. She gasped and bent down, looking under the table. "Holy shit." She jumped up, grabbed the table, and pulled. Considering it had monitors stacked on top of it, it was lighter than she would have guessed. The monitors didn't wobble, as if they were all bolted to the table. When she pulled one side away from the wall, a giant hole behind the monitors came into view.

"Fuck. Unbelievable." One monitor had a giant grip attached to the back of it, making it easy to pull into place should someone hop in the hole and disappear. She slammed the table back in place, ran back to the main room, grabbed a flashlight from the storage boxes, and ran back into the monitor room.

Her heart was racing again, but this time it was from excitement. Nerves, sure, but also excitement.

She pulled the table away again and a thin current of cold air came into the room, hitting her in the face. A musty smell like old clothes and mold seeped out. She shined her light in and the beam revealed a crude, small tunnel. There was enough room for her to crawl in, but it wasn't enough to quell her claustrophobia.

"Holy shit. What the fuck do I do?"

The circular structure was all stone, rough and jutting, and she knew crawling in would be painful and gross. She could always try to block the entrance, stop them from coming back in, but it wouldn't stop them from torturing her and loudly harassing her when she tried to sleep. She'd spend whatever short portion of her life she had left worried they'd get through the vents and kill her.

She had no food. No sleep. Her only option was to kill them. What other choice did she have? But what the fuck was she about to walk into? A nest of them? How many were in there, and how trapped would she be once she was in the tunnel?

"Fuck. Fuck. Fuck."

Before she went into the cave, she headed to the hallway to glance at the folders she dropped during her exchange with Spot. Most of them were covered in blood, ripped, and crumpled. She flipped John Adam's folder open. The pages inside listed a series of surgeries first.

TOOTH EXTRACTION: REGENERATION EVEN AFTER EXTENDED FASTING.

JAW REMOVAL: REGENERATION EVEN AFTER EXTENDED FASTING.

From there, it listed experiments, but Dr. Renard had coded them with numbers and letters, giving Cassie zero insight into what the tests entailed.

TRIAL QR45GoI: NO REACTION

TRIAL FRT67B9: NO REACTION

She flipped through a few other files to compare. For Jefferson and Madison, it stated: no regeneration after one day of fasting. For trial QR45GoI they both said, "SUBJECT UNRESPONSIVE

UNTIL GIVEN BLOOD." For trial FRT67B9 they both said, "SUBJECT DECEASED."

"John Adams, you're a tough son of a bitch, huh?"

Back at the tunnel, she tucked a stake into her pants and tossed the other into the tunnel. Biting the flashlight between her front teeth, she crawled in.

Chapter 27

Where We Once Smiled

Names and dates. For all we do, this is all we will be known for. Names and dates.

––––––

The tunnel's sharp, stony floor dug into Cassie's lower arms and legs as she slithered through the maw. A gentle dripping came from somewhere in front of her, but she couldn't find the source. All the stones were wet and slick, their slimy surfaces cold on her flesh.

For a while, the tunnel only went in one direction - forward. It didn't tilt or turn or slant. She crawled for so long she worried it would never end. The more she traveled away from the monitor room, the more her chest constricted. If something came at her, she couldn't turn around and run. She'd have to slither backwards, warding off any attacker with her stakes. It wasn't optimal.

The further in she went, the more going back felt impossible. The size of the tunnel changed, getting smaller. She had to lie flat, ear to the stone under her, limbs stuck in front of her to flatten herself as much as possible.

"Oh god. I can't do this," she whispered to herself.

She felt the oxygen within the cavernous tunnel disappear. As she squeezed through, the surrounding walls only clenched tighter. The idea of being stuck in the middle of this place made her dizzy. She used her yoga training to keep hyperventilation at bay and continued to push through.

The knife slipped out of her pants when it rubbed against the low ceiling. With no range of motion, she couldn't retrieve it. Luckily, she had pushed the stake far enough down it stayed in place, although the tip kept poking her upper thigh.

At one point, the tunnel split, continuing forward or turning left. She considered her options, but with no idea where either could lead, she just kept moving forward.

After a little while longer, she reached a point where the tunnel finally turned slightly to the left. When she turned her head, flashlight still stuck between her teeth, the beam shined on markings on the stone. Cutting up her arm, she wiggled it upward until her hand reached her mouth, and then she moved the flashlight over the anomaly. Names were carved into the rock. Miller. Mary. Zeke. Kelly. They were each etched in with sharp lines. There were other names, too, but she couldn't make out what they said.

Who were they? What kinds of stories did they have?

She guessed the scribbles were decades old, but that was only a guess. It made her wonder what this place was before, where it had led to, how children had access to it.

She took a deep breath, put the flashlight back in her teeth, and continued on, digging her toes into the rocky floor and used whatever strength her lower legs could muster to shimmy forward. Her upper body didn't have the movement to provide any help. One of her arms was stuck laid out in front of her, while the other was jammed on her side, her lower arm cramped under her belly. It had no freedom to move. As she bent around the corner, her shoulders caught on the wall. With the small amount of wiggle room she had, she shook back and forth, trying to get her shoulders to move forward an inch, or even back, anything to get them unstuck.

The stones dug into her chest. She officially couldn't move. Completely stuck. She closed her eyes, couldn't look at the cave anymore. Pictures of rock crumbling on top of her head sent waves of terror into her guts.

"Breathe, Cassie. Breathe. Long pulls in through the nose. Big outs through the mouth. Slow. Slow. Slow."

She dug her toes in again but couldn't find the strength to pull herself forward, not another centimeter. She opened her eyes, accepting this might be the place she died. The closed-in space gave her only one movement, craning her head. She turned it left to right, and the beam caught more etching. KENDALL AND MICHAEL 4/8/23.

She smiled. Someone's happiness was written on the wall, etched so strongly it survived the end of the world. And how powerful was that? It was there in that cave before she had ever stepped foot in it, and it would continue to tell its story long after she was gone.

She imagined them, Kendall and Michael, carving their names into eternity, smiling at the idea of forever. Cassie might not make it out of here, might spend the last minutes of her life next to their names, so the least she could do was share it with them, to think of them, to give them the life she never truly had. If she could, she'd send a message to them, giving them thanks for helping her find peace in the end.

The idea of someone finding so much happiness that they felt the need to dig into stone, to remind the world of its existence, sent a shiver down her spine. Had she ever had that? Had she even recognized happiness when it came? It wasn't just that she kept herself busy, but even when she had some downtime, she couldn't remember ever being in the moment enough to say, "This moment matters."

Fuck. Had she ever been happy? Ever?

She honestly didn't know the answer.

Tears trailed down to her temples. "Thank you, Kendall and Michael. I hope your joy together was enough for all of us."

Thinking of them renewed her anger at the world for exploding. How unfair it was for those who relished their lives.

"If I don't die here, I swear I will find at least one minute to enjoy my life. After I kill these fucking vampires. Deal, Kendall and Michael? What do you say?"

She turned her head away, dug her toes in, and gave it one more shot. Once again, she couldn't shave an inch in either direction.

More tears. "Fuck. I'm going to die here." She couldn't believe, after all that happened, she'd die stuck in a tunnel. Would it come from starvation, dehydration, or would the sharp cuts of rock digging into her chest eventually suffocate her?

"I don't want to die this way."

Something made a sound like the hissing of a radiator. It grew louder and with it, the pitter-patter of something crawling her way from behind. It must have come from the split in the tunnel she'd passed. Either way, without the ability to move, the thing could rip her to shreds and she couldn't do anything but take it.

"Come on," she said to herself. "Don't let it get you."

It moved quickly, drumming closer and closer, knees and hands slapping against the wet rock.

"Please. Please. Please." She sucked in her belly, twisted her lower legs so her toes struck purchase on the side walls, and gave it one more try. But before it might do anything, something grabbed her foot.

Chapter 28

Luggage

CASSIE, AGE 6

Cassie sat in the chair obviously designed for adults. She felt the cushions might swallow her whole as she sunk deeper into it. With her hands tucked under her butt, she kicked her feet out one at a time, letting her heels thunk against the chair on their return.

Thunk, thunk, thunk.

The voice inside her bubbled on the surface, ready to leap out of her, which meant it sensed danger for Cassie. But Cassie saw nothing in the room worthy of her anxiety. Besides, her mother suggested this appointment, and Cassie's mother would never put her in any danger. Still, she'd learned to trust that other voice and knew it foolish to ignore its warnings. The voice had always done such a good job of shielding her, she never felt the need to protect herself. If something happened, the voice would come out and the situation would get handled.

The room was comfortable, with bland colors on all the furniture, shelves of books too big for Cassie's liking, and a neat coffee table with lots of puzzles. She liked the one with the pegs. She'd played that one before at a restaurant with her family. They were very impressed when she hopped the pegs around until only one was left. Of course, the voice helped her with that, but when her brother and father acted so awed by it, she didn't want to tell them the truth.

A woman walked into the room, running her hands through her red hair and sighing. "Hello, Cassie. Sorry to keep you waiting." The woman plopped a small stack of manilla folders on the coffee table.

Cassie sat and watched as the woman opened the files one by one, breezing through their contents.

As if the woman realized she'd put her focus in the wrong place, she shifted her glance to Cassie and smiled. "How are you today?" she asked as she continued to flip through the pages.

"I'm good." Cassie suspected the woman wanted more of an answer, but she didn't know what else to say.

"Good. How's your mom?"

Cassie shrugged. "Good, I think."

The woman stretched her smile a little more. "Your mom used to be a patient of mine as well, just like you're going to be. I helped her a lot, and now I am going to help you. How does that sound?"

Cassie filled her cheeks with air and slowly let it out of her tightened lips. "Help me with what?"

"Feel better."

"Like a doctor?"

The woman laughed. "I actually am a doctor. Dr. Renard. You can call me Lisa."

"But I feel okay. I'm not sick."

Dr. Renard said, "You are correct. You are not sick. Has anyone ever told you there is something wrong with you when you didn't feel like there was?"

Cassie nodded. "Yes."

"Who?"

Cassie turned away from the doctor and stared out the window. "My dad. Kids at school."

"What do they say?"

"That there is something wrong with me. That I'm scary. That I am bad."

"Do you feel like you're bad?"

Cassie shook her head.

"So, how does it make you feel when people say those things?"

"It hurts my feelings."

Dr. Renard leaned forward, commanding Cassie's attention. "Well, you're right. There is nothing wrong with you, and you aren't bad. I want you to do me a favor. Close your eyes and picture the story I am telling."

Cassie smushed her eyelids together.

"Imagine everyone in the world carried around luggage wherever they went."

Cassie shook her head, imagining a busy street with folks walking down the sidewalk, all carrying a heavy bag at their side.

"Now imagine you get on an elevator with a bunch of strangers. Everyone has their luggage next to them. What are people carrying with them?"

Cassie shrugged, keeping her eyes closed. "I don't know."

"Why don't you know?"

"Their bags are closed."

The doctor snapped her fingers, the gentle pop of it infiltrating Cassie's mind.

"Exactly. You can't see what they are holding. So, you couldn't determine if what they have is good or bad stuff, right? Maybe one of them has treasure, and maybe another has rocks to throw at people. But you can't tell because you can't see in their bags, right?"

"Yes," Cassie said, unsure where this was going.

"But, what if while you were in the elevator, you smelled some-thing really strong and gross in one of the bags, and you could tell which bag it came from?"

"Ew."

"Exactly. Ew. You would wonder what was wrong with that person, right? Why are they carrying around something so stinky?"

169

"Yeah."

"What would you think of that person?"

Cassie shrugged again, trying to think of a suitable answer. "I don't know. Maybe they don't wash their stuff very well."

"Now, what if you found out he was carrying around some fish because he liked to feed the neighborhood cats?"

"That's a nice thing to do."

"You can open your eyes now."

Cassie opened them, the bright light from the window blinding her for a second. Then Dr. Renard came through the whiteness, her smile still in place.

"You see, we all have luggage in our brains. No one can see what it is. But people think they can based on how we act sometimes."

"Do I act stinky?"

Dr. Renard laughed. It was a gentle noise, not harmful or mean-spirited. "No. You don't act stinky. But you sometimes do things that make people scared. But your luggage isn't bad. I've known your luggage for a long time. I've seen inside the bag, and it's wonderful. It cares about you, and that's a good thing, isn't it."

Cassie's lips snarled and the other voice came out, rough and angry. "Lying bitch."

Dr. Renard showed no concern over the appearance of the second voice, only offered it another smile. "I'm going to help you train the other voice. Make it so it still protects you but also doesn't harm other people. How does that sound?"

Cassie was surprised. Whenever the other voice came out, people either ran away or for those few that knew the voice, like her mother and father, stopped talking to Cassie and shifted their conversation to the other voice. But Dr. Renard ignored it and kept speaking directly to Cassie.

The voice didn't like being ignored.

"Cassie, she's giving you a false sense of security. Don't trust her. She doesn't want to help you. She wants to strip you of your spirit."

Dr. Renard crossed her legs and hit a button on a small box beside her chair.

A second later, a woman's voice buzzed through. "Yes?"

"Hi, Kathy. Can you bring me the table I left out there?"

"Be right in."

Dr. Renard hit something that shut the box off and tilted her head as she stared at Cassie. "Cassie, will you tell the other voice to stop talking now, or does the other voice not trust you to speak for yourself?"

The other voice growled at the insinuation, but Cassie's voice returned to her own. "Okay. What do you want to talk about?"

Kathy opened the door, wheeling in a rectangular table with two shelves under it. Each shelf was filled with bottles of different colored liquids. She made a wide arc around Cassie, as if afraid to come near her, and stopped the table by Dr. Renard's side. Without a word, she left the room and closed the door behind her.

The other voice snapped back. "What is this now?"

Dr. Renard didn't answer it, only scooped up one of the top bottles, examined it, and leaned forward, waving it in front of Cassie's face.

Cassie frowned, watching the colorless liquid splash inside the bottle. "What's that?" she asked in her own voice.

Dr. Renard put the bottle back, took a pen from her pocket, and jotted something in one of her folders. "Ethanol."

"Why?" Cassie wasn't sure which voice asked.

"No reason." Dr. Renard grabbed another bottle and did the same thing. Then another and another.

From the second shelf, she pulled out a smaller bottle with blue liquid. When she put it in front of Cassie's face, something happened. All of her muscles felt as if they were tearing, like putty torn apart by a child.

The second voice screamed from Cassie's lungs, and then an emptiness swallowed her, devouring her. She felt incomplete, broken. Her head ached. Her soul shattered.

Dr. Renard moved the bottle away, and Cassie lurched forward, tossing up a black liquid. It streamed from her, pouring out forcefully. So much of it spilled from her throat she couldn't find the time to inhale, to get oxygen. She was drowning in her own fluids.

Dr. Renard's eyes grew two sizes bigger, and she ran to Cassie's side. "Okay. You're okay." She patted the girl's back. "Just relax. Let it all out."

Eventually, the throw-up stopped and Cassie rocked in the chair, wiping the ooze from her face. "What did you do to me?"

"Nothing. You'll be fine."

After a minute, she felt better. The emptiness dissipated and the headache cleared. The other voice returned. "If you ever do anything like that again, I will fucking rip you to shreds!"

Dr. Renard sat back down, unmoved by the threats. "Cassie, tell me more about The White Wolf."

Cassie looked at the black liquid soaked into her dress, the chair, the floor. "Aren't you going to clean me up?"

Dr. Renard chuckled. "Of course! Eventually. Not yet though. Tell me about The White Wolf."

"Don't answer her," the other voice said.

Dr. Renard sighed, reached for another bottle from the second shelf, and sloshed it in front of Cassie's face.

Cassie flinched, nervous the same thing would happen again, but nothing occurred. Same as all the bottles before the blue one.

Dr. Renard moved fast, grabbing another bottle and shaking it, then another. When she reached a bottle with an amber liquid, flecked with shiny spots, Cassie flopped back.

Her mouth opened wide and a creaking sound left her lungs. Her whole body shook, convulsed. She felt it all happen but couldn't look; her eyes were rolling behind her lids.

When Dr. Renard pulled the bottle away, she righted herself and felt fine again. "Why do you keep doing that?" Cassie cried.

"I'm sorry. I know it's not fun."

Cassie's fingernails gripped into the chair's fabric sides. "Not fun? I could chew your tongue off. Let's see if that's not fun!"

"Will you let the girl tell me about The White Wolf now, or should I get another bottle?"

Cassie tilted her head. "Why aren't you scared of me? You know I could kill you in seconds."

Dr. Renard cleared her throat and eyed the doorway, as if considering an escape route. "Yes. You could. But you won't."

Cassie's upper lip curled. "Why would you think that?"

Dr. Renard sat forward. "Because we want the same thing." She sat back, relaxing, showing no fear at all. "Now, Cassie, tell me about The White Wolf."

Chapter 29

Old Friends

"I've heard when someone loses a limb, they can still feel it. Do you imagine that's true? That you get so used to something being a part of you, when it's gone, your mind can't accept it?"

Cassie squirmed as something took hold of her shoe, and somehow it gave her enough leverage to shift forward. The thing kept a tight hold on her, wrapping its hands on her ankle, but with the slight freedom she received in the closed quarters, she shimmied forward and kicked her free foot at the thing. It struck purchase, although she couldn't be sure where. She hoped her heel landed right in the thing's face.

It growled and slashed at her leg.

A burning sting hit her calf. She didn't care, hardly noticed, was too busy worming forward, moving as fast as she could. She wished she could turn back to see the creature, but she still hardly had enough room to move forward, let alone look back.

She tossed the stake ahead, and her palms hit the rocky floor. With all her strength, she pushed forward. Then again. And again.

The noises from the creature stretched farther and farther away, and Cassie hoped that meant it also got stuck in the turn.

She reached a point where the tunnel opened into a four-way turn. While she planned to continue forward, she used the opportunity to shift into one of the side exits so she could turn around. She wanted to see the creature. Had to.

When she'd shimmied her way into facing the opposite direction, she shined her light down the tunnel, hoping for her first sight of John Adams. But what she saw was an eyeless beast. Spot. He was indeed stuck in the same place, but he was flailing and would probably free himself quickly. Part of her wanted to crawl back to him and jam the stake into his face until he died, but she didn't have the courage, and the claustrophobic need to get the fuck out of the tunnels was too great.

She slung her legs into the side tunnel and slid her upper body back around. *Crawl. Crawl.* After getting stuck, having the little room to move opened her airwaves and made her feel lighter, but she still needed to get the hell out of the tunnel. She hadn't imagined it would be so damned long. What if it collapsed? The idea made her feel faint.

As the dim glow of the flashlight bobbed with the movements of her head, it shined on something different ahead. It wasn't totally different, and with the faintness of the glow, she couldn't quite determine what it was, but the colors differed from the walls surrounding her. It was a light grey as opposed to the darker ones enveloping her. It also looked smoother. She stared at it as she moved forward, the light revealing more details as she closed in on it. Before she could figure it out, her hand hit nothing. Nothing. She dropped the stake and it clanked below, probably about five feet. She shifted forward, and her arm hung over a ledge. A little more and she could get her head into the clearing. The flashlight dangled from her mouth, revealing a floor below. A normal floor. Cement, but smoothed.

"Oh, thank God," she whispered to herself. She didn't have the clearance to prepare for a clean drop, so she dangled her upper body over the ledge until her hips cleared and then her weight pushed her down, crashing onto the floor. The second stake in her pants fell out and clanged about.

Cassie groaned and stood up, wiping her dirty hands on her cardigan. She felt rips and holes all over the garment from her tunnel trek. With all the horror surrounding her, the monsters, lack of food, end of the world and all, she still let the little things get to her. Maybe that was human nature to hone in on minor annoyances when the big catastrophes lurked. A paper cut while dying of cancer. But she loved that cardigan, wore it like a spring jacket whenever a light breeze came in. She'd wrap the open sides around each other and squeeze herself warm. Frustrated tears built in her eyes.

With the flashlight in hand, she scanned the room. Splashes of red streaked the walls. There was a rolling chair in a corner, but not much else other than a door to her left. She picked up her stakes, tucked them into the back of her pants, and crept toward it.

As she neared the door, something made a hiss from the tunnel.

Her heart plunged, and she grabbed the door handle.

Spot found his way out and was moving fast.

The door opened and she peeked out, flashing her light left and right. A long corridor stretched farther than the light would shine. Another door stood opposite the one she stepped out of. Spot thumped behind her as he fell out of the tunnel.

With her pulse pounding, she ran for the other door, praying it was unlocked, praying more it had no occupants, and praying further still she could lock it once inside.

The second and third prayer proved unnecessary because the first wasn't granted. As she twisted the handle, it stayed stubbornly in place.

Without thinking, she kicked the door in frustration, creating a loud bang. The door behind her slid open and she lost her breath as Spot stood across from her smiling. Her back pressed against the door, its locked handle digging into her lower back.

"I toooooold you. I don't need eyes to kill you." His unnatural

176

smile slithered up his cheeks. "And once I do, your magic blood will grow me new ones."

"You found me but killing me is a whole other journey." Her words came out shivery, and she knew she couldn't portray the confidence she feigned, but she kept it going anyway. "The question is, without your eyes, what should I pluck out of you this time?"

He growled and charged, slamming into her.

Her hands gripped his temples, keeping his chomping teeth from gnawing into her. They both fell to the ground, Spot on top of her. Her back pressed into the two stakes resting in her pants. While she held Spot's head away from her, he dug his claws into her side. She screamed out in pain, trying to figure out what to do next. If she reached for a stake he could bite her, but if she kept her hands on his head he'd keep clawing her stomach until he'd ripped her apart. Instead, she drove her knees up into his groin.

It, apparently, had the same effect on vampire men as it did human ones, because Spot rolled off her, howling as he clutched his crotch. But he rolled to the right, which was where the corridor went. To the left was only a wall. She'd have to hop over him to get by. It was a stupid waste of time, but she tried to turn the doorknob again, hoping to find she just hadn't pulled it hard enough on the first go.

It remained locked, but as she jiggled it, a pair of eyes showed up in the small door window. Terrified eyes. Green eyes Cassie recognized. The latch unlocked and Cassie spilled into the room, falling to the floor as the door opened. She rolled over as the door shut behind her, the lock clicking into place.

The woman turned to her. "Cassie?" Dr. Renard said.

Chapter 30

Reunion

"Sadly, I don't trust any of them. I'm not sure that's good for either of us."

———

Dr. Renard's eyes darted wildly around the room, as if she couldn't look at Cassie directly. Red streaks lit across her eyes. Her face was gaunter than the last time Cassie saw her only a short while ago, and her skin had the pallor of a ghost. Most noticeably, her clothes were soaked in crimson. She still wore the fancy black dress she left the house in, but even against the dark fabric, Cassie recognized blood. Her pearl necklace no longer draped around her lithe neck, and her feet were bare, caked in dried blood.

Before Cassie could ask where Mr. Renard was, Dr. Renard asked a one-word question. "James?"

Cassie's heart sank. She couldn't form the words necessary, so she just shook her head.

With that simple action, Dr. Renard crumbled, falling to the floor in a fit of wails and sobs.

Cassie wanted to tell her to shut up, that she could attract the vampires. More so, she wanted to ask a million questions, none more pressing than, 'What the fuck were you doing down here?' But she knew she'd never yank a coherent answer from beyond the wall of grief she'd just built around the woman.

As Dr. Renard continued her crying, Spot came to the door, pounding his fists against the window.

Each thump made Cassie flinch.

Dr. Renard rocked on the balls of her feet, arms wrapped around her legs, head buried in her knees, not reacting to the heavy thumps a few feet above her.

While Dr. Renard poured her grief out in loud moans, Cassie slid backwards until her back was in the far corner, away from the door as much as possible. She hoped if Spot broke in he'd go for the nearest target first, giving Cassie some time to run.

With a growling belly, a head full of anxiety, and a body battered and bruised, each second felt like a day. Time wasted, time they could be planning their survival. Maybe she could divert the grief. She had a feeling Mr. Renard was equally dead, but his wife probably had some time to acclimate to life without him. "Dr. Renard, where's Mr. Renard?"

Dr. Renard wiped her hands on her shirt, directly where the pools of crimson were. "Mark's dead." She looked up and finally planted her eyes on Cassie. "With James," she swallowed hard, "was it the bombs?"

Cassie shook her head again.

Dr. Renard cringed, her mouth drooping like a Dali painting. "Was it them?" She waved her thumb toward the door behind her.

Cassie nodded. "Specifically, him." She tilted her chin toward Spot.

The scream that left Dr. Renard's mouth shocked Cassie into stumbling backwards and clunking her head into the wall. It was the loudest, shrillest yell Cassie had ever heard. A boiling pustule of grief and hate exploding into the atmosphere. It shook Cassie to her core, penetrating so deeply it reached her soul and squeezed.

"Dr. Renard, you have to tell me what's going on here."

The doctor wiped her face. "What does it look like, Cassie?"

"It looks like there's fucking vampires down here."

Renard stood up, but immediately fell back against the wall as if too weak to stand. "You always were smart."

"But something is happening to me, too. The one in the kitchen... What was his name? William Harrison? He came at me, and I was so strong. I killed him. I was throwing up black stuff, and I was so strong and confident, but then I threw up more of it, and I was back to feeling normal. Like, weaker. I know I need to kill these fucking things, but I keep thinking I don't have the power to." She glanced at Dr. Renard. It didn't look like the woman was paying any attention. "But I did, because I killed one."

She didn't know why she was rambling about this. She had so many more important questions. Why were the vampires chained up the way they were? What experiments were the Renards doing? Was there more food down here? Could they survive? But Cassie always turned flustered when faced with conversation.

She waited for the doctor to respond, but before she could, someone yelled, "Sssshhhhhhh," in the hallway, causing Spot to stop his pounding.

All went still, as if another bomb had just exploded. An eerie silence captured the atmosphere, fraying Cassie's nerves.

"What is that?" Cassie whispered as a low tapping noise came from the hallway.

Terror washed over Dr. Renard's face. "It's John Adams."

Cassie's eyes moved from Dr. Renard to the door window.

Spot stopped looking in and was staring off at something coming his way down the hall.

A giant hand with long, veiny, pale fingers gripped the side of Spot's face and pushed him away. A set of gold and red eyes pressed against the window. The colors swirled in his eyes, dancing around each other like tidepools. Gold and red, both beautiful and horrific. The skin around his eyes looked like white plastic, smooth and lifeless. "Hello, Cassie."

She couldn't see his smile but saw the way his eyelids moved and the skin wrinkled around them. He was smiling. This was joyous for him.

Dr. Renard's breath came out in shivers. "We have to get out of here. Now."

"How?" Cassie asked.

"There's a secret corridor. Follow me."

But before Dr. Renard could move, her head pushed back, her eyes squinting. "Where's your necklace?"

John Adams stepped back and kicked the door. A hard crack.

Cassie flinched again. She couldn't fathom why the doctor would ask such a stupid and unimportant question at a time like this. "What?"

"Your necklace. Where is it?"

Another crack at the door.

Cassie put her hand to her neck, feeling the absence of the jewelry. It had driven her mad before the world exploded, and ever since, she hadn't the time or mental capacity to even think of it.

"It's in my pocket. A link broke on it." She reached into her cardigan and pulled it out. Once it dangled from her fingers, she realized how miraculous it was that the necklace had remained in her pocket through all she'd dealt with.

Another crack, and this time, it sounded like some wood split.

Dr. Renard cupped her hands over her mouth. "Oh my god. You said you killed Harrison? The... the one in the kitchen, right? But you struggled with the rest?"

"Yes." Cassie said, but it sounded more like a question. She wanted to shake the doctor and say, 'Snap the fuck out of it. We need to go,' but she also sensed the importance of these random questions.

"Were you wearing the cardigan in the kitchen?" Dr. Renard ran to her, ignoring the slams in the door.

Cassie had to think about the question, not remembering something so minor when her life was flipping upside down. "No. No, I wasn't." It felt like a revelation to remember that detail, but she didn't know why it mattered.

Crack. Another kick. It wouldn't be long now.

"What about when you struggled with the rest? Wearing it?"

Cassie shook her head, then nodded, not really sure how to react at all. This time, she knew the answer immediately. "Outside of when I took a shower, I've been wearing it pretty much the whole time."

Dr. Renard put her hand out. "Give me the necklace."

"Why?"

"Just do it."

Crack.

Cassie tossed her the necklace, thinking of the poor girl she'd assaulted in the bathroom at school for touching it. Dr. Renard took the necklace and threw it in the room's corner. "Let's get the fuck out of here."

"Wait, I want the necklace." She turned back to it, but Dr. Renard grabbed her arm.

"No. Trust me. I'll explain later." Dr. Renard pulled Cassie to the opposite wall, pressing on a stone. It moved. She wiggled it back and forth until finally it pulled out like a baby tooth.

Crack. Crack. Crack.

"Shit," Dr. Renard said, as she pulled out another stone.

"Faster," Cassie shouted, eyeing the door.

When the second stone came out, Dr. Renard reached into the wall, putting her arm behind a line of stones, and pulled. She grunted and her arm muscles tightened until the entire stack of them fell down, revealing a thin, dark tunnel.

"Let's go."

Crack.

Pieces of wood shattered and splintered across the room. Cold air spilled in. John Adams stood at the threshold of the newly opened space, five other vampires behind him.

182

Cassie nearly froze at the sight of him.

He was tall and gaunt, his spiky teeth swooshing down like tiny sabers. Despite his thin frame, he exuded power, confidence, and strength.

"Now," Dr. Renard yelled, yanking on Cassie.

She turned to the dark corridor and ran. Enveloped in darkness, she booked it, trying her hardest to follow Dr. Renard's silhouette. The dark swallowed them, wrapped around them, and squeezed. From behind, the echoes of multiple footsteps charged.

Chapter 31

Something Wicked

"Cassiopeia, you're the only friend I've got."

———

The further she ran into the tunnel, the thicker the darkness grew. She couldn't see Dr. Renard at all anymore and followed solely based on the sounds of the doctor's footsteps. She made the mistake of looking behind her. Even in the pitch blackness, she could see the glowing red eyes and pale white skin of the vampires.

John Adams ran toward her on all fours, galloping like a hungry coyote. His vampire friends were trotting in the same way, but two of them were on the walls and one on the ceiling, defying gravity, yet running feet to surface. There was more behind them, but she couldn't make anything out.

As she ran, her stomach lurched and that familiar feeling of bile moving up her lungs took over. She swallowed hard, knowing a vomit session would equal death right now. She hoped she could fight it off until Dr. Renard led her to wherever the hell they were going.

Ahead, Dr. Renard yelled, "This way."

Cassie couldn't see which way was 'this way.' Instead, she slammed into a wall in front of her where her path ended. She swatted her arms on each side to feel for walls, and when couldn't find purchase, took a chance and darted left. She quickly realized her mistake when she lost the sound of Dr. Renard's footsteps. Not only did she lose the person giving her directions, but she very well could run herself into a dead end.

Behind her, John Adam's shouted, "Follow the girl, not the doctor."

Fuck.

On top of everything, she was slowing down. She couldn't hold a steady speed, not with her body in such terrible shape, so unfueled, with her stomach threatening to toss up the nothing she had in her belly, and without sight and a proper leader. Her hands remained outstretched, which she hoped would be enough to stop her face from breaking if she went face-first into another wall.

If the vampire's noises, the slapping of palms on ceiling and wall, feet hitting cement, and their venomous hissing were any indication, her pursuers were very close behind. The hissing reminded her of the coyotes that roamed the woods behind her house as a little girl, the way they would howl while chasing their prey. The sounds would reverberate throughout the forest, making it seem as if they were surrounding the house. The hisses were everywhere, echoing all around her, behind her, on her sides, in her fucking ears.

Everywhere.

The tunnel turned sharp right, and she hit the turn perfectly, without bumping headfirst into the wall. It was as if instinct took over, learned the route for her, and planned her steps. In a way, instinct felt right, like something primal had taken hold, knew how to protect her, kept her right. Some aches had gone away, too, and her breathing stabilized. Her body wasn't screaming for a break, wasn't punching her ribs with sharp pains. But boy did she still need to throw up. In fact, the need for it only intensified.

Acidic liquid shot up her throat. She coughed, but kept it

contained in her mouth, and swallowed it back down. It burned coming up and going down, but she kept fighting it back because once she let a little escape, it would flow out and she'd keel over, puking in her final moments as the undead ate her for a snack.

John Adams whistled. A taunting little call. "Cassie. Cassie. You know we'll find you. There's nowhere to go."

She slid her hands down the wall, hoping to find a cut-through, some kind of secret passage or door. Anything.

With a quick glance behind her, she noticed the ceiling vampire clearing the front of the line, a few steps ahead of John Adams.

"Good job, Nick. Use your speed."

The slapping of hands and feet on the ceiling grew closer until it was right above her head.

More bile burned its way up her throat. Up ahead, she caught a faint glimmer of light. The closer she moved toward it, the more it grew. Her heart sang with hope. The light came from a room. The beam cut through the bottom and sides of a door. Now, she just had to pray the door was unlocked. But before she even reached it, Nick jumped down from the ceiling, landing right on top of her. His weight collapsed her body, and she slammed into the cement floor, still propelling forward from the speed of her run.

Her face scraped against the uneven terrain, cutting deep into her cheeks, banging her nose and left eye. She rolled over to fend off the incoming attack and saw the streaks of red on her hands and arms, as tendrils of blood dribbled down them.

Before she could do much of anything, something hot hit her upper arm. It was Nick. His teeth were fully inserted into her flesh. His head shook as he dug in deeper. With her free arm, she punched him in the temple and he released, but they both knew it was too late. He'd taken a bite, and that meant she was fucked. She was one of them. The feeling she had carried with her since childhood was now a reality. Dead and gone. No longer human. Not fit for the world. Something *other*.

His victorious smile mocked her as her blood ringed his mouth. A crimson outline. His trophy.

John Adams and the rest of the vampires stood around her, staring in awe at Nick's win.

Adams kicked him away, wanting a full look at her. "Did you taste it?"

Nick wiped his lips, glaring deep into her soul. "No. A little. But she's not fully ready yet."

John Adams sighed. "Well, she's one of us now. Grab her. Take her to the cells. We'll finish the meal once her blood is good and seasoned." Then John Adams turned to Nick and put his hand on his subordinate's shoulder. "You must be proud. You're a god now."

Cassie rolled over and let the vomit spew from her mouth.

Chapter 32

Unraveling

"My favorite days are the ones where we are alone, where the world goes still, and nothing else exists besides us."

———

The vampires gave her a wide berth while she fired out black gunk all over the floor.

Cassie couldn't do much while she puked her guts out, but she tried to assess the situation unfolding around her. She didn't know why. She'd already lost. Soon, she'd be a vampire too. Only a matter of when. But the instinct to fight never left her. Once she went through the tunnel, knowing she'd go to war with the vampires, she'd decided she would be the last living thing in the bunker. She planned to keep that promise to herself, even if she was a vampire instead of a human.

One thing that surprised her about the brood of vampires was that a few of them were women. Until this point, she'd only witnessed male vampires. Of course, it made sense female vampires would exist, but her mind had only accepted what it had seen.

John Adams grabbed one woman by the shoulder. "Allyson, bite into her while she's weak. Fiona, you take a bite after Allyson. Build up your strength. Once she has recovered, she won't be easy to kill. But it's her own strength that will give us what we need to split her in two."

Every time Cassie felt better, like the vomiting was done, her chest heaved and another round poured from her mouth and nose.

As more came from within her, Allyson bent down, careful not to step in the mess, and dug her teeth into Cassie's upper arm.

As more throw-up expelled from her throat, Cassie ripped her arm away. She tried to scream in pain but couldn't with a lung full of liquid.

Fiona fell to her knees in dramatic fashion and yanked Cassie's arm back, forcing her to fall face-first into her own spew. The woman dug into Cassie's wrist with her razor-sharp teeth.

Cassie rolled over, back against the wall.

Fiona stood up and roared, bellowing a war cry. Blood dribbled down her chin, and she wiped it onto her fingers before inserting them into her mouth, unwilling to lose a drop. "Jesus, that's delicious." She put her head on John Adam's shoulder. "You told me she was special, but I had no idea. I've never had anything like this. I feel like I could live a million years on this blood."

Cassie closed her eyes, ignoring the multiple wounds searing her arms. The vomiting finally stopped and she had a second to catch her breath. Footsteps moved closer to her.

"Can I, sir?" a voice said.

"Haven't you had enough? I should punish you for your greediness. You nearly ruined this for all of us. No. You've already had a bite. Let the others get their fill."

Cassie opened her eyes. Her vision had adjusted to the darkness, and she could clearly define the pitiful expression brewing on Spot's face as he looked down at her with deep hunger. Her heartbeat picked up. She saw an opportunity and the window for it was closing as Spot sighed and took a step back.

Cassie took her twice-bitten arm and grabbed the stake from the back of her pants. With one swift motion, she lunged up and fell into Spot, pushing the wooden spear into his chest. He screamed as his blood showered out like a lawn sprinkler, covering Cassie's face and the surrounding vampires.

The two female vampires came at her from each direction. She dropped low and avoided their grasp before running as fast as she could down the hall, toward the light. The group chased close behind, their footsteps pitter-pattering in unison.

"Don't let her get to that room. We have to time this right."

Once again, the feeling something else controlled her took over, removing the pain, the normal human fatigue.

One vampire grabbed her arm.

Cassie responded by spinning around. On the spin, she kicked out one foot and knocked the vampire on its ass. It was Nick, the one who bit her first. She had no time to gloat about a minor victory. She went back to running.

She closed in on the light. It came from the slivers of space on the edges of the door, and not from a window, and as she approached, she could see the door was metal, a much sturdier door than the previous ones. Now, if only it was unlocked.

She crashed into it, turning the latch, and the door swung open. As she slid into the room, she slammed the door behind her, closing it right on Allyson. The last thing she saw in the hallway before the door shut was her own blood decorating Allyson's face like war paint.

The locking mechanism was a long, thick, metal bar that slid across the door jamb. When it struck purchase, it bolted with a satisfying *thunk*.

The vampires banged their fists and feet into the door, but Cassie felt confident it would keep them out for the time being. She turned to examine the room, catching her breath. There, in between a series of glowing computer monitors, stood Dr. Renard with her hands over her face.

"Cassie, thank God. I thought I lost you." The doctor ran to her, but before she embraced her in a hug, she noticed the multiple bite wounds and stepped back. "Oh no. Oh, no. They got you."

Cassie noticed the door on the other side of the room from which Dr. Renard must have entered. She stared at it for a minute, still working her lungs.

"I'm so sorry. Do you know what this means?"

Yes, she wanted to say. *I know because it happened to your child and I had to kill him.*

Instead, she grabbed the doctor by her throat and slammed her into a wall. "It means I don't have time, so you better give me some fucking answers as to what the fuck is going on here." She dropped the doctor, who clutched her throat and wheezed. An icy chill spilled down Cassie's spine. The girl who struggled to talk back to anyone was once again showing her ferocity, and it both pleased and horrified her.

Once the doctor was back on her feet, she glanced at the ceiling, deep in thought. "I'm not even sure where to begin. Tell me what you know first so I can avoid wasting time."

Cassie shot her a look like the woman was insane. She yelled, pointing her finger in Dr. Renard's chest. "I know there's fucking vampires. I know I keep puking out more black liquid than my body could possibly hold. I know you were doing experiments or some shit on those things. I know you have bunker up there with one bed for a family of three, no clothes, a nice kitchen, but not enough food to last for any extensive amount of time."

Dr. Renard nodded. "Okay, that's good, so you're not in denial about what you're seeing. Those are vampires. You understand that."

Cassie shook her head and threw her hands up. "Yeah, kind of obvious."

Dr. Renard rubbed her hands all over her face. "Look, I don't know how to say any of this without sounding crazy to you, but hopefully the fact you know there are vampires will make this a little easier to swallow. I'm a regular psychologist. I deal with normal patients all the time, normal as in not vampires. But I've become quite known to people who believe in other things."

Cassie waved her arms like a traffic officer telling the cars to keep moving. "Like vampires. I get it."

"Well, not *just* vampires. Other things too."

Cassie scrunched her brow. "Like what? Werewolves?"

Dr. Renard slowly nodded her head. "Yes, like that. And many, many other things."

Cassie widened her eyes. "Lampposts? You gonna tell me lampposts are real?"

Dr. Renard laughed. "No. Don't be ridiculous. Those only exist on that stupid Kevin Bacon show. But other things like..." she paused, struggling to get this out, and that made Cassie's stomach drop. "...like demons."

Cassie laughed. "Okay. What does that have to do with our current situation?" As soon as the words left her mouth, she thought she understood. It all hit her like a baseball bat to the gut.

"You, Cassie. You're possessed by a demon."

Cassie bent over laughing. It wasn't funny, not in the slightest, because it was either nonsense and a ridiculous thing to kid about at a time like this or it was real and terrifying. She wasn't stupid enough to wash it away as false but couldn't place the pieces in enough, couldn't fathom something so bizarre.

"It's not your fault that you're in the dark about this. It took a lot to chisel it from your mind."

She fell to her knees. It all flooded back. The necklace. The doctor's appointments. And, of course, "The White Wolf." She whispered it, speaking more to herself than anyone else.

"Yes, The White Wolf. I could never figure out what that meant. I know it's what you called the demon, but I never understood why." She said this as if Cassie would suddenly provide the answer, to give her the last piece of a puzzle she had never completed.

Tears flooded Cassie's eyes. "You did this to me. You stole from me. You're a fucking monster."

Dr. Renard stepped back. Her eyes bulged. Her mouth dropped. "Cassie, no. That's not what happened."

Cassie screamed, drowning out the sounds of the vampires pounding on the door. "You fucking monster."

Chapter 33

A Chance to Break Free

CASSIE, AGE 7

Cassie stepped into Dr. Renard's office, prepared for another day of the woman waving weird chemicals in her face, begging her to reveal the meaning behind The White Wolf, and asking her a series of inane questions. Part of her hated these visits, but a part of her loved to see the frustration brewing on Dr. Renard's face as Cassie avoided giving her an inch.

The doctor was already waiting for her when she entered, which made Cassie uncomfortable. And not *just* Cassie, but The White Wolf, too. She felt the demon rumbling in her chest, ready to lash out. Something was up. The doctor always walked into their meetings late, frazzled, and eager to begin. To see her sitting calmly in her leather chair, legs crossed, unsettled Cassie, as if she had already lost the upper hand for the day.

There were no files strewn about on the coffee table. Dr. Renard always had files out, papers with scribbled notes. She spent the entire hour jotting down information. Today, nothing.

Cassie sat in her abnormally large chair and stared, waiting.

Dr. Renard smiled. "How are you, Cassie?"

The White Wolf answered. "Fuck you."

"Ah, you're coming right out today, huh? Don't want to give the girl a chance to speak for herself?"

"Fuck you again."

Dr. Renard released a cartoonish sigh and rolled her eyes. "I have something for you." She held up a fist, disguising her present in the clutches of her fingers.

Cassie's eyes widened. Her voice overtook The White Wolf. "What is it?"

"Catch." Dr. Renard tossed a shiny object into the air.

Cassie didn't catch it. Couldn't if she wanted to. The shimmering thing snaked across the room, and as soon as it neared her, her entire body seized. Her back arched, fingers and toes curled, everything tightened. A noise poured from her throat like a train horn. It more than hurt. It felt like her life force, her *soul*, was ripping away from her.

The necklace landed on her chest and, through the seizing, it wormed down to her belly. She could look at it, could see it causing all this pain, but could do nothing to remove it. Eventually, it slid off her and onto the floor. As soon as it fell, Cassie gained her faculties back. She heaved, gagged.

Dr. Renard, who sat there watching the whole time, no intentions of helping, kicked a bucket toward Cassie. Cassie grabbed it and retched for what seemed an endless amount of time.

Once she finished, she placed the bucket over the necklace, not even wanting to look at it. She still felt its power over her, though not as strongly. Still, she felt an emptiness, a missing part of herself.

"Now, let's talk Cassie. I'm going to guess your friend has nothing to say right now?"

Cassie paused, waiting for The White Wolf to chime in, but she didn't. In fact, Cassie couldn't even feel her in there. No more volatile bubbling in her chest.

"What do you want to talk about?" The words came out in a whimper, tears frosting her eyes.

"Why do you call the demon The White Wolf?"

Cassie lifted her legs, crisscrossing them on the seat cushion, hoping to keep them as far from the necklace as possible. A growl escaped her, but it was pathetic, one last flailing from The White Wolf, who seemed powerless inside her. "I don't want to talk about it."

Dr. Renard signed. "Week in and week out I placed chemicals in front of you. Do you know why?"

Cassie shook her head.

"Once upon a time, another young girl came to visit me. This girl also had a demon in her. In fact, she had the very same demon. That woman, as you have probably guessed, being the smart girl you are, was your mother. Now, your mom, she didn't have the opportunity you're about to have, because we didn't know how to remove the demon from within her. In fact, we got so desperate to figure it out, we called a priest to do an exorcism." Dr. Renard cackled. "Can you believe that? No, but your mother was powerful, and she learned to adapt over time. The demon was always there, and it did some awful things, but ultimately, she learned to contain it, or at least to control herself. Then, unfortunately for you, when you were born, the demon passed down to you. We don't know why. The White Wolf doesn't like to talk to us, so we can't be sure why she didn't go to your brother first, but nonetheless, here we are." Dr. Renard paused and bit her lip, staring at Cassie as if waiting for her to say something, anything.

Cassie felt dizzy, sick to her stomach, and had no intention of formulating words.

"Anyway, one day when your mother came in, I noticed something. She seemed weird. And I don't mean possessed weird. I mean, out of it. Her demon wasn't throwing in her usual snide answers and your mom was more reserved, tired, and maybe a little weak. For the life of me, I couldn't figure out what was wrong with her, and she seemed not to know either."

Cassie could hardly listen. The room spun around her; her temples throbbed.

"As we were chatting, I realized I had left something on the floor. See, my office at the time was smaller and less professional. I had a metal shelving unit in a corner of the room, and when our ceiling leaked, it got a little rusty. So, I picked up some rust remover and sprayed it down about half-hour before your mom's appointment. When I finished, I left the can under the coffee table by her chair. So, I picked it up, and as it crossed by her face, The White Wolf flipped out, and your poor mother looked like she was having a seizure."

Cassie looked up, understanding now why Dr. Renard placed stuff in front of her face.

"When I removed the can, your mom returned to her normal self, although The White Wolf was extraordinarily cruel that day. I ran a little test, and right before your mom's appointment ended, I put the can back in front of her, and wouldn't you know it, it caused the same reaction again."

Cassie hated listening to this, didn't want to hear the doctor's stupid methods for causing her current predicament, but couldn't help her need to know.

"This got me thinking. Maybe there are chemicals that are upsetting to the demon, and if there is one, maybe there are many. And while one was only enough to annoy it, maybe a combination of a bunch could diminish it entirely. We may never learn how to remove the demon from you, Cassie, but I found a way to make it stop. Thanks to the trials I have run with you, I learned it was hydrofluoric acid in the rust remover that caused the reaction, if you were wondering."

Cassie put her head down and cried.

"Cassie, this is good news. You can be free. I know change is scary, but after years and years of studying the demon, I finally learned how to give you a good life. You were hurting people, Cassie. You were scaring everyone around you. You don't have to live alone anymore. You can have peace."

Cassie raised her head, glaring at Dr. Renard. "No."

"No what, Cassie? All you have to do is wear that nice necklace I gave you, and you will never have to worry about the demon again. Your brother can sleep soundly at night. Your parents won't fight all day and night about what to do with you. You can make friends without worrying about hurting them. Cassie, you ripped a girl's toenails off. You know that right?"

Fury bubbled in Cassie's belly and it wasn't from the demon. It was entirely her own. "You said my mom learned how to manage it. Why can't I?"

Dr. Renard scoffed, shook her head angrily. "Because in the meantime, you could kill someone. You could really hurt another person. This isn't a part of you worth growing into. It needs to be shut down."

The coating of tears turned into a deluge. "It's not a part of me. It *is* me. You're telling me I need to remove myself from myself."

Dr. Renard hopped off her seat and got onto her knees, approaching Cassie. "I know it feels that way. I understand. You were born with it, so it's going to be hard to find your own identity, but it is *not* you. You are you, and nothing can change that. In fact, the demon was keeping you from being you." Dr. Renard put her hands on Cassie's knees.

Cassie knew right then the doctor was wrong. If The White Wolf was still active, she would have ripped Dr. Renard's hands right off her body. But without the demon, Cassie couldn't do anything except sit there and accept the doctor's cruel, smug smile and placating gestures. But Cassie *wanted* to. She wished for nothing more than the ability to make Dr. Renard scream in pain. The White Wolf was her. They were the same. They wanted the same things. They needed each other. The demon had always taken care of Cassie. What kind of person would she be to stuff the demon in a box within herself? What kind of betrayal would that be?

When the doctor moved away, giving Cassie some space, a fresh wave of nausea came over Cassie and she spent some more time with the bucket.

Dr. Renard sat and watched, not giving her a word.

When Cassie finished, the session was over.

The doctor picked the necklace up and handed it to Cassie. "Just take it for now. You don't have to wear it yet, but just take it."

When Cassie stepped out of the office, Dr. Renard told her mother everything. Cassie watched her mother's facial expressions turn to glee, and she'd never felt so betrayed in all her life.

They got in the car and drove away from the office in silence.

Eventually, her mother broke the quiet. "You seem sad."

Cassie looked at the floating colors in the necklace's pendant. "Yeah."

Her mother put her arm on Cassie's shoulder. "You're not ready to say goodbye, are you?"

"I never want to say goodbye."

Her mother sighed and turned up the radio. Until they reached their road, they stayed in silence. Before turning into the driveway, her mother spoke up once more. "Listen, give me the necklace. I'll tuck it away somewhere. If you ever decide you are ready for it, let me know. But I have to tell you, and make sure your friend is listening too - if you do anything dangerous or harmful to anyone else, or yourself, I will force you to wear it. Understood?"

Cassie beamed, nearly jumping out of her seat. "Yes, mom. I promise. Thank you so much."

Her mother put the car in park and ran her hands through Cassie's hair. "And keep this from your brother and father. If they know we have a cure and aren't using it, they will go apeshit on both of us."

Cassie put her index finger and thumb to her lips, pinched them together, and ran them across her mouth like a zipper.

Her mother reached over and hugged her. With her lips pressed against Cassie's ear, she whispered, "Remember that I always love you."

Cassie wasn't sure if her mother was talking to her or the demon.

Chapter 34

No Coming Back

"Cassiopeia, are you awake?"

———

Cassie shoved Dr. Renard, knocking her to the floor. She yelled, "All this time, you stole from me. You ripped my whole life away from me."

Dr. Renard slid back on her butt, putting space between her and the angered girl. "Cassie, you've thrived. You're in college, and you're incredibly intelligent. You have a bright future. We helped you."

Cassie shook her head. She felt sick again. While her body washed away the aches, she could feel The White Wolf breaking free, and it hurt her all over. "You have no idea. A bright future? Every single day is suffering. I hated my life. Hated it. It was the life you wanted for me, my parents, everyone else. It wasn't the life I wanted."

Dr. Renard stood up, putting one hand out as a protective shield. "Let's not forget who made the choice. As I recall, your mother didn't make you wear the necklace. *You* eventually put it on."

Cassie turned around and punched the wall, letting out a frustrated yelp. When she turned back to the doctor, blood dribbled down her fingers from her knuckles. She calmed her voice. "It's amazing how little you know."

She'd been so focused on the doctor, and all the memories washing up shore, that she had failed to realize the vampires had spread out and were now pounding on both doors. Eventually, they'd get in and this would all be over. Cassie placed a hand over the bite wound on her wrist, remembering it would be over soon for her whether or not the vampires got in.

Dr. Renard stumbled, bumping her back into the wall. "All I ever wanted to do was help you."

Cassie squinted her eyes. "Bullshit. I'm sure you tell yourself you're helping the world by what you did to the vampires, too."

Dr. Renard laughed, and then her face turned stern. "Don't you dare try to humanize them. I watched those creatures rip my husband to pieces for pleasure. They killed my son. My son!"

Cassie moved closer to her. "Oh, I know what they are and I'm going to fucking kill them. But what I wouldn't do is chain them up and rip their jaws off, keep them separated by a few yards to test their communication abilities, see how they adapt, see if they turn on each other or cooperate to gain freedom."

Dr. Renard smiled. "See, you are so brilliant. You understood the trials perfectly. And you're letting your emotions block your smarts. You know damned well why learning that information is important. Those fucking things lived on Earth. They killed people. Nightly. Studying them was important." She put her head down, and the volume in her voice decreased with it. "I guess it's not anymore."

Cassie took one more step, but as soon as she did, she dropped to the floor, head smashing on concrete. Her whole body seized. She felt herself kicking, shaking. Dr. Renard dropped to Cassie's side, putting her hand under Cassie's head to protect it.

The seizure ended a minute later. "What's happening to me?"

Dr. Renard helped her sit up and leaned her against a wall. "The demon is coming out. You've worn the necklace for so long, it's good and buried. As soon as the necklace comes off, the demon can free itself a little, but if the chemicals in the necklace stayed close by, it would still protect you from the demon fully coming out."

"Stop saying 'protect.'"

Dr. Renard rolled her eyes. "When you described what happened up there, being able to kill one vampire but not another, I sensed the necklace had something to do with it. The demon is deep inside, imprisoned, but when you move away from the necklace, it's able to release its anger through you."

Cassie thought about the showers, about how it was the one time she felt free to release her rage. She always removed the necklace before washing. It explained so much. The memories of her friend were coming back, but in bits and pieces and it was a struggle to put them all together, especially with a vicious pack of monsters outside the doors.

"Fuck. It hurts."

Dr. Renard rubbed Cassie's arm. "I know you're going through a lot right now, but we need that demon to come out. Fast. Our only hope of surviving the vampires is if you can lure out The White Wolf."

Cassie put her head on her knees. Her muscles felt like someone was tearing them to pieces. "I don't know how to help it out faster."

She wrapped her arms around herself and screamed. The pain was unbearable.

Dr. Renard stood up. "Okay. Okay. While we are waiting, I'll tell you what I can about the vampires, maybe it will help." She paced and chewed on the inside of her cheek. "The leader is John Adams. We named them after presidents for a while. Before that, we named them after famous actors, and before that, it was pop stars. Anyway, John Adams was always a special one. Most of the vampires drain after not having blood. They weaken, get more animalistic, more brutal, but also kind of dumber. They just act without thinking."

The pain moved from Cassie's stomach to her chest, as if the demon was working its way up.

"But it never happened with John Adams. Some vampires would deplete within a day. Without blood, they'd just fall apart into what you saw upstairs, almost like zombies in movies. But we had John Adams in a cage for over a year. *A year!* And he never changed. Always remained sharp."

Cassie's eyes rolled back and a low guttural noise rumbled in her throat like an idle motorcycle.

The metal doors bent in with each kick and punch. Vampire strength proved enough to warp the thick doors.

"The crew he has with them were new. We hadn't even named them yet. Their human names were Allyson Flickinger, Nicholas Beishline, Fiona Adams, no relation to John, and..." She paused. "Jeez, I forgot the other one."

Sweat leaked down Cassie's face. Was the demon coming out or was the vampire poison seeping in? She imagined she looked just like James had right before he turned.

The doors had warped so heavily, the space between lock and jamb was growing by the second. It wouldn't take long before it fully separated.

"They were all in cells. Somehow, John broke out. We still can't figure out how. That was the emergency my husband and I needed to take care of when you came to babysit. When we got down here, the world fucking ended. Jesus, that's crazy to say out loud. Anyway, John chased us around and got us trapped in a pantry. At least we had food for a little while."

Cassie noted there was more food down here; hopeful she could survive all this and eat a meal, but then, once again, had to remind herself they'd bitten her. There was no coming back from that.

"While they had trapped us in the pantry, John Adams found his way to the control room, where he released the rest of them. They didn't group together and come after us the way they are now, though. It was almost as if they wanted to leave us alone, as if we weren't important to them. My husband had a plan to sneak into the control room where we could use the electronic locks to keep them wherever they were hiding. I knew it was stupid, but he was right. We couldn't hide out in the pantry forever."

Cassie rolled over, walking on all fours. Waves of pain drilled up her spine, into her brain. She thought her skull might explode.

She craned her head back to Dr. Renard.

"Besides the wooden stakes, what kills them?" It wasn't Cassie that asked the question.

The sound of the voice shattered her heart. "I missed you so much," she whispered to her long-lost companion.

"What kills them?" the voice yelled.

Dr. Renard stood up. "Just the wooden stakes I'm afraid."

The other voice laughed as a door smashed open.

"We'll see about that," it said. "I already helped Cassie kill one with a knife. Maybe the best weapon against them is me."

Chapter 35

With Sword in Hand

"When you were a wee little thing, I remember you crawling into a chair leg. Your head slammed hard into it, and later you developed an egg on your forehead. But at the time, you burst into tears, cried for about thirty seconds, then laughed. You laughed. Children are the most terrifying things."

———

Before Cassie could stand, the vampires were on her.

Nick pinned her arms down, and Allyson sat on her stomach, smile still caked in Cassie's blood.

While all this was going on, Dr. Renard slipped back into a corner, keeping as low a profile as possible.

There were four vampires in the room, and the rest continued to pound on the other door.

"Is your little friend out yet?" Allyson said. "She was so delicious before. Come out, come out, little demon. I want a taste."

A vampire behind her said, "You've already had a taste. It's my turn." His nose bent down like a parrot's beak.

Allyson licked her lips. "Fine. Take just a little snack." She dismounted Cassie's stomach.

Bird Face giggled as he sat on her.

Cassie said nothing, didn't try to break free. She wanted to. She wished for nothing more than to kick and scream and run away, but she felt The White Wolf moving around inside her. It placed a gentle hand on her raging heart and whispered, "Sssssshhhhh," in her ear.

Bird Face moved his head closer to Cassie's. His hot breath smelled like a sack of dirty pennies. A forest of blackheads on his nose became visible. His receding hairline dripped sweat. Against her stomach, his body trembled with anticipation. With his eyes closed, he whispered, "I've been feeding on small tastes of the bitch's husband for days. God, I need something new." He opened his mouth, getting ready to dig his teeth into her neck. A line of saliva drove from his top teeth to his bottom.

As he inched closer, The White Wolf pulled Cassie's head up, as if giving him his prize. Then she bit his nose, wiggling her head back and forth until it broke clean off his face. His blood splashed on her as he fell off her, clutching the space where his nose used to be.

Nick's grip loosened, so to further distract him, Cassie spit the nose at him. He used a hand to block it, which gave her the space she needed. With her free arm, she slashed at his face, scratching down his cheek. Now she had both arms free.

Before she had much time, Allyson and Fiona were on top of her.

While she struggled to free herself from them, Nick recovered and gripped her hair, keeping her head in place as he pulled it.

Fiona punched her square between the eyes.

Her vision went blurry and her ears rang. As soon as she recovered, Fiona took another shot. A red pool seeped from her nose into her eyes. She had expected more from The White Wolf, but then again, the demon had years of rust to clean off.

"No more playing around," Allyson said. "Take her to John's room. Follow the plan."

Fiona and Nick each took an arm and dragged her toward the door.

Through the fog in her vision, Cassie saw a blurred Dr. Renard still hovering in the corner.

Bird Face and Allyson followed behind Cassie, and out the door they went.

"John, we got her," Allyson yelled, no shortage of triumph in her voice.

Her bravado sent The White Wolf tumbling inside Cassie. "Have you ever..." Cassie's voice faded away, swimming in a sea of confusion.

"Shut up, girl."

"...ever played tic-tac-toe?"

Bird Face laughed, the noseless fuck. "I think you knocked her silly."

"It's such a stupid game," Cassie said, her back grinding against the cement as they dragged her.

They ignored her rambling.

"If one player knows the game..." she broke out into hysterics, laughing so hard it hurt her head, "...winner is always the first to go." She yanked an arm free and with strength and agility she never possessed, jumped to her feet, only using her lower legs to get her there. Fiona still clung to the other arm, which was bent painfully behind her, but she couldn't focus on that. With her free hand, she grabbed Bird Face by the neck and slammed his head into the wall. A powerful bang reverberated through the corridor.

Allyson dove for her, and Cassie used the vampire's momentum against her, grabbing the back of the vampire's head and driving her knee into Allyson's face. A satisfying crunch. Blood sprayed all over Cassie's pant legs.

Nick jumped on her back, wrapping his arms around her torso. She spun, getting her other arm in front of her.

Fiona still gripped her wrists tightly, unwilling to let go. Instead of fighting to free the grip, Cassie drew her arm in, forcing Fiona closer. When she was close enough, Cassie bit her cheek, tearing a hunk of flesh from her face. The taste of sweat and blood stayed in her mouth, even after she spit the hunk out.

With Nick still on her back, she fell hard into the wall behind her, slamming him into the cement. She drove her head back, smashing the back of her skull into his face. His arms slid off her, and she stepped forward, his body flopping to the ground.

None of them would be out for long. They were vampires. They'd recover easier than a human, and Cassie was pretty sure John Adams gave them each a taste of Mr. Renard, which would offer them strength for a little while. But she gave herself a few moments, or The White Wolf did.

She ran back into the room where Dr. Renard stayed hovering in the corner, rocking and shaking. The vampires weren't pounding on the other door, which meant John Adams was probably making his way around to her. Cassie bent down to Dr. Renard's level. "Tell me there's more stakes."

Dr. Renard looked up at her and winced, presumably from the massive amounts of blood on her face, a combination of her own and the vampires. She probably looked like the girl from *The Descent* after swimming in a pond of gore. Dr. Renard lifted a trembling finger and muttered something under her breath.

Cassie thought the woman might have snapped. After witnessing her husband's death, finding out her son died much the same way, and then seeing a combination of her work bloodying each other up in front of her would probably do the trick.

Cassie huffed and pried open the door she had come in, the one John Adams had been pounding at, and checked the hallway. Nothing. He was probably closing in on the other side of the room. The vampires Cassie had attacked were also surely licking their wounds and planning their revenge.

She ran to Spot's dead body and gripped the stake still in his chest. His agape mouth appeared crooked thanks to his lower jaw shifting to the side. His flesh turned rubbery and purplish-blue.

She ripped the stake out. It left his body with a squelch.

As she headed back to the room, prepared to fight to the death, The White Wolf chimed in. "Cassie, wait."

She leaned against the wall, trying to keep her bearings. Even with The White Wolf's power running through her bloodstream, she felt exhausted, feeble, broken. She also wondered when she'd turn, when the vampire bites would take hold. "We don't have time to wait," she said.

"It's been a long time since I've been able to speak to you. I've seen your suffering and could do nothing but watch."

She sniffled. "I know. I know. That's why we have to hurry and finish this."

"Cassie, that's what I need to tell you. You remember me from childhood. Maybe I seem mythical to you, but I am not. I am scared. I can help you, sure, but I am not all-powerful. Those vampires can kill us both."

She fell to her knees, sobbing. "It doesn't matter anyway. I'm going to turn into one of them." She rubbed her hand on her bitten wrist.

"No, you won't, Cassiopeia. That part I *can* help with. I am in your blood. I am part of your DNA. They can't turn you as long as I am in here, but they can kill you. Because of me, your blood is more valuable to them. It's what makes them so strong. Just a sip of your blood could keep them satiated for centuries."

Cassie stood back up. "Well, let's go finish this or die trying."

The White Wolf growled. "Okay."

Before she stepped back into the room, Cassie's heart dropped. "Wait. Did you call me Cassiopeia?"

Chapter 36

The Day Cassie Died

CASSIE, AGE 8

After school, while Cassie's father worked at the restaurant, her mother sat in the basement typing away at her computer, and her brother hung out at his friend Jordan's house, Cassie explored the backyard. The family had a nice, clean-cut yard with a picket fence blocking the woody hills behind. Those hills were part of their property, but the terrain was too dangerous, too filled with wild animals and angry hornets for Cassie's comfortably suburban parents. Her family was often too busy to know Cassie spent time there.

Her father built a latch gate on the corner of the yard, leading right into the woods, so he could pitch yard debris back there without having to heave it over the fence. He, basically, gave Cassie the invitation to explore.

Today, she planned to cross a small stream at the bottom of the hill, something she'd promised herself she would do at some point, but required gumption because when she got close to the stream, she lost sight of the picket fence. It was uncharted territory, a faraway planet, a new world. Even The White Wolf stirred inside her at the idea of going down there. Her hidden friend knew something about those woods, about the things lurking in the foliage. But what was life without a raised heartbeat? What was the point otherwise?

The hill was relatively steep, so Cassie had to walk sideways to avoid stumbling all the way down. When she reached the bottom after a slow descent, she peered up toward where the picket fence should be. It hid behind the peaks and elms, and the absence of it in her vision sent a fun chill down her spine. The White Wolf grumbled.

The stream was a shallow thing, barely clearing the stones at the bed as the water chugged by, but it was quick, moving so swiftly it made a nice, chaotic swishing sound.

Across the stream, she caught movement. At first, it scared her, but then she recognized the figures. Chris and Jordan. Her brother was laughing as Jordan waved his arms around, telling some kind of yarn.

Cassie ducked behind a tree, not just so she could snoop, although that too, but because she worried her brother would flip knowing she crossed into his world somehow, even if it was accidental. The snooping proved boring. They mainly just tossed rocks and talked shit about their classmates.

Jordan was a beefy kid and when he talked, his cheeks grew redder by the second. He and Chris had been friends for as long as Cassie could remember, and she hated it because Chris always acted like a dick around Jordan.

Chris walked across the stream, the water dribbling against his feet as he crossed.

Jordan followed with a little less grace.

As they neared where Cassie hid, a wasp landed on her arm. Without thinking, she swatted at the foreign invader, killing it instantly. After the distraction, she peeked back to find her brother and his friend already across the stream and walking around the tree she hid behind.

Then, she heard the buzzing. She turned in time to see a cloud of wasps swarming around her. A burning prick hit her leg, then another on her arm. She fell over and screamed, startling Chris and landing on Jordan, knocking him over, too.

"Oh fuck, wasps," he yelled, flailing his arms and legs.

Chris said, "What the fuck are you doing here, Cassie," before realizing the swarm of stinging bugs. He stumbled backwards and ran a small distance away.

Cassie swatted with fury, fighting them off as best she could, but they were all over her. The White Wolf took over, slamming and slashing. She rolled over, trying to get to her feet, and Jordan slapped her in the face while attempting to get the wasps off himself.

The White Wolf reacted to the threats all around, punching. Cassie's fist slammed into Jordan's face, and then she extended her fingers like talons and drove them into Jordan's throat. She wasn't human anymore, nor was she a demon. She was just a ball of energy, an electrical current trapped in a box. She was movement, reaction, but no thought. None at all.

She bit into Jordan's neck, ripping away skin. Her fingers dug into his nostrils and pulled upward until his nose had come away from his face with a clean snap. Her elbow drove up and down into his mouth until he choked on his teeth.

Slowly, the world came back.

The first sign of life came from her brother, who screamed for her to stop from across the stream where he retreated, thanks to the wasps. "Cassie! Stop! What the fuck are you doing?"

Then the pain from the wasp stings kicked in. They were all over her, continuing their assault. Red welts and bumps covered her legs, arms, and presumably her face, too. She stood up, seeing the damage she had done, the brutal remains of her work. Jordan's face was nothing more than mush, a tree stump of viscera.

Chris turned and ran up the hill yelling, "Mom! Mom! Mom!"

Cassie charged after him, running with all her life. One by one the wasps fell off her, until Cassie had run through the already-opened gate into the yard. Her skin was free from the wasps, but the craggy, welted flesh from their assault would remain for God knew how long. Meanwhile, Cassie knew their venom was flowing through her bloodstream, probably enough to kill her.

She came in through the back door, her mother already at the scene. Chris stood in front of her, belligerently screaming and trying to tell her the story but not making much sense.

When Cassie's mother shot a glance at her and saw the sloping hills on her daughter's flesh, she did a double take. Her eyes widened, and she left Chris to scream his story to no one.

"Cassie, what happened?"

She tried to talk to her mother over the sobbing and freaking out. "I'm so sorry mom. It wasn't on purpose. It was the wasps."

"What are you talking about, honey?"

"I was just trying to get away from the wasps."

Chris shouted something. At first, it sounded like a muffled thing, but as he continued to repeat the same words over and over, they grew in strength and clarity. "She killed Jordan. She killed Jordan. Mom, she killed Jordan."

Cassie's mother looked to Chris, to Cassie, to Chris, to Cassie, and in that moment, where the information seeped into her mother's brain, Cassie got the rare experience of witnessing her life turn to dust. In her mother's eyes, through the glossy reflection, Cassie saw herself and saw the shifting shape of her mother's eyelids, going from concern for her daughter to absolute terror. This was it. Nothing would ever be the same again.

She didn't know how yet, but Cassie knew the blood from the body in the woods would travel as swiftly as the stream. It would come up the hill, into the yard, into her house, her bed, her closets, into her mother's heart, her father's hands, her brother's spine. It would kill them all. They were all as good as dead.

Her mother stood up and looked around, navigating a plan of

action in her mind. "Cassie, go upstairs and take a shower. Wash all of that blood off." She turned toward Chris. "Go stand outside the bathroom door. Keep your ears peeled. Call for her every thirty seconds to make sure she responds and is breathing."

Chris threw his hands up. "You're crazy. I don't want to be anywhere near her."

Her mother stiffened and spoke loud and clear. "Do what I fucking tell you, Chris."

Chris stepped forward. "Where are you going?"

"I'm going to Jordan." Without leaving room for conversation, she stepped around Cassie and barged out the back door, letting the screen slam on its way back home.

Chris crossed his arms. "I'm not going up there with you. I don't give a fuck if you die. You hear me?"

Cassie put her head down and went alone up the stairs. In the shower, she cried and scrubbed at the stings, wishing the soap would make the redness and bumps go away. At least Jordan's blood came off nice and easy. She didn't mean to kill him, and neither did The White Wolf. It was an accident. It was just an accident.

She turned off the water when she heard the back door slam again. After wrapping a towel around herself, she crept down the stairs where her mother whispered something to her brother. She said nothing as she made her way to them in the kitchen.

They both turned to her, staring.

Her mother's hands shook, and Jordan's blood covered her shirt, face, and arms. "I need to know you're both listening. And Chris," she looked him square in the eyes, "I don't want to hear your objections. You're doing what I tell you."

Cassie's heart beat faster. The blood on her mother, the way her mom's eyes flickered and darted like an excited gnat, it all portended to something dark, something that would shift the balance of their household, toppling it into an upside-down world.

"I'm going to call the police."

Chris's face lit up.

"I'm going to tell them I did this. When I was a kid, I went to a juvenile detention center for violent things, so they won't question it, especially after what I just did while I was down there. My DNA will be all over him."

Chris went to speak, and his mother put her blood-soaked hand in his face. "Chris, I love you. I know you can't see that, but it's true. And I don't mean to snap at you, but this is not the fucking time. If they ask you questions, you will lie and tell them I did it, you will tell them you saw me do it, and you will tell them I have been acting scary for weeks."

"No. Fucking, no. I won't do that," Chris said.

"Chris!" Her nostrils flared. "I am not having this conversation. You will do what I fucking tell you. This isn't a debate."

"Why? Why would you continue to defend her and make my life a living hell? She's evil, Mom. Now you're going to go to jail so I can be even more alone with her?" Tears dribbled down his cheeks, and his upper lip trembled.

"Because your sister made a promise to me." She turned to Cassie, "Didn't you?"

Cassie stared in bewilderment until it clicked. She shook her head. "What? No. Mom. I'll go to jail. I don't care. You shouldn't take the blame for something I did."

Her mother punched the wall and screamed.

Chris and Cassie flinched.

"I am not having this conversation. Both of you, listen to me. Cassie, you can't go to jail for something you didn't do. You didn't do this. You understand? It wasn't you. It was your friend. You're a fucking kid, and jail will ruin you. You have no idea. It will follow you forever. Forever. That's if they ever let you out. For what happened out there, I wouldn't be surprised if you'd be the youngest kid in history to be tried as an adult."

"Good, let her," Chris chimed in.

She turned to her son. "Listen. I know this is going to be hard to believe, but we have a cure for your sister. A real cure. It's my fault this happened because I didn't make her take it. But Cassie promised me," she said those last two words sternly, "that she would take the cure if anything else happened."

"But mom," Cassie pleaded.

"And I would certainly fucking say this qualifies."

Cassie hugged her, wrapping her arms around her mother's waist and placing her head in the crook of her mom's shoulder. "Please, mom. I don't want you to go."

Chris stood still, sobbing, looking on the verge of shattering. "Mom, don't do this."

"He's right, mom. You can't do this."

Her mother gently pried Cassie away from her, went to the old-style kitchen phone that hung on the wall, and dialed 911. With an eerie calmness, she simply said, "Hello, I need police officers to come to my house right away... Yes, that's correct... Yes, that's our address... Because I just killed a child in the woods behind my house." She hung up.

Chris and Cassie broke out into hysterical sobs. For the first time, they shared a mutual pain.

The next ten minutes were a blur of begging and pleading to stop the inevitable. The wheels had been set in motion and nothing good could happen from that point forward.

Her mother forced Cassie upstairs to change out of her towel before the police arrived.

While she changed, Chris screamed throughout the house, angrily throwing any random object he could find.

The police came. While they spoke to Cassie's mother, other men and women trounced around the house into the woods.

Cassie stood in a corner, watching everything, holding in her breath, and wishing she had the strength to hold it until she died.

The police asked her some questions, and Chris, too, but they seemed uninterested in their answers. They had their murderer wrapped up with a solid confession. Chris and Cassie kept to their mother's story as they'd been instructed. Cassie was sure Chris would break, but he never did.

All the while, her mother acted out a character, an unstable one who shouted and whispered and broke into frenzied hysterics. It all felt so cartoonish to Cassie, but if the police could see through her acting, they weren't showing it. Besides, she doubted anyone would believe a child did what happened to Jordan.

As the police dragged Cassie's mother out of the house, she tossed the necklace at Cassie and yelled, "Wear that fucking thing, Cassie. Remember me as I was before this."

Cassie slid out of the way, letting the necklace drop to the floor. She moved to another corner, keeping as much distance as she could. At first, Cassie didn't know what her mother meant by that. Of course, Cassie would remember her as she was before. She knew the hysterics were all an act.

A sole officer remained until Chris assured him their father would be home soon. No one seemed concerned about Cassie's welt-ridden skin. The house emptied, but their father was due home soon with a brand-new hurricane to weather,

Chris stormed up to his room and shut the door.

Cassie went upstairs and cried into her pillow.

"We should have listened, Cassiopeia," a voice whispered in her ear.

Cassie sat up, wiping her face. "Shut up."

"Cassiopeia, you know I'm telling the truth."

"You didn't mean to do it. You were protecting me."

"I know that. You know that. But I will forever be a liability to you. My job is to protect you. Look around, I have failed. I have destroyed your life."

"My mother just left me. Now you want to leave me too?"

"Cassiopeia, you know well that I don't want to do this."

"Then don't."

"When your father gets home, let your brother talk to him. He won't lie to your father. They will both be angry with you. Once they've had a little time, go downstairs and I will talk to them."

"No. I won't let you leave me. I won't do this. You're all I have left. Who will protect me?"

The White Wolf growled in her ear. "You stop that. You have you. You will protect you. You will be your biggest friend. You're just like your mother. Never knew when to defend herself, to fight for herself. What she just did for you was the proudest of her I've ever been because she finally acted. And she did it for you. I expect you to do the same. For yourself."

Cassie whimpered again. "No. I don't know how to be without you. I can't."

"You are stronger than you give yourself credit for. You will do it because you love me and I need you to do it. I demand it. I don't have your morality. I want to hurt things. I want to taste blood. You will never live a normal life with me and I will not let you suffer anymore by my hands. You've done too much already.

"Here is how it will go. The necklace will make me go away more and more each day. I'll never fully be gone, but I'll be buried. On my way out, I will infect your brain. I will change things. You won't remember me anymore, so you can't miss me. Instead, all your important memories of me will go to someone else. You'll know they happened, but they won't be with me. I will make myself disappear completely. I love you so much, I would erase myself from history for you."

Cassie went from sobbing to full-on bawling.

The front door slammed open and Chris came barreling out of his room.

Cassie listened from the top steps as both her brother and father shouted. When she crept down the stairs, both men were standing in the hallway.

Chris moved behind their father, arms crossed smugly.

Cassie's father stood with a bag of groceries felled at his feet. His jaw had dropped so much it looked like it could separate from the rest of his face. Tears built in his eyes.

He looked to Cassie and pointed to the door. "Get out of my house," he said. Sense seemed to kick in. "I'm going to call the police."

The White Wolf took control and walked around them, not to the door, but to the living room where the necklace sat in a corner. Together, she and Cassie stared at it. Then, they turned back to Cassie's father. "And they'll believe a child capable of what happened? Don't be a fool."

"Give me my wife back!"

Her upper lip snarled and she charged. Cassie couldn't believe what The White Wolf was doing. "You're in no place to make demands, old man. Sit down, the both of you." The White Wolf's voice was so deep, so filled with fury, it surprised them all.

No one argued. Her father and brother sat next to each other on the couch.

"I won't live in the same house as you," her father said with as much backbone as he could muster.

"And you won't have to. I am leaving."

Her father and Chris lifted their heads at the same time, eyebrows raising with them.

"Her therapist found a cure for me. A necklace filled with chemicals that keeps me bottled up, unable to manifest within Cassie. She refused to wear it. Until today, I argued in her favor, and so did her mother, who hid the necklace from you both."

Chris looked like someone punched him in the gut.

Cassie's father made a pained sob.

"I am going to force Cassie to wear it. I will be gone. I know that's hard to believe, but it's true. You are free to call Dr. Renard for proof. I will be gone and Cassie will stay."

"No," Chris said.

Cassie yapped and chomped her teeth. "This is not a request. Cassie will wear the necklace, always. You will treat her with respect, or if you can't manage that, you will at least stay clear of her."

Her father threw his hands up. "You've got to be kidding. That's it? And you get away scot-free from all you've done to us?"

The White Wolf had full control of Cassie, and now its anger trapped her even further. Cassie couldn't move, talk, or do anything but watch things unfold. She knew it was over. The White Wolf would enforce the rules and she'd fall into a seizure as The White Wolf picked up the necklace. When she came to, she'd have no memory of the only friend she ever had.

"I will be trapped in the girl's belly for eternity, you damned fool. Is that not punishment for you?" The White Wolf snapped.

"Not enough of one if you ask me," Chris said.

"There are rules." The White Wolf stared hard.

"Here we go," her father said, standing up and pretending he was going to walk away. No one in the room believed he would, probably not even himself.

"*Sit down!*"

Her father listened.

"Why do you humans pretend you have a backbone? There are rules," The White Wolf snapped, "and you will obey them."

Cassie's father rubbed his forehead. "Can I get even one minute to absorb what's happening here? I come home from work, ready to put some groceries away, and I find out my life has been turned upside down. My wife is gone." His voice broke. It took a second for him to bring it back. "In jail for murder. All because of you and you have the nerve to give me demands? You know what? I don't have a backbone, you're right. But I would have to be the biggest sap of all time to keep listening to you. Fuck you. How's that?"

The White Wolf forced Cassie's body to jump, landing right on her father. She pinned her father's arms to the cushions. "That was good. Nice spine. But here's the problem. If you kick us out, I will sneak through the window and gut you while you sleep. If you tell the police the truth and Cassie goes to jail, I will come through the window and gut you while you sleep. If you do anything other than what I tell you, I will gut you while you sleep." She turned her head toward Chris. "Then I will eat your son for fun."

The White Wolf waited for any objections. None came. "You fear your daughter. That is my fault. Mine alone. Once she wears the necklace, I will slowly disappear. Over time, it will be more and more difficult for me to come out, even with the necklace removed. Once a day, you will grant me freedom. You will make Cassie take a shower and the only time she won't have her necklace on is during that shower. I'll be so locked up I won't be able to fully manifest, but it will help her release the rage she bottles. It's the only action I will perform. Helping her rage. Once the shower is over, she will put the necklace back on. You won't need to tell her. It'll be instinctual for her." The White Wolf looked from her father to her brother, making sure they followed. "Number two, you will understand it is me you hate, not her. Your fear may remain, but your hate is not allowed. You will not be cruel to her, or I will whisper in her ear, 'remove the necklace, Cassiopeia.'" Again, she waited. This time, their silence wasn't enough to satisfy. "Understood?"

They both nodded.

"Chris, I am going to erase Cassie's memory of me. She won't remember what happened to your friend, nor will she remember any other violence we have done together. But she will remember all the happiness. She will remember our bond, but she won't know it was ours." Cassie's hand moved to Chris's, causing her brother to flinch. "She will believe it was all with you. You can use that as an opportunity to bond. I'm sure you won't take it, but if you so choose to move on from this, the chance is there." Cassie sat up. "You lost a wife today, a mother. Your hate and grief will boil for days. You can let it fester, or you can put the blame where it belongs, on me, and recognize you have a beautiful daughter who wants nothing more than to love you and be loved in return."

The White Wolf guided her toward the necklace. Cassie couldn't yell, couldn't fight, because The White Wolf had taken full control, but she screamed at her inside her head. *No! No! No!* Her body bent down and snatched the necklace from the floor, causing her to convulse.

When Cassie came to, she had a deep need for her family. She needed to hug them, to find out the world was still in order, but she found the house empty. Empty, dark, and full of hidden recesses.

Chapter 37

To See Her

"I sometimes fear who I am. I would hate to see myself from someone else's perspective."

———

The thin corridor spun as all the memories flooded back. The White Wolf. It had always been The White Wolf there for her, giving her affection, fighting for her. And it told her to defend herself, taught her how to be strong, and she failed to listen. For all these years, she had failed. When she believed the advice came from her brother, as opposed to a voice inside herself, it seemed so fragile, especially given what happened to Chris.

"I can't believe it. You made me forget you."

"Things done. Things regretted, Cassie. Can we discuss this after we finish our current situation?"

She shook her head, but she'd lost all her verve. When she had too much to feel, how could she concentrate? She stepped into the room where Dr. Renard still stayed cradled in the corner, rocking herself mad.

The doctor noticed Cassie and stood up. "Cassie! We made a mistake. It was the demon they were after the whole time. Not you. We never should have let it out."

The White Wolf took control of Cassie, grabbed Dr. Renard by the throat, and pinned her to the wall.

Dr. Renard gasped and choked, her feet kicking a few centimeters off the floor.

The words that came from Cassie's mouth were not her own, but in so many ways, they were. "You convinced me what needed to be done. Just like Cassie's mother, brother, and father. You were wrong."

Dr. Renard spoke in a whisper, unable to produce anything louder with a hand wrapped around her vocal cords. "You're a demon. A fucking demon. How could you believe you were good for her?"

The White Wolf growled. "Yes, and every time a woman gnashes her teeth, it must be a supernatural evil, right?"

"Don't be ridiculous. You killed people."

"Yes, I did. And only sometimes was it regrettable." She tossed her out of the corner.

Dr. Renard's body hit the cement floor with a sickening thud. She lay on the floor staring at the ceiling. "You asked about the bedroom." The doctor sat up, groaning. "The bunker on the other side of the tunnel was always just for show, a place for us to do experiments without raising eyebrows. Zoning and building regulations and all that shit. Our real bunker is down here, same as the prisons. We found the tunnels by accident, so we built all of this down here. There's an exit that goes into the middle of the woods. This is where the real bedrooms are, the pantry, kitchen, bathrooms, and yes, the vampire prison. It's all a fucking secret. We didn't even tell James about it. Half the time we said we were going to work, we just drove down a dirt road in the woods a few miles behind our house and did work down here. Not that we didn't have real clients to work with in our offices. I can't think of the last time we went through the bunker doors in our yard. We always came from this side."

"Why didn't you dig out the tunnels more? I nearly got stuck."

Dr Renard shook her head. "You went straight. Yeah, we always meant to make that bigger, but there's a side tunnel that's much easier to get through, so we just never got around to it. The other tunnel pops out right in the main living quarters."

Main living quarters. Beds. Pantry. Kitchen. Maybe she could still find a way to live down there. A thought came to Cassie. Where were the vampires? Why weren't they attacking her? It must have occurred to The White Wolf too, because she turned toward the second door, sharp-eyed, eager to fight, but nervous. Cassie knew The White Wolf's fear by the way it affected her own heartbeat, just a slight uptick in beats; small, but noticeable. They drifted to the door, then peered their head out in the hallway.

Nothing.

No movement.

No noise outside of a low dripping.

She dipped to the opposite side, away from the door, and leaned her back square on the wall. From there, she slid down the hall, stake at the ready. The dripping sound grew louder with each step she took.

Drip. Drip. Drip.

Just as before, as she moved away from the room the hallway's darkness suffocated her. She tried to steady her shaky breath to listen for any sound. She'd traveled far enough from the room that she was no longer sure where she was, what directions the hall would take, and where it all led. At some point, it had to cross where she had once run from the vampires since Dr. Renard found her way to the same room where she ended up, but Cassie didn't know if the hallway had any other turns that would confuse her sense of direction.

Far down the hall, something skittered from one side of the hall to the other before disappearing. It laughed on its way. Allyson or Fiona, she guessed by the sound.

She stared in the direction, trying to pick up any visual, a nook, something to explain where they could have come from or where they went.

Then, something moved behind her.

She jolted at the sound.

Something else skittered from one side to the other before disappearing.

It made no sense. She had just been over there, and the hall had offered no turns. Where could they have come from? Where could they have gone? As far as she knew, they didn't possess the ability to move through walls.

She kept sliding forward but turned her head back and forth, keeping sentry from all sides.

As she slid, her foot hit something, or rather, hit nothing. She bent down and put her hand where the wall should have been. Nothing. A hole, a crawl space really. Her eyes were focused at eye level, so she hadn't noticed the hallway was pockmarked with small crevices to crawl through.

"Shit," she whispered.

As the word left her mouth, something latched onto her hand.

She screamed.

It pulled her forward, banging her head into the wall. A sharp sting hit the meaty part of her hand between her thumb and forefinger as the creature bit into her.

She yanked her hand away and fell backwards as the thing slid out of the crawl space with unnatural ease, as if it had done so a hundred times. Even with limited sight, she recognized Bird Face.

He jumped on top of her and bit her, carving his teeth into the skin around her lower jaw.

With The White Wolf in control, Cassie gripped her weapon tight. The stake penetrated Bird Face's neck so smoothly the tip came out the other side.

His eyes went dead. Before he fell off her, he coughed a spattering of blood on her face.

She ripped the stake out and let his body flop to the side. As she tried to sit up, something tackled her and held her down while something else grabbed her legs.

Hisses came from all around her. Lots of them. She recognized Nick. He tried to hold her arms in place, but Cassie proved too quick. The stake went into his chest once, twice, three times. She kept pounding it in, making sure it finished the job.

As Nick's dead weight landed on top of her, Allyson bit into her calf. She didn't have time to react before another vampire pulled her hair.

She took the stake out of Nick and drove it upward, hitting the unfamiliar vampire gripping a chunk of her hair right in the front of his neck. As she pulled it out, she brought it down on the top of Allyson's head. The stake went right through her skull. Pieces of brains oozed from the tip as she removed it. She stood up, covered in blood and unable to walk beyond a hobble thanks to the newly formed calf bite.

Two vampires stood on each side of her. The only one she knew was Fiona. John Adams was nowhere to be seen. The four remaining vampires circled her, one in front, one behind, and one to each side. North, East, South, and West.

Cassie turned her wrist, holding the spike of the stake out. She inhaled deeply and spun around. The stake drove through one neck, then the next. On the third, she had to stop her spin and correct her positioning. That one got the sharp end of the stick right in the temple instead. That left only North.

He pounced, jumping on her back and wrapping his hands around her torso.

She stabbed at his arms until he loosened his grip and they both fell backwards, Cassie landing on top of North. Staring up at the ceiling, she saw the source of the dripping sound. Mr. Renard hung from the ceiling, his stomach cut open. Jesus. They must have just done this; otherwise he would have bled dry by now. They did this for her. It was for show, more psychological warfare.

As Mr. Renard's dripping body took her focus, North bit into the back of her skull.

She pulled away from him, tired, losing blood, stung by too many wasps. He scratched at her, but she didn't change her speed, didn't care about a few more wounds. She faced him, staring, and his eyes widened with fear.

"The demon," he whispered. "I can see her."

"No," Cassie said. "You're seeing me." She slammed the stake into his eye. When she pulled it from his skull, the eye dropped to the floor. She stepped on it and drove the stake into North's chest. Hobbling forward, no longer keeping her back to the wall, she trekked down the hallway, confident no other vampires existed in the bunker outside of one. John Adams.

As if on cue, he stepped into the hall far down from where she was.

They stared at each other.

"Come now, Cassie. Let's finish this." He stepped away from where he had originally come, and a light clicked on.

Another room.

She stepped forward, her left leg dragging. Her eyes were swollen. Each bite throbbed. She was in no shape to fight, but The White Wolf would help. One way or the other, this ended now.

When she reached the room's threshold, she held the stake out, ready to stab.

John Adams dashed from her peripheral.

A sharp pain hit the side of her stomach before taking over her whole body. She fell over, convulsing. Every muscle in her body burned at once. An unbearable pain shot from head to toe, as if stabbed by a million pins. And then, emptiness. Complete emptiness.

She rolled over to see the live wire zapping, wriggling like a snake.

John Adams kicked it away from her, its job done.

The pain was worse than electrocution. It was something else, something familiar, but long since forgotten. She rolled to the other side and her heart sank.

A woman sat curled and naked on the floor, her silver hair spilling down her back. Slivers of smoke curled around her body, a scrim of grey like a thin protective shell.

Cassie knew immediately who it was.

The White Wolf.

John Adams had ripped The White Wolf from her body.

Chapter 38

The Night Chris Died

Chris cranked his music up, as he did most nights. He hoped it would signal Cassie to leave him alone. As much animosity as he had for her, he didn't want her to find him. His father wouldn't handle it much better, one more loss for the poor man, but at least his father had an adult mind. Cassie was too young, had been through the same horrors Chris had, and adding one more to the list felt cruel. But Chris couldn't keep going. He couldn't.

While Cassie buried her face in her schoolwork, Chris snuck upstairs and set up the rope, the chair, the table, all he would need to make it happen. As he mentally prepared, something flashed in the attic window. He squinted, trying to make it out.

A figure moved through the fog in the yard, coming through the thick mist and revealing itself.

Chris wept at the sight, something he'd heard about so many times, but had never seen. It was the thing which haunted his nightmares, the thing always there for a tragedy. The White Wolf. He knew his sister called the demon The White Wolf, but he hadn't imagined it actually looked like one. But there it was, a giant beast in snowy fur, waltzing through the yard.

Chris tightened the slipknot and pushed it, letting it swing wildly from the rafters. He crept down the stairs, sneaking past Cassie's bedroom, down another flight, and stopped at the back door. The White Wolf sat patiently on the lawn, waiting for his arrival.

He opened the door, and The White Wolf stared up at him.

Chris's heart pounded wildly. "What do you want?"

"Come sit with me before you go." The White Wolf shifted, as if making room for Chris.

Figuring he had nothing to lose, Chris obeyed the thing he hated most in life. As he sat, he said, "I thought we buried you."

"The part of me in Cassie is buried."

"So what part am I talking to?"

"The part in you."

Chris buried his face in his knees, tears flowing. "If you've been with me all this time, why haven't you helped me? Where have you been?"

"I'm not possessing you, Chris. Never was. I stayed with your mother when you were born and left with Cassie later. But I put a little piece of myself in you, just a piece."

This made Chris cry harder. He had hated The White Wolf for years, but maybe a part of him hated that he never had one, that yet another thing let him down. "Why didn't you choose me?"

"Choose. Not choose. Things are not so simple. Your mother still needed me when you were born. By staying with her, keeping her strong, I was choosing you."

"My mother didn't still need you when Cassie was born?"

"No."

"Why?"

"Because of you, Chris. You fixed your broken mother."

Chris listed his head, resting it on The White Wolf's furry neck. He wasn't sure why he did it, but he needed to. "Is this the 'you have value' speech?"

"No."

"Then why are you here?"

"To tell you that I love you. You say I didn't choose you, but I did. I chose you when I made Cassie forget me, when I rearranged her memories to make them all about you. I tried to give you something, to help you. You didn't take it."

"So, this is my fault? Got it." Chris took his head away but didn't move otherwise, not yet willing to leave the conversation.

"Nothing is your fault, Chris. Nothing is anyone's fault. You suffer. I didn't help with that. But it doesn't matter. If your life was all roses, you'd still be here."

Chris sat back, letting his head land softly on the freshly mowed grass. He stared up at the stars. "Are you saying I'm destined to kill myself?"

"No, Chris. If I thought that, I wouldn't be here. You are, however, destined to be you. You have problems. I can't fix them. I'm a demon, not a therapist. But they can be fixed."

"Yeah, by who?" The sky seemed closer, not a faraway series of mysteries but a touchable, breathable universe, the lights to a festival, a home.

The White Wolf sighed. "I wish I was good at this. I don't have all the answers. Humanity's greatest strength is its ability to change, pivot, adapt, transform. Its greatest weakness is its inability to recognize that."

"What?"

"You all convince yourselves that you are what you are, unchangeable. You are clay to be molded repeatedly, yet you consistently opt to throw yourselves in the oven and call yourselves done. You can choose to go through with your plans for the evening, or you can wake up tomorrow and reshape yourself."

"I'll still be depressed."

"Yes, and you'll still suffer. You can change yourself, but you can't change what's broken, within you and without."

"So, we aren't so malleable after all."

"Suffering isn't so bad, Chris."

Chris laughed, a small smile stabbing through the surface. "How could you possibly say that?"

"A pearl comes from an oyster fixing a wound."

Chris laughed, a manic sound. "That's it? That's your big pitch? Oysters?"

The White Wolf turned her head, red eyes landing deep within Chris's soul. "Fine, Chris. How's this? A gravitational pull sucked in gases and solid matter, creating the world, an uninhabitable rock. An asteroid crashed into it, ricocheting debris, and creating the moon. It also tilted the axis of the Earth, but all this stupid rock had was carbon dioxide, methane, and water vapor. Any oxygen created from the vapor mixing with sunlight was quickly defeated by the methane and trapped into the Earth's crust. Yet, life formed regardless. Single-celled bacterium used the minerals at the bottom of the ocean to generate energy. Through this, cyanobacteria evolved. They used water as a source of power. How did they do this? They oxidized it. These little fucking things gave oxygen to the oceans, which eventually seeped into the air, overtaking the methane. We exist because of those cyanobacteria."

Chris sat up. "What's the point of this?"

"All of life is suffering, all of it is flaws. Being perfect, fitting the status quo, means never changing. It means no massive explosions that create a universe. It means no asteroids crashing in your mind to tilt your axis. It means losing the perfect conditions to grow life. Flaws, Chris. Life exists because of flaws, because of suffering. Because of pain and anger, and a deep desire to survive. Your genes are nothing without alleles. Mutations. Mistakes."

Chris put his hand up. "Okay, I get it."

"You were born with mistakes, Chris. And everyone around you is better for it. Unfortunately, one of your mistakes is an inability to see that. But there are doctors who can help you navigate it, to make you feel better. You don't have to suffer always."

Chris stood up, dusting his pants off. "I'm going to go inside now."

The White Wolf nodded.

"But thank you."

The White Wolf tilted his head. "For?"

"This conversation was probably the most alive I've felt in a long time."

As he opened the screen door, he stopped himself, turned back to The White Wolf, and chuckled.

"What's so funny?"

"I can't believe you're actually a fucking white wolf. I thought it was just something my sister called you."

The White Wolf smiled. "I am not. I thought it would be less distressing if I appeared this way, since it's how you knew me all these years."

Chris put his head down, staring at his feet. "Before I leave, can I see the real you?"

The White Wolf nodded. She transformed.

Chris wept.

"Are you afraid?" she asked.

Chris nodded. "Yes. It's beautiful."

He turned and went inside, snuck up to the attic, and wrapped the slipknot around his neck. The demon stared from the window, and while it was too far away, Chris thought he saw tears trailing down her inhuman and horrifying face.

Chapter 39

Everything Ends Eventually

"Fighting is the universal truth."

———

Cassie couldn't take her eyes off The White Wolf. As a child, the only friend she'd ever known was one she couldn't see, and here the woman was, separated from her. Completely ripped out of her. She felt like a carapace, a hollow shell, missing the inner part of herself, thin and fragile. And like a molting lobster, The White Wolf was most vulnerable without a hardened shell wrapped around her.

John Adams bent down, rubbing his hands on the various wounds on Cassie's body.

The White Wolf told her the demon could protect her DNA from the vampire's poison, but now that they were separated, she wondered how long she had before she turned.

"It'll be interesting to see if you die from these wounds before turning into one of us," John Adams said. He licked his lips. "Funny, don't you think? Your therapist spent years throwing chemicals in your face to find out how to bury the demon when all she had to do was give you a little electricity and she could have ripped the thing right out." He laughed at his own joke.

Cassie eyed the stake she'd dropped when the electricity hit.

John Adams caught her glance. He picked up the stake and snapped it in half before sliding it across the floor and away from her. "You're too weak to do anything now, but why risk it, am I right?"

Without the stake, she turned her attention toward the only other weapon she knew, The White Wolf. But her old friend hadn't shifted from the fetal position, facing away from both of them.

John Adams, once again, caught her stare. He smiled and stood up. "Oh, your little friend isn't going to be much help. She's nothing without a host." He kicked The White Wolf.

A horrendous squeal came from her as her lifeless body flopped over. For the first time, Cassie saw her face. It was almost alien. No nose, just two nostrils on a smooth surface. Her skin was yellow, taut, and plastic-like. Her mouth drooped down on one side and her eyes were uneven, one practically level with her nostril holes. This had lived inside her for her entire life.

At first, the sight was jarring, but not scary. It was like she had only seen herself in a grime-covered mirror and, for the first time, wiped the surface clean. Because the demon was her, and she was it. They were the same. The face she looked at was hers.

John Adams lifted The White Wolf by her hair, and the demon did nothing to fight back. He sniffed her hair. "Do you know why I'm so strong, Cassie, why I could endure your psychotic doctor's cruel trials? Because one hundred years ago, I bit into the flesh of a demon. His power kept me satiated all this time. Since you humans are so hellbent on destroying the world, and each other, I would love to have something that can keep me going for another hundred. Imagine the entire world up there, mine. All mine. All alone. You can relate to that, can't you, Cassie?" He dropped The White Wolf. "I feel attached to you. The time I spent hiding in the walls, reading all about you. The doctor was, if nothing else, an excellent note taker."

Cassie stared at her counterpart, unable to help. Even separated, they were one; their histories intertwined for better or worse. They'd done horrible things, things she couldn't ever pay the toll for, but if given the chance, she could have tamed it. No one had given her a chance to be anything else. And who was the world to judge? They'd gone and killed each other until nothing was left.

That was the great lie of childhood, to think that one day you'd grow into a role where no one controlled you, no one could rule over you. But that never ended. Someone always pressed their fingers down telling you to work harder, to sleep less, to be different. There was always someone to answer to, and the world squeezed that power so tightly it imploded. Exploded. Imploded and exploded. Humanity needed no demons to reveal its evil.

But Cassie *did* need the demon to act. Her whole life she hid behind a wall, afraid to put attention on herself, too nervous to stick up for herself. Even down here she only pushed back out of necessity.

The White Wolf always urged her to fight, and she'd let her down. One of her last words to Cassie before the necklace was, "You have you." And she'd ignored it.

No more.

No more.

Before she had time to act, John Adams cleared his throat. "Well, no more wasting time. It will be fun to see your face while I kill your friend. Oh, you'll want to kill me for it, but then you'll either die from your wounds or turn into my slave."

He lifted The White Wolf, the entity that once existed within Cassie that made her feel invincible, and he pulled.

The White Wolf's body split in two, ripping apart at the waist. Black blood poured from her.

"No!" Cassie screamed. The radio static in her brain disappeared. Even after having all memories of The White Wolf removed from her mind, a piece of her knew she was there, or that something was. A noise, a hum, the feeling of a gentle hand on her chest, something always remained. She'd lost The White Wolf as a child, and felt

240

it, but now she knew what it truly felt like to lose the demon. It was a curtain closing in her brain, blacking out the world. It was a fist clenching her heart until it popped. It was a knife to the spine, rat poison in the blood, plastic wrap around her mouth and nose. It was total loss.

And now, she understood the ramifications of her actions, how Chris must have felt when she tore his best friend to shreds in the woods. How her father must have felt when her mother went to prison for life, a life that ended in suicide in her prison cell just a few months later. All of it Cassie's fault, and while she loved the people she'd hurt, she never loved them like *this,* because they never loved her like *this.*

John Adams hung the woman over his head and let the blood coat his face. He stuck his tongue out and drank the rain.

You have you.

You have you.

You have you.

And now, she understood why she never took the advice. She had her, sure. She could have defended herself, but it didn't matter if she *could,* she had never wanted to because a piece of herself had been removed. She never needed the strength to defend herself, she needed something to defend. They forced her to remove The White Wolf and then told her to love herself. They broke her. They stole from her. They forced her to be something other than who she was and then expected her to care. She did care. She cared about The White Wolf. What she needed all this time was something to defend. Something bigger than herself.

And now, she felt like fighting. Ignoring all the pain, the imminent death, she stood up, blood-soaked and hell-bent on revenge.

John Adams was too busy enjoying his shower of blood to notice.

She picked up the sizzling and snaking live wire and hobbled toward the vampire. Cassie realized as she walked why she had truly held back all these years. Because deep inside, she knew she had done awful things, been awful things, thought awful things, and she worried if she spoke up for herself, fought for herself, the villain would come out again. She'd hurt everyone she'd ever loved, and now she did nothing while the biggest part of her got ripped in half. Cassie was the villain, and for the first time, she embraced it.

As John Adams kept his face skyward, swallowing the drizzles of demon blood, Cassie shoved the live wire down his throat. He shot across the room, a spectacular display of pops and sparks coming from his mouth. The White Wolf's upper body dropped on top of her lower half.

Cassie hoped the electricity would provide her enough time to arm herself with the stake, but the vampire crashed into the wall and came right at her.

He pounced on top of her, pinning her to the floor. His smarmy charm wiped from his face, all he showed was violent intentions and rage. He spread his lips, revealing his black-soaked teeth, and brought his face down to hers.

"Hey!" Dr. Renard shouted from the doorway. She ran to them. On the way, she kicked the top portion of the stake toward Cassie.

John Adams stood, and with lightning speed, grabbed Dr. Renard by the throat and tore her head clean off her body. The woman's body dropped hard, and John Adams tossed her head behind him like it was nothing more than old gum. When he turned back to Cassie, she was standing and ready for him.

A small fragment of the stake went into his left eye. She hardly gripped the end where the wood splintered, but she used her forefingers to pull it out. As she drove it into his right eye, the left had already started the healing process.

She understood the value of the demon blood now, and wondered how much influence it had on her, too. When The White Wolf was locked away, Cassie was always in pain, but when she freed it from the necklace, her body felt good, strong, able to weather whatever came her way. She'd never experience that feeling again.

She clenched her teeth and stabbed John Adams in the neck, then the other side, then the front. When he fell over, clutching his injuries, she leaped on top of him and plunged the stake into his chest, right above his heart. She hoped it was enough to kill him because the stake took its final toll, too, breaking in the wall of the vampire's ribs.

Unwilling to presume, she crawled over to the top portion of the stake that sat on the floor near the door. She crawled back, and with the blunt end where it snapped, jammed it on top of the first stake, pushing it further into his chest.

John Adam's eyes and mouth opened wide. He gasped.

Cassie knew he'd die then, that soon, a geyser of blood would shoot from his throat, but she wasn't ready to accept that. She'd dealt with him for too long, and never got to return the favor.

He deserved torture, a lifetime of pain.

She wrapped her hand around the stake's blunt end and slammed her fist into his nose, his cheeks, his teeth.

His bones snapped, popped. Those violent, poisonous teeth cracked and fell down his airways. He gagged and choked, and she kept on smashing.

She'd never felt so free, so happy.

His face turned to mush at her doing, and she refused to stop. Crimson rain decorated the floors and walls, Cassie's face and clothes. Small bone fragments shot away from John's face. He screamed in pain, and the sound was beautiful, palpable. It echoed through the room, reminding Cassie of Chris's rap thumping through the hallways of her childhood home.

Eventually, he stopped screaming, and his blood did geyser from his throat, but she continued to slam until his skull was so broken and destroyed, the bottom of the stake clanked against the cement floor.

Cassie stood, winded and exhausted. Her heart banged, pleading. She was going to die now, or worse, turn into a vampire. She felt the poison flowing through her. It was powerful, but gross, as if it were turning her blood to swamp water.

She rejoiced at the horrid sight of John's dead body and mutilated face. A tinge of sadness crept up her spine for Dr. Renard. The poor woman had lost her husband and son and died trying to protect her old patient. Cassie hated her for so much, for the life the doctor forced upon her, for her experiments gone wrong that caused all of this, for never fully understanding the things she attempted to study. The doctor was flawed, but she had the best of intentions.

John Adams and Dr. Renard were the only bodies Cassie could assess. She refused to turn toward The White Wolf. She wanted nothing more than to fall on top of her felled friend, to say her last goodbyes before the hand of God dropped the final curtain on her life, to hug the corpse of the demon and thank her, tell her how much she loved her. But in the end, Cassie couldn't. Just as the cruelty of the fates didn't allow her to make John Adams suffer more, it also kept her from sharing her final thoughts with the only thing that ever truly knew her. She just wasn't strong enough in the end.

But there was one more thing to do before this all ended.

Just one more thing.

Chapter 40

A Day in the Sun

CASSIE, AGE 4

Despite her parents swearing off the stroller six months ago, they lugged the thing out of the trunk and plopped Cassie into it. The sun-drenched the parking lot bringing blinding light and sweltering heat. Steam waved off the pavement.

Chris took his hat off and wiped his brow. "Maybe we should come back another day," he said.

His father huffed. "We've already driven all this way."

Cassie's mother pushed the stroller, and Cassie's father and brother flanked each side. The wheels made a satisfying rattle against the uneven cement. It nearly put Cassie to sleep and would have if the wheels didn't stop at a booth where a loud woman told them about how tickets to the dino exhibit were separate.

After her mother shuffled through her purse and gave the loud woman her plastic card, they were off and running in the park. After three exhibits, giraffes, elephants, and prairie dogs, Chris's complaining became a running theme. It was too hot for him and he wanted to make sure everyone knew that.

Her father relented and bought bottles of water for each of them, but Chris didn't even crack his open. He didn't want relief, he wanted to go home. Anything else was half-measures and he wouldn't stand for it.

Meanwhile, Cassie had her own complaints. "Mama, I want out." She kicked her feet until her mother relented, unbuckling her and putting her down. Cassie could tell by the way her mom folded up the stroller, all rough and fast, that Cassie had upset her, but she couldn't get a good view of the animals from inside the cart.

After everyone had some water, except for Chris who remained stubborn on the subject, they went into the Tropical America exhibit. Sloths sat lazily in trees, bats hung from branches in their glass enclosures, and snakes coiled around mini shrubs. The humidity tripled in the indoor exhibit, and Cassie noticed her brother's deepening breathing. She stared at him as his eyes rolled up and his body collapsed to the floor.

A flash of panic hit everyone around. Cassie's parents dove to the floor, surrounding Chris. Cassie's father poured water onto his son's lips, while her mother held his head up and yelled his name over and over.

Strangers began surrounding him, too, and medical personnel rolled in.

Cassie's pulse quickened at the sight of so many people. She hated large gatherings. While she waited for the action to settle, she wandered over to the sloths, passing a weird, lanky woman staring at the ceiling with sunglasses on.

The sloths were cute, and Cassie wondered why she'd never heard of them before. They looked like the kind of animal someone would keep as a pet. The silly voice came to her then. "Cassie. Go back to your family. Look at those sloths. They aren't going anywhere." Cassie giggled, but before she could take the voice's advice, her mother grabbed her shoulder and ushered her out the door.

She didn't know what was happening, but her mom was walking

fast, and she had trouble keeping up. They marched along the paths toward the Arctic exhibit, toward the zoo exit.

"I don't want to leave. Where's Chris?" she said.

"Hush."

Cassie's heart slammed on the brakes. That wasn't her mother's voice. She looked up and saw the strange woman with the glasses. The entire world froze, icing Cassie's body.

The voice inside her took control. "You made a mistake," it said to the woman and bit hard on her fingers.

The woman screamed and ripped his hand away, driblets of blood speckling the hot cement. "You fucking psycho."

Cassie smiled, and the voice spoke for her again. "Go tell the police how you tried to kidnap a child. Maybe explain to them how a four-year-old nearly ripped your fingers off."

The woman's eyes widened at the power within that voice. "I was just trying to help her," she said as she wrapped one hand around her bloody fingers.

"Sure you were, away from security and toward the exits."

The woman opened her mouth to argue but thought better of it and ran away.

Cassie looked around, alone. Suddenly, every human passing by was a potential threat, someone trying to steal her. The size of the zoo expanded and the vastness of it threatened to swallow her whole.

"Shhhhhh," the voice said to her beating heart. "I've got you. You are never alone."

Cassie wanted to believe her, but she didn't even know how to get back to her parents. What if they left without her? What if she never found her way home?

"Shhhhh," the voice said again. "Let me show you something."

Her feet stepped forward as if pulled like a marionette. She followed until they reached a fenced-in area of green lawn. A few groups of people were close to the fence, pointing at nothing, all waiting to find whatever lived inside.

After a few seconds, a large, white dog exited a small cavern. The people shouted, "There she is!" But the white dog ignored them. Instead, it headed right toward Cassie. It showed no signs of animosity.

"This is the white wolf," the voice said.

The white wolf came to the fence and stared at her.

She stepped forward, resting her head on the metal fence.

The white wolf stepped forward and put his forehead to hers.

People watching gasped.

"The white wolf runs in packs. When the alpha couple has babies, the entire pack works together to feed and protect the children. When the children are older, they protect the elderly wolves. It's a genuine community effort. The pack has one mission: protect the pack."

Cassie put her fingers to the fence, letting the white wolf's thick fur touch her fingertips. "I don't have a pack." She thought of her family, their complex dynamic. They loved her. They avoided her. They fed her. They never played. They kissed her good night. They walked around her.

"You have me. I am your pack."

The white wolf licked the fence, her wet tongue slopping on Cassie's skin.

"Will you play with me?"

"Forever."

"Will you be my friend?"

"Always."

"Will you save me?"

"With my life."

"Can I call you The White Wolf?"

"As if it were my name."

Cassie leaned away from the fence, and the white wolf turned back to his cavern. "Does that mean I will also save you when you get old?"

The voice laughed. "I do not get old, but trust me, you save me every day."

"How?"

"By being you."

Cassie's nerves settled. In the distance, her mother and father shouted her name, panic in their voices.

"We should get back to them now, my little Cassiopeia."

Cassie laughed. "I like that name."

Chapter 41

Last Woman on Earth

"One day you will take your throne as queen of the world."

———

Cassie walked to the doorway, turned, and examined the carnage. Blood soaked the floor, decorated the walls, coated her face and clothes. She promised herself she'd be the last one standing in the bunker, and there she was, living her legacy. If only she'd known that would mean the death of her only friend, that she would have to watch a piece of herself be shredded in half. She still couldn't look that way, couldn't see the remains of The White Wolf.

She turned and walked down the hall, past the pile of dead vampires. More of her legacy. She walked through the room where Dr. Renard unleashed her memories and broke free her past. From there, she hobbled down the hall to where Spot lay dead with holes for eyes and a cavity in his chest.

Cassie's wounds throbbed, and the animalistic DNA of the vampires seared in her veins. She didn't have much longer.

She found her way to the tunnel where she had once been stuck, but on her return trip, she made it through just fine. Probably because she didn't care, wasn't riddled with tension anymore.

Back in the main bunker, she stopped at the bedroom, giving a moment of silence to James. Poor James.

In the main room, the theme from *Friends* played again. She couldn't remember if she left it on or if this was the last remainder of vampire torture, psychological warfare left on a loop.

When she opened the bulkhead, she squinted, unsure if she'd be met with blinding sunlight or the empty blackness of night. Instead, the world offered a low-hanging cloud of grey, a blizzard of ash flecks buzzing within.

Her heart shattered, and an audible disapproval left her mouth. Where once stood a house she envied, only razed earth remained.

Again, she was reminded of the great lie told to the youth, that one day they'd be in charge of themselves. We were all at the mercy of a few powerful men. Men with great weapons who hung bombs over our heads to keep us at heel. And even when we obeyed, they turned us to dust, just because they could.

She coughed as she crossed the wild abyss that once was a neighborhood, sucking in the chalky death. Which poison would win? The manmade one or the vampire one? She inhaled deeper, sucking in tendrils of war, coughing out charcoal mists. She marched on, waiting for, praying for death.

A twinge of sadness shot up her spine, a mourning of her own life. Maybe she, too, was like those powerful men, always concerned about herself above all else. But the sadness dissipated like the floating ash as she brushed it aside because Cassie had something most other people could only dream of. She had, for a short while, known herself fully, and what greater gift could life provide than that.

She inhaled another dose of airborne poison and stepped into a road. God, how her feet had grown to hate concrete. She laughed as she imagined a tractor-trailer breaking through the fog and crushing her body under its weight. How beautiful would that be? But no trailer would come because nothing was left. Nothing but her, queen of the world for another few minutes until the nuclear gases and world debris suffocated her.

She bent over and hacked up more black soot. *Let it come quickly*, she prayed. *Let it come quickly*. Let it win over the vampire poison. She fell to her knees and stared at the gray sky. Her heart skipped a beat. As more smoke entered her lungs, she felt herself dying, felt it deep within. She didn't fear it; not anymore.

As she finished another coughing fit, she whispered, "Are you ready?"

And then something grabbed her by the shoulder and dragged her backwards. As she was pulled, a voice whispered in her ear...

Chapter 42

The Response

"..."

———

"Not yet."

If you or someone you know is in crisis, please use the following resources:

988 - Suicide and Crisis Lifeline

1-800-273-8255 - National Suicide Prevention Lifeline

Text HOME to 741741 for Crisis Counseling

You've heard it a million times. Reviews make the world go round for indie authors. I would love to hear what you thought of this story. If you'd like, drop me a line or leave a review on your favorite review site. Or don't. Totally up to you. No pressure. Reading is a hobby, and you should enjoy it however you want.

For a five day free trial to my Patreon, use this QR code, or go to www.patreon.com/gagegreenwood Depending on the tier you sign up for, we have everything from access to group chats, monthly zoom meetings, access to all of my writing as I write it, and tons of exclusives, including Patreon exclusive variant covers for all of my books.

Sign up for my newsletter to receive updates, hear my weird ramblings, and find out inside info before everyone else, or go to www.gagegreenwood.com

Lastly, one of my favorite readers, Kylee Jones, made a playlist for this book on Spotify. If you'd like to check it out, you can do so here, or go

to https://open.spotify.com/playlist/3ZTdhQjpGGqoQ2H-W73ESIz

Acknowledgments

Becky and Nolan were instrumental in getting this book published. Without their support, my career would be in retail management and not publishing.

Catie McGuinness messaged me while reading an early version of this story with, "Is this about vampires?" At the time, it was not about vampires, but her idea was much, much better. I offered to make her a co-author on the book if she let me run with it. She refused the credit, but let me take the concept. The version that existed before her text message was far inferior. She deserves all the credit.

Megan Stockton and Jaxon Lee Rose were diehard fans of this book before all the changes that turned it into what it is now. They liked the raw concepts, and they urged me to keep writing it, even when I felt backed into a brick wall. Without them, I never would have made it to, "The end."

Mary Danner makes all my novels prettier than when they started, but she's more than an excellent editor. She's also one of the coolest people I've ever met.

Whenever I posted on social media about this book, the number one comment I'd get was, "Damn, that cover is beautiful." I agree. We can thank Luke Spooner for that. He's one of the best artists working on book covers today. He also did the interior artwork, my logos, and the DreadPop logo.

Nick Roberts, John Durgin, Jay Bower, Felix Blackwell, Sammy

Scott, and Duncan Ralston were all instrumental in giving me advice and helping me prepare the launch of this book.

My Patreon family, who will all be listed on their own page, were all a huge help in getting this book made. I couldn't have done it without their financial support.

All the people who rush out to buy my special editions, you have no idea how much that helps me continue to write.

Heather Ann Larson and Chandra Greco gave early eyes to this story and came to me with problem areas they needed fixing.

Kendall O'Connor has been a diehard Gagent of Chaos, and when I found out about her upcoming wedding, I had to give a shoutout to her and her husband in the pages of this book. It was a pivotal moment for our protagonist, Cassie, just as her support has been pivotal in my career.

Kylee Jones spent a ton of time curating the perfect playlist for this novel, and I think she did a fantastic job. I highly recommend you check it out. (You can find it a page back from these acknowledgments).

About the Author

Gage Greenwood is the best-selling author of the Winter's Myths Saga, and Bunker Dogs. He's a proud member of the Horror Writers Association and Science Fiction and Fantasy Writers association.

He's been an actor, comedian, podcaster, and even the Vice President of an escape room company. Since childhood, he's been a big fan of comic books, horror movies, and depressing music that fills him with existential dread.

He lives in New England with his girlfriend and son, and he spends his time writing, hiking, and decorating for various holidays.

Find out more, or contact me: www.gagegreenwood.com

Also by Gage Greenwood

THE WINTER'S MYTHS SAGA

Winter's Myths

Winter's Legacy

SHORT STORIES

Through Flickering Lights, a Silhouette

Grackles on the Feeder

NOVELS

Bunker Dogs

COMING SOON

On a Clear Day, You Can See Block Island (2023)

I Have Always Loved Taylor Swift (2024)

Forever Between Us (2024)

My Patreon Supporters

Terri Lynn Hudson, Susanne Stohr, Sally Feliz, Michael Casey, H.L. Holston, Gail Casey, Tiffany Riggs, Summer Smith, Shannon Ettaro, SP Somtow, Roth Schilling, Kelsey Stokes, Jodi Souza, Jaxon Lee Rose, Chiara Cooper, Brooke Conley, Tina Coley, Sara Ferrarese, Sarah D'Ambro, Osana Bolger, Nicole Laudij, Natasha Holley, Molly Mix, Kelly Kujawski, Kelli Hahn, Kate Forsman, Justine Manzano, JL Courtney, Jae Mazer, Bryan Walsh, Ali Sweet, Adrian Mathis, Matt St. Pier, Melissa Timmann, Leah Cole, Kylee Jones, Jason Artz, Janalyn Prude, Emily Morash, Crystal Cook, Chandra Greco, Ashley Harvey, Rhonda Bobbitt, Megan Stockton, Lisa Vasquez, Kristina Lee, Kristy Williams, Kendall O'Connor, Hope Haugstad, Engilbert Egill Stefansson, Deven VanKirk, Christopher Knickerbocker, Angie Valentine.

The White Wolf Army

Jennifer Henderson, Derek Thomas, Brittany Fox, Tessa Yerger, Heidi Sheehan, Lisa Lucania, Clifford T. Long, Chandra Greco, Matthew St. Pier, Shannon Ettaro, Alejandra Garcia, Mandee Quinn, Ashaway Free Public Library, Gillian Speicher, Sara Ferrarese, Laurie Cross, Cowgirl Mandy, Cathy Joy, Ronni Lowery, Christine Wright, Wendy Greve, Michael E. Casey, April Jernigan, Emily Morash, Christa Mouser, Frederick Bruce, Leah Cole, Terry LaRiccia, Amber Judge, Meghan Burns, Robin Ginther Venneri, Stephanie Huddle, Kate Foreman, Catie McGuinness, Christopher Knickerbocker, Bryan Walsh, Nicole Laudij, Tracey Nudd, Gabriel Wandersee, Osanna Bulger, Kristy Morey, Ami Gieselman, Kaylee Lawrence, Debbie Alder, Paul Davis, Mallory Elliott, Megan Stockton, Jason Arts, Erica Fields, Adrian Mathis, Angelina Valentine, Sarah D'Ambro, Kristina Lee, Elyn Noble, Nicholas Beishline, Tiqua Lovett, Heather Ann Larson, Rhonda Bobbitt, Lisa Vasquez, Jessica Gregorius, Lisa Eckrem-Weewie, Ashley Harvey, Holly Horror, Kendall O'Connor, Hope Haugstad.

Printed in Great Britain
by Amazon

24740634R00158